TILE M FOR MURDER

FELICIA CARPARELLI

TILE M FOR MURDER

FELICIA CARPARELLI

BELLA
BOOKS

2024

Bella Books, Inc.
P.O. Box 10543
Tallahassee, FL 32302

Printed in the United States of America on acid-free paper.

First Edition - 2024

Editor: Ann Roberts
Cover Designer: Kayla Mancuso

ISBN: 978-1-64247-512-8

PUBLISHER'S NOTE

Acknowledgments

To my family, Tina, Davy, Pete and Jen—you are always there for me.

For Dan, my literary advisor, I thank you. For Gwen, Megan, Maureen and Melinda, thank you for your support and years of friendship.

Thanks to Bella Books and to Ann Roberts, for her most illuminating and excellent edits.

Dedication

To Ellie and Johnny, the lights of my life

Tile M for Murder

(A Jayne Marple Scrabble Mystery)

Place: Chicago
Time: The present—spring

THE PLAYERS

Jayne Marple: Retired golf professional, scrabble team organizer, ex-punk rock singer, hors d'oeuvres expert

Arnolda (Arnie) Palmer: Retired english and special education teacher, scrabble fan, owner of elsinore detective agency, mixologist, Jayne's new girlfriend

Robin York: Tax attorney, pianist and philatelist, passionate scrabble player, husband to Marion

Marion Wayne: Interior designer, long-haired, glamorous, prone to hyperbole, reckless scrabble player

Fred Woods: Retired mortician, active tap dancer, beer drinker, devoted husband

Ethel Woods: Homemaker, fond of vintage clothes, loves rhinestones and satin, makes award-winning pies, dedicated caregiver

Nick Pappas: Gym owner, health conscious and sober, red-haired and mellow, plays scrabble to keep his partner happy

Noreen Charles: Princess Diana lookalike, avid skier, brewery owner, introduced partner Nick to scrabble, yoga, and culture

Vanessa Harding: Ageless femme fatale, has had numerous spouses, smokes cigarettes, owns Tutu (a pomeranian), botoxed diva, into jewels, martinis, and vamping men and women

David Harding: previous husband of Vanessa, wanted by police for fraud and for trying to throttle ex-wife

Donald Harding: Twin brother of David, also ex-spouse of Vanessa, convicted felon

Sarah York: Older sister of Robin, widow, horse trainer

Tanya: Personal assistant of Vanessa harding

Detective Perry (Pericles) Schultz: Chicago PD detective, closet knitter, lives on tums, coffee, and donuts

CHAPTER ONE

Diva—8 Points

Jayne Marple, one half of the Elsinore Detective Agency, stared in disbelief at their client Vanessa Harding. Vanessa's age was anywhere between Medicare and death.

Femme fatale extraordinaire, she lounged in bed, surrounded by marabou feathers, ice packs, a carton of menthol cigarettes, and a box of dark chocolates. As she dropped ashes over the head of Tutu, her little dog, Jayne thought the animal resembled an oversize tangerine powder puff.

She tried not to stare at Vanessa's bleached-blond hair and ample bosom, displayed and arrayed in a silk negligee with a diamond pendant dangling between her breasts.

Jayne's partner, in both business and pleasure, Arnolda Palmer, or Arnie, as she was known to friends, was staring. "Arnie," Jayne said, kicking her in the ankle.

She snapped to. "Mrs. Harding—"

"Vanessa," she cooed in a husky voice. "Call me Vanessa, Arnolda dear, after all, we do have a working relationship, don't we?"

Arnie nodded with round eyes and a silly grin, and again, Jayne wanted to kick her. "Mrs. Harding," Jayne said, "we're very sorry your ex-husband, David Harding, broke in last night and tried to hurt you." She studied a recent photograph. "How did he come to have the house keys?"

"Hurt me?" She tugged on marabou feathers to expose a red, chafed throat. "That idiot tried to kill me! If it hadn't been for that car alarm going off and the lights in the yard going on, he would've murdered me. I guess I forgot to change all the locks after our divorce," she added. "And now, some of my jewels are missing!"

"We don't want him to be able to break in here again. Did you call the security people?" asked Arnie.

Vanessa assumed the look of a little girl, twisting a blond curl around a jeweled finger. "Oh, Arnie, I forgot," she said in a baby singsong voice. "Could you pwease do that for me now?" She pulled a paper out of her cleavage and squinted at it. "These numbers are so small." She pointed to an enormous, old-fashioned push-button phone, pink with rhinestones and French poodles painted on the receiver. "Isn't my phone so pretty?"

Jayne sniffed and shot Arnie a look.

Arnie took the phone in one hand and made a "What can I say?" motion with the other.

Jayne walked over to a wall of photos, all framed with sparkly crystals and gemstones. Vanessa embracing celebrities from the past. Vanessa in a flowing gown with a tiara on her poufy hair. Four different wedding photos, showing Vanessa at various ages, smiling provocatively as she clutched the arms of her willing marital victims. Vanessa poured into a gold lamé gown, embracing a very famous blue-eyed Italian singer.

"What a pretty daughter," said Jayne.

Vanessa stopped listening to Arnie long enough to hiss, "I don't have a daughter, that's me."

"Miss St. Patrick's Day Parade Queen, 196—"

"Yes, well, that was a long time ago," she snapped. "The date doesn't matter."

"That's a great honor to be chosen as the queen," Arnie said smoothly. "I didn't know you were Irish."

"Maloney was my maiden name. One hundred percent Irish, that's me. County Cork."

"Delightful. Isn't it, Jayne?" Arnie asked.

"Absolutely fantastic," she said, trying to find any resemblance between the dewy-eyed, red-haired colleen in the picture to the dyed blond in the bed, with her mean Botoxed face, huge goldfish lips, and wide eyes stretched like a taxidermist's owl. She could not stand Vanessa Harding. The woman reminded her of the mean girls in high school who'd made fun of Jayne's six-foot height, and being a jock. They also had guessed correctly she was gay and they were brutal about it, leaving nasty notes on her desk and pointedly avoiding her in the locker room during gym class.

"Did you marry the same man twice?" Jayne stared at the face of David, younger and with more hair.

"Twins," Vanessa chuckled.

"Excuse me?"

"I married twin brothers. That's Donald's picture you're looking at. I married Donald about five years before David. In between, I dated Frank Sinatra. What a guy." She paused, sighing, and Jayne expected a drumroll.

"Twins?" Jayne repeated.

"What can I say? I liked their faces. I had hoped that David would have a better personality than Donald. I was wrong. Donald was outgoing and a divine dancer and a great kisser. But he was a con artist. Always had a scheme going. Always borrowing money and getting into trouble with the mob and the cops. He was very good at finding out stuff about people." The diva stubbed out her cigarette vigorously in a flamingo ashtray.

"And David? Jayne asked.

"David was more solid, quiet, and romantic—or so I thought. He kind of bored me after a while. Very nervous guy."

"May I borrow these pictures?" Arnie asked. "For our investigation."

"Sure, go ahead," Vanessa said.

"David and Donald aren't exactly alike," Jayne commented. "David's chin is more pointed, although they both have diamond-shaped faces."

"Really?" Vanessa coughed and Tutu growled. "I never noticed."

"May I ask why you're so sure that it was your ex who broke in last night? It was dark in here and you—"

"I, what?"

"Do you wear glasses?"

"I most certainly do not." The diva scowled.

"Okay, copy that." Jayne needed escape. Vanessa Harding was getting on her nerves. "Arnie, I really should get home and set up for our game tonight," she said.

"Game? What game? Can I play?" Vanessa broke into a wheezy laugh.

"Scrabble," Arnie told her.

"Word games?" Her face fell, not far, but it shifted, Jayne noted with amusement. "I prefer other…entertainments."

"Give me a break," Jayne muttered under her breath.

"What did you say, Jill dear?" Vanessa asked.

"I said, I'm going home to cook steak. For the snacks tonight."

Arnie coughed. "Good idea, Jayne."

Vanessa inspected Jayne with a skeptical look and lit another cigarette. "Are you still on hold, Arnie, with the company?"

"They're checking your files," she said. "Do you have an inventory of your jewelry and what's missing?"

"Somewhere." She waved her hand in the direction of a French provincial desk.

"The police will want to know if you filed a report," Arnie said gently.

"Will they?" She inhaled deeply and coughed. "I know I'm missing a huge sapphire I was going to have set into a brooch, a pair of diamond earrings, and an emerald ring that belonged to my mother. She turned to Jayne. "How long have you been Arnie's assistant?"

"A while. Since I retired from being a full-time golf pro."

"Golf pro? How interesting. You sure are tall enough."

Jayne raised her eyebrows. "It was very nice to meet you, Vanessa, but I've got to run. I hope you get all your issues sorted."

"Likewise," Vanessa said, stubbing out the cigarette in an empty candy box.

"I'll let myself out," Jayne said.

"See you later, Jayne," Arnie said. Arnie's forehead glistened with sweat. Being left alone with the black widow spider was going to make her sweat buckets, Jayne thought. Serves her right for taking on such an outrageous client.

On the way out, Jayne paused to open a few drawers in the hallway armoire. Parking tickets, receipts—and whoa. A small, pink .38 Smith and Wesson lay under a stack of lace hankies stinking of musk perfume.

"How appropriate, baby pink," she said to Tutu the pup, who had followed her downstairs. "Too bad the ex-husband missed this last night."

CHAPTER TWO

Hors D'oeuvres—19 Points

It was only a mile and a half from the luxurious townhome on Chicago's gold coast to her lakefront condo. Jayne was happy to walk, to think, and to breathe fresh air.

The Magnificent Mile, as the most wealthiest street in Chicago is called, was late-afternoon peaceful. Rush hour was an hour away. Shoppers strolled with designer bags. A well-dressed woman around Jayne's age walked out of a jewelry shop with a tiny box under her arm. She was slim and chic. Jayne looked down at the grass stains on her khakis—a result of inspecting Vanessa's damp backyard for clues—and her scuffed gym shoes.

"Hard to be glamorous with this job," she told a pigeon on the Michigan Avenue bridge. The bird with its beady orange eyes was unmoved by her comment. She arrived home a few minutes later. Her building faced the Chicago River and had spectacular views of Lake Michigan and the city. After her daughter married and moved to London five years ago, she'd sold the house and moved downtown. She'd been divorced for a long time, came out in her forties, and enjoyed a single life.

Her life alternated between intense love affairs and stretches of celibacy. It was exhilarating being retired—a new home, more time for golf games, and now, a new lady in her life, who was having a great effect on her outlook on life. She was more positive, less stressed and definitely more loving with Arnie at her side.

She grabbed her mail and took the elevator to twenty-four. After she entered her home and the door clicked shut, Lucia, her tiny Chihuahua mix, rescue pup extraordinaire, jumped off her cashmere doggie bed to greet her.

"You little silly." Jayne tossed a few soft chicken treats to the pup. Lucia only had five teeth after two major dental surgeries, so she liked soft, gourmet dog food. Due to the lack of teeth, her little tongue often hung out of one side of her mouth, giving her an adorable but "woe is me" canine look. She was spoiled and liked to be adored. Lucia was still getting used to Arnie, and she wasn't always happy when she slept over.

Jayne tossed her mail on the granite counter and gave it a quick look. Electric bill, grocery store ads, Scrabble newsletter, golf magazine, and an expensive-looking cream-colored envelope. It was addressed to both her and Arnie, in care of the Elsinore Detective Agency. The envelope gave off a scent of sandalwood and sage.

"It's addressed to Arnie and me," she said to Lucia. "So, I will be a good assistant and wait to open it. And, you're the third animal I've talked to today. Maybe Arnie's right. I retired too soon." The Chihuahua princess sniffed the air as Jayne took out ingredients for bacon wraps, deviled eggs, salmon mousse and onion dip. She tied on a chef's apron and got to work.

Arnie finally showed up, as Jayne finished frying bacon and onions. "Smells great in here."

"Thanks for leaving me stranded, sweetie." Jayne chopped celery with precision.

"I'm sorry, but she wouldn't stop talking," Arnie sighed. "I think she might be lonely."

"Lonely? That man-woman eater?" Jayne sliced a hard-boiled egg.

"She didn't take to you very well," Arnie admitted. "I don't know why."

Jayne pointed the paring knife at Arnie with a mock smile. "Clueless."

"We've got a half hour, so put me to work. Forgiven?"

"I'll think about it," Jayne said. But how could she stay mad at Arnie, with her lovely auburn hair, deep blue eyes and sweet smile? "Did you get the diva's issues sorted out?"

"I had to wait for the security people to come and fix her alarms and change the locks," she said, mopping her face with a fresh, white, linen handkerchief.

"You only sweat when you're upset," Jayne remarked, wrapping bacon around a water chestnut.

"She's a very demanding client."

"I have to agree with you. She must have driven her four husbands bonkers. And marrying twins? That's unbelievable. That woman sure has a lot of nerve. Of course, with her bad eyesight, maybe she couldn't even tell them apart. Except in the sack."

"Now be nice," Arnie admonished.

Jayne scooped salmon mousse into a cobalt-blue Fiestaware bowl. "This bowl matches your eyes, Arnie. So pretty." She admired the contrast of pink salmon against blue ceramic.

"I forgot your golf clubs are in the trunk of my car," Arnie said, her cheeks pink with pleasure. "Shall I get them now?"

"No rush, we can get them later."

"They're very expensive clubs, Jayne."

"The garage is safe and the clubs are insured. Don't worry, honey. And you played very well this morning."

"I've got a good teacher," she said. "You've helped my golf game tremendously."

She diced onions for the sour cream chive dip and wiped away a tear. "Arnie, we got some mail today."

"We did?"

"Yes, on lovely notepaper, smelling of sage and sandalwood. Addressed to you and me at the Elsinore Detective Agency. It's on the edge of the counter there."

Arnie picked it up and sniffed. "Very elegant," Arnie said. She slit it open, read it, and frowned.

Jayne looked up. "What is it? What does it say?"

Arnie read it aloud.

SCRABBLE TEAM KILLER?

CHECK OUT THE FIFTH HOLE FRIDAY

NO ONE IS SAFE HERE!

"What?" Jayne put down her knife. "May I see it, please?"

"What could it possibly mean?" Arnie asked. She stood looking over her shoulder. "Someone is literary."

"What do you mean?"

"It's a haiku. A form of Japanese poetry. Five-seven-five syllables," Arnie said.

"Trust an English teacher to spot that. A threatening haiku? Hmm. We have a client who is a poetic assassin?"

"Or one of our Scrabble buddies playing a joke? What team? Hard to believe that one of our friends is a killer," Arnie said.

"I agree," Jayne said. "I don't see any of our Scrabble mates writing strange poems. Fred is a retired mortician, Ethel a homemaker, Noreen owns a brewery, and Nick owns a gym."

"And Robin is a tax attorney," Arnie said. "Now Marion—"

"Marion has an over-the-top sense of humor. He loves to dress up and be dramatic—and he has a temper."

"The world is his stage," Arnie agreed. "He likes to show off and be noticed. Since he was a model in his youth, he's always walking the catwalk."

"Should we show them the note?"

"Confront them and see what happens? I don't know. After Marion stabbed Robin with the pencil last time, I'm not sure if I trust this group to behave," Arnie said.

"Let's play it by ear," Jayne said. "If we think we should bring up the note, we can try it." She buried it in her knitting basket for now.

"Sounds good. Check out the vibes first. Now, back to work. What is the theme for tonight's snacks?" She, like Lucia, sniffed appreciatively.

"1950s hors d'oeuvres," Jayne said. "Deviled eggs, onion dip and chips, bacon-wrapped water chestnuts, and salmon mousse with Ritz crackers."

"I am in charge of the cocktails?"

"Yes, please. Your summer bartending jobs are really paying off, pleasing this group. Do you know any appropriate cocktails?"

"Tom Collins?"

"A tad too summery," she said, stuffing eggs with the deviled mixture, bright yellow yolks mixed with red pimento.

"Singapore sling?"

"Too pink."

"Martinis?"

"Too predictable," she said, and tossed Lucia a bit of bacon.

"How about a sidecar?"

"Refresh my memory about the ingredients?"

"Cognac, lemon juice and triple sec. Then a vigorous shake in the cocktail shaker." She looked in the liquor cabinet. "You've got it all here. Maybe I'll add some shaved ice."

"Sounds good. The tart drink will balance all this gooey, dippy, mayonnaise-y food."

"And some beer for Fred, of course."

Jayne looked at the clock. "I'll change my clothes," she said and dashed into the bedroom. She emerged in minutes, tucking a chocolate-brown silk blouse into slim black trousers.

"You look great," Arnie said, smiling. "You always do."

"Thanks, my dear." Jayne gave her a full body hug just as the doorbell rang.

"Ignore it," Arnie groaned, nuzzling her neck.

"Can't," Jayne sighed. Lucia barked, ferociously. "Damn it. I'll get the door."

Jayne opened the door with a big smile on her face. "Nice to see you, Fred and Ethel. Right on time."

"Always good to see you Jayne," Fred said, pulling down his Hawaiian shirt over his ample middle. "And Lucia, too."

"I brought coconut crème pies, Jayne," Ethel said, handing Jayne the heavy whipped crème-laden desserts.

"Thank you, Ethel, these look amazing. As do you. I love your dress."

"It's a bit old-fashioned but I thought this cocktail dress would go with the '50s theme," she said, smoothing out the puce satin over her petite, plump figure. On her shoulder was pinned an enormous rhinestone brooch, shaped like a crescent moon.

"Hi, Fred and Ethel, how you doing? Here's a beer, Fred," Arnie said, handing him a cold bottle.

"Thank you." He opened the brew with a gold coffin-shaped bottle opener.

"What's the cocktail du jour?" Ethel asked, exuding Midnight in Paris perfume.

"Sidecars," Arnie said, holding up the Art Deco cocktail shaker.

"Ooh, delicious," Ethel sighed. "Fred, you don't know what you're missing."

"I only drink beer, my love," he said. "Sometimes imported, sometimes homebrew and sometimes the good old cheap stuff."

"You're an equal opportunity guzzler," Jayne said. She placed trays of food on the long, granite kitchen island.

"You always have such beautiful food," Ethel said in a tinkly voice like sleigh bells skimming over icy paths. "How are you tonight?" She eyed the hors d'oeuvres with deep satisfaction. "Did you play golf today? And I just love your hair! How do you get it to stay up that way?"

Jayne patted her platinum-blond, spiky hairdo. "We did golf this morning, very early. The weather was fabulous. And my hair? Lots of hair gel. Maybe I should change the style. What do you think?"

"If it ain't broke, don't fix it," Fred said, pointing to the picture of Jayne, circa 1980, hanging over the fireplace. Lead singer and bassist for The Pink Bohemians, a Chicago fixture of the punk and new wave scene, Jayne had been a golfer by day and a musician by night, way back when.

"It suits you, Jayne," Arnie said, concentrating on a one-two-one Rhumba shaking motion. "Highlights your high cheekbones."

"Thanks, Arnie." She waited until her shaking was over and then handed her a tray with cocktail glasses.

"Who are we playing against tonight?" Ethel asked.

"You and Fred are playing against Nick and Noreen," Jayne said.

"Good." Ethel frowned. "I don't want to play with Robin and Marion. Last time was too much."

"It upset Ethel terribly when Robin stabbed Marion with the pencil," Fred said.

"It upset me too," said Jayne. "I couldn't believe it."

"Just because he couldn't spell rutabaga correctly," Arnie said.

"I think there was more to it than that," Jayne mused. "Those two were touchy from the moment they walked in. Marion was making wisecracks and Robin was doing a slow burn."

"Marion has a big mouth," Fred said. "Maybe it's time to find new Scrabble players."

"I hope we can all be friends tonight," Jayne said. The doorbell rang again and Lucia barked, this time with less vigor. "I'll get it."

"Jayne, my beautiful rock 'n' roll star." Marion Wayne sailed into her foyer and filled the room with air kisses. He removed his Irish tweed cape with a flourish, while his husband, Robin, waited patiently behind him. A scarf fluttered to the floor. Jayne picked it up, appreciating the luscious, silk fabric pattern with persimmon tulips and teal and burgundy doves.

"Hi, Marion, how are you tonight? You're looking amazing as always."

"I am absolutely fabulous." He looked her up and down. "You look great, my love. Your mama might have named you after a British spinster sleuth, but to me you will always be my Jayne Mansfield."

"I am hardly a blond bombshell sex goddess from the fifties," Jayne protested.

"Don't say that, darlin'. You will always be a goddess to me. You were so hot in that rock band from the eighties. Hotter than Blondie." Marion removed fine taupe calfskin gloves, revealing milk-white hands.

"You are too kind. That's me, hot stuff."

Lucia ran up and sniffed and barked at Marion. "My little love, Lucia!" He patted her head. "Congratulations on turning eleven last week. Muzzle tov! Jayne, I just adore your home! It's like the Taj Mahal!"

"You should like it, Marion, since you decorated it for me," she said.

"I did a fabulous job, didn't I? All the chrome and leather reminds me of golf clubs," he said, taking out a comb to arrange his beautiful shoulder-length ebony hair in front of the oval mirror. He frowned at a gray strand on his fifty-year-old head. A small bandage covered his right palm, where his husband had stabbed him with a pencil two weeks ago. He sighed with satisfaction.

"Mirror, mirror on the wall," Jayne said.

"Who's the fairest of them all?" Marion finished. "Why I am! Now where is that woman of yours? Arnie Palmer, you famous golfer you, I need a drinkie!"

"In here, Marion," Arnie called out. "Cocktails shaken not stirred."

"Just like James Bond, how thrilling," he said to Jayne and his husband. "I am ready for my cocktail, Sherlock," he sang out to Arnie as he floated into the living room. "I am parched like the Sahara. I could drink gallons!"

"Hello, Jayne," said a voice behind Marion.

"Hello, Robin," she said to Marion's soft-spoken husband. "It's good to see you."

"Good to see you, too. How's it going?"

"Great, thanks. I had a very busy day, but a productive day. Marion seems in a good mood, as always. I always get a kick out of his enthusiasm." Jayne took Robin's leather jacket and hung up the coats.

"Marion does have a tendency to speak in clichés and to quote old movies," he said, with a frown.

"That's part of his charm." She paused. "How are you doing?"

"Don't worry," he said. "We won't have a repeat of last time. I will behave."

"I never doubted it for a minute," she assured him. "Although I was a bit surprised you got so excited last time. I didn't know you could get so emotional."

"I didn't either," he said. "I must be under more stress than I thought. The new tax laws are tricky. And sometimes Marion won't quit making comments. He knows how to upset me." He looked at his husband who was telling a joke with wide eyes and extended arms. "He likes to be the center of attention. I didn't mean to stab him, but the pencil was in my hand and before I knew it—"

"It just slipped? Still waters run deep, I think," Ethel said, coming out of the small bathroom room in the hall. "My mother always said you had to watch the quiet ones. You had better keep the pencils away from him tonight, Jayne."

Robin's fair skin became rosy. He removed his glasses and polished the lenses with a pristine white linen handkerchief. Without his glasses, Jayne noticed his face looked angular and a bit predatory.

"That was very wise of your mother, but I am sure we won't have any problems tonight." Ethel smoothed her skirt and walked into the living room, leaving a trail of perfume fumes. "She means well, but doesn't know when to keep still," Jayne said. "Have you acquired any new amazing stamps, Robin?"

"I was able to acquire a very rare stamp. George Washington, 1867, I was very pleased that my bid was accepted."

"That's great, Robin. You know so much about history and philately. See? I remembered that word."

"You are a very bright lady, Jayne."

"For a golf pro, right?" She squeezed his elbow. "Now, how about a cocktail?"

Ethel and Fred sat at their table, sipping their drinks. Marion plopped down next to Ethel. "Ethel, my dearest Ethel, can you ever forgive me for behaving so badly last time? I don't know what got into me. I don't usually behave like that."

"Marion, you scared the life out of me," she said. "I was so afraid. I thought Robin was going to go crazy and stab us all!"

"Ethel was very upset," Fred said. "You shouldn't provoke people like that."

"I know, I know, I'm so sorry! I was so edgy." He dropped his voice. "To tell you the truth, I was trying to reduce for a charity gala where I was asked to model and I was starving! And that made me so irritable, isn't that so, Robin?"

Robin, staring into his sidecar, shook his head. "Starvation and amphetamines. Not a great combo for happiness."

"Pills?" Ethel asked. "Aren't they dangerous?"

"My dear, Ethel, it was temporary," Marion said. "I am clean and free of all chemicals tonight. I will behave. You won't be ashamed of me."

"I hope so."

"And may I say, you look amazing in puce and the sparkles in your brooch match the sparkles in your eyes," Marion gushed.

Ethel giggled, Fred patted her hand, and Jayne noticed that even Robin was smiling. She gave a thumbs-up to Arnie.

"Let the games begin," she said, and Lucia barked in agreement.

CHAPTER THREE

Haiku—12 Points

"Detox." Noreen Charles put down the first word of the night. Forty-two points. She smiled at her opponents, Fred and Ethel.

"Are you sure you wanted to use your X on the first turn?" Nick, her partner, asked.

"I got a double letter score and a double word," she said with a frown.

"Very good word," Fred assured her.

"Doesn't that word upset you, Nick?" Ethel asked, her eyes wide behind her rhinestone glasses.

"I've been sober for ten years, Ethel. The word doesn't bother me, if that's what you're referring to?" Nick, tall, lean, red-haired, with a sleepy but freckled Huck Finn kind of face, arranged his tiles on the wooden tray and did not look at Ethel.

At the other table, Jayne looked at Arnie with concern. Arnie gave a thumbs-up.

"Ethel, darling," Marion said, from the next table, "you should *fermez* your *bouche*, once in a while."

"Yes, keep your pretty lips closed, Ethel," Fred agreed, staring at his own tiles. "Why even mention it?" He smiled like a Cheshire cat. "Ooh, this is going to be good." He put down an I, F, Y, after Noreen's word. "Detoxify. Triple word score," he beamed, putting down a four-point Y on a red triple word square.

Jayne handed Ethel a tissue. Her big baby-blue eyes, coated with heavy mascara which gave her a Lamb Chop look, filled with tears. "I didn't mean anything by it," Ethel sniffled.

Noreen patted her hand. "Of course, you didn't. If Nick can live with me owning a microbrewery, then a word like that isn't going to upset him."

"Sixty-six points! Most excellent. Great set-up word for me, Noreen," said Fred.

"Perhaps you shouldn't use X so near to a triple word square," Nick commented with a frown.

"It's okay," Noreen said. "The game just started."

"That was a great play, Fred," Nick said. "I'm up next." He rolled up his sleeves, revealing tanned, muscled forearms as was befitting a gym owner and personal trainer. A tattoo on his left wrist said, *strive*, and on the right wrist it said, *for excellence*.

"Don't take too long, honey," Noreen said, looking at the five-minute timer.

"I won't," Nick muttered, without glancing at the clock. "Give me a chance, Noreen, I'm the newest member of the group."

"And the youngest," Ethel said, sipping her cocktail.

"Don't remind him," Noreen said. "He's quite sensitive about being thirty-five."

"And you forty-five, isn't that so, Nor?" Marion walked over and stuck his long nose into their game. Like a bunny, his elegant, long hooter twitched.

"Why, Grandpa, what a good memory you have," Noreen said, but her hazel eyes flashed.

"I just love your hair," Marion gushed. "So totally Princess Di."

"Why don't you follow your own advice and *fermez* your *bouche*, Marion," Fred said, opening another beer. "What woman wants to be reminded of her age?"

"Well, be that way." Marion tossed his locks and went back to his table. Again, Jayne looked at Arnie with wide eyes. Was this evening going to self-destruct as badly as the last game?

Nick put down D, E, R. "Deer," he said. "Eight points."

Ethel put down H, A. "Had and ad," she said. "Count it for me, Fred."

"Thirteen points. Good one, Ethel." Ethel beamed and Nick gave Noreen a glance that said, "Don't say anything about my little word," and Noreen turned her attention to her tiles.

At the next table, words were flowing easily. Arnie opened the game with TABLE, sixteen points. Marion built off his word with SHAM, also sixteen points. Jayne made SCAN for twelve points, and Robin made YAWN, twenty points with two double letters. As he was leading after the first round, he was smiling.

During the next round, Marion built off Arnie's POMP with an OUS. "Pompous," he said. "Now who does that remind us of?" he asked, ignoring his spouse.

Jayne gave him the stern, "I'm going to pop you one" look.

"Oh, all right," he said, and jumped up. "Jaynie, if I can't speak, how about you give me something to eat?"

"Go help yourself, Marion. It's all out on the island. My turn now."

While thinking of her next word, Jayne watched Marion fill a plate with hors d'oeuvres, heavy on the deviled eggs, and wander around the room, looking at photographs and gazing out the floor-to-ceiling windows. "You really were a hot chick, Jayne," he said, looking at an old band picture. Jayne had on a vinyl miniskirt with plaid tights and Doc Martens on her feet. Her bass guitar was hot pink. "Very punk."

"Why, thank you, kindly, sir," she said. "Those were the good old days."

"These are the good old days," Marion said. "The view here is amazing. I can see right across Lake Michigan. I love our condo but it faces south. Why, we can see Indiana!" He shivered. "I hate the thought of winter coming." He sighed. "Time change. Cold weather. So, dreary." He bit into a deviled egg. "Divine, delicious, delectable," he sighed. "And pink eggs! How did you accomplish that, my love?"

"I soaked the eggs in a little beet juice," Jayne said, putting down the word ZOO off Marion's O in POMPOUS. "Triple letter for the Z."

"Good job," Arnie said. "We're ahead now."

Robin scowled while Marion topped up his drink and then trotted to the bathroom. Robin rubbed his chin as he stared at his tiles. Jayne thought his pointed little chin gave him a foxlike look. When Marion returned, his husband was making a very respectable, OXEN and AXE for thirty-seven points, using the X twice in both directions.

"Happy, baby?" Marion looked at his tiles and his drink. Robin smiled a small, cautious smile.

"Early days, yet," he said. "Your turn, Arnie."

"How is the Elsinore Detective Agency doing, Arnie? Flourishing?" Marion's eyes widened innocently. "Or is something rotten in the state of Denmark?"

Robin's eyes widened. "Be quiet, Marion, how can Arnie think with your incessant chatter?"

"Temper, temper, my love," Marion said. "I just think it's so dang cool she named her agency after *Hamlet*."

Arnie looked up from her tiles. "Didn't know you were so literary, Marion."

"I have many hidden talents." He smirked and ate another deviled egg.

Jayne studied the other players while Arnie plotted her next move. What did she really know about them? They had met about a year ago when Jayne, after hiring Robin to do her taxes, discovered they both loved Scrabble. Robin knew Ethel and Fred as clients and Marion knew Nick from the gym. She'd met Arnie six months ago on a social media group for lesbians. She was sorry her Scrabble partner and golfing friend, Sue, had moved to Alaska, but Sue had met a woman online and wanted to try another life up north. Jayne couldn't blame her, new beginnings were exciting but very difficult to achieve after a certain age. Jayne had met Arnie when she had posted a message for new Scrabble players in the area. It had been love, lust—or both—at first sight. Hope springs eternal and love can come to anyone, like the old song said, she thought. She never dreamed she could meet a fabulous woman like Arnie at this stage in life.

Robin and Marion were charming, well-educated, affluent and a bit hard to figure out. Were they happy together? Was that feeling of underlying tension and stream of bitchy comments a sign of affection or dissatisfaction?

Fred and Ethel were almost too good to be true. Fred, a retired mortician, liked to dance. Ethel, a homemaker, liked to cook, eat, and dress up. She took care of her ninety-six-year-old mother in their home. Outside of a few awkward comments that she was always truly sorry for, Ethel was a sweet lady. Fred, good-natured, regardless of his views on cremation, was a good sport when he played Scrabble and never complained.

Nick and Noreen were more difficult to fathom. She was elegant and always impeccably coiffed and dressed. She was making a fortune by running the microbrewery her brother left her when he unexpectedly passed away. Noreen looked like she would be more at home creating fine wines, but she'd surprised everyone by rolling up her sleeves, learning the ins and outs of brewing and promoting her merchandise. She had met Nick when he was a part-time bartender at the brewery. After six months, they had moved in together and she had floated him a loan to start his own gym.

They all seemed so polite and pleasant for the most part and were good Scrabble players. Jayne had to reign in her temper at times. Arnie, always kind and adorable, said she needed more nerve to stand up to her foes. Didn't they all have some baggage to deal with? She watched Ethel move her tiles around with little white fingers, her long red nails adorned with rhinestones. Jayne always hosted the bimonthly games, but each team took turns bringing snacks and booze.

"Your pies last time were amazing, Ethel," Jayne said. "Shepherd's pie, quiche Lorraine, pizza rustica, and lemon custard. Totally delicious and so much work."

"The Italian pie stuffed with eggs, sausage and cheese…I was undone," Arnie said, clutching her heart. "Astounding."

"Thank you," Ethel said, glowing. "I'm half Italian."

"And the other half fabulous," Fred said, patting her hand.

Jayne felt her fears dispel. This group couldn't have sent her that note. They were all too nice, right? After an hour of play, Jayne and Arnie were slightly ahead of Robin and Marion. Fred and Ethel were almost tied with Nick and Noreen, as Noreen seemed to have lost her initial enthusiasm, much to Nick's consternation. Jayne refreshed the snack trays. The others rose for cocktail refills. Robin sat down at Jayne's vintage upright Baldwin piano and started to play a medley of Gershwin tunes.

"Break time," Fred said, filling a plate. "I got rhythm," he sang along.

"I got music," Ethel chimed in.

"I got cocktails, who could ask for anything more?" Marion sang off-key and loudly. "I just love bacon," Marion said, nose twitching appreciatively. He popped a bacon-wrapped water chestnut into his mouth. "Totally decadent and bad for you."

"Very Betty Crocker cookbook," Fred said. "Reminds me of my mother and my youth."

"That's yout' to you," Marion said.

"Marion," Robin said. "Quit it." He segued into "'S Wonderful."

Jayne picked up the deviled eggs. "How about an egg, you devil?"

Marion snickered and took another egg. He wrinkled his nose at his husband. Robin had a dangerous look on his face. There was a sharpened pencil on the table and Jayne moved it to her desk, hoping no one had noticed.

Fred, oblivious to the tension around him, broke into an impromptu tap step. "That you should care for me…" He shuffled over to Arnie for a beer.

"You dance so well," Jayne said.

"That step is called the Shirley Temple," Fred said proudly.

Marion opened his mouth but Arnie cut in. "That's a great name for a dance step. Loved her old movies. Didn't you say you had something you wanted to share with us, Jayne?"

"Yes," she said, looking at her friends. "Did anyone send Arnie and me a cryptic message in the mail?"

"How positively Gothic," Marion said. "What kind of message? About buried treasure? A secret love note from someone who adores your backswing?"

"It was a haiku," Jayne said, ignoring Marion. She scanned their faces carefully. "Sort of a warning for us to be careful."

"Careful?" Fred dipped a chip into the onion dip. "Careful of what?"

Robin stopped playing and picked up his drink. "There was no return address or any indication of who sent it?"

"None at all," she said.

"Can we see it?" Nick asked.

"You didn't dust it for fingerprints, Arnie?" Marion chugged half his cocktail and held out his arm for more.

"No, I didn't," Arnie said, topping up his glass.

Jayne pulled out the note from her knitting basket. "Very good hiding place," Marion sniggered into his drink.

"Maybe you should slow up on those," Robin murmured.

"Oh, pooh," Marion retorted with a toss of his hair. "Robin, you are really turning into an old fart. You know I have a hollow leg."

"That's enough now, Marion," Jayne said sternly. "We expect you to behave better this time, please."

"The royal we?"

"Marion," Robin groaned.

"Okay, okay, I'm sorry that I'm such a bitch," he said. "I'll shut up."

"It's about time," Noreen sighed.

"Princess Di speaks," Marion said and stomped off to the bathroom.

"Glad he's gone," Fred said. "He's got a mouth on him."

Ethel steadily ate hors d'oeuvres. "I would comment but I don't want to be misunderstood," she said, looking at Nick.

"All is forgiven," he said. "How is your mother adjusting to living with you?"

Ethel brightened. "She's doing okay, thanks. Much better than we expected. She likes her home aide, is sleeping and eating well and we watch *Wheel of Fortune* together every night. She's in great shape for ninety-six."

"That's wonderful," Nick said.

"Ethel takes the best care of Nana," Fred agreed. "So, back to the note."

"It came in the mail today, no return address, no clue what it's about," Jayne said.

"So, show us the note, please, Jayne," Robin said. "The suspense is killing me."

Jayne took out the note and handed it to Robin. He read it aloud.

SCRABBLE TEAM KILLER?
CHECK OUT THE FIFTH HOLE FRIDAY
NO ONE IS SAFE HERE!

"Let's see that," Noreen said. He passed it to her. "Strange."

Fred looked at it over her shoulder. "Must be a joke, yes?"

Ethel sniffed. "Not very funny."

"But effective," Nick said. "We're all taken aback and thinking about it."

Marion came back and Ethel handed him the note. "What's this?" His eyes sparkled. "Scrabble team killer? Is one of us a killer? Or is one of us going to get killed?"

Ethel gasped. "Don't say that!" She grasped Fred's hand in horror. "Don't joke, Marion."

"I am deadly serious," he said. "Fifth hole? What hole? Clues on a golf course. How positively Sherlockian. That's your department, isn't it, Arnie? With Jayne's help, of course." He ate another deviled egg. "No one's safe?"

"I am sure it's just someone's idea of a joke," Fred said.

"Not my idea of a joke," Robin said. "And not very funny either."

"Will you go to the golf course tomorrow?" Noreen asked. Jayne and Arnie exchanged glances.

"Maybe," Jayne said, folding the note and putting it in her pants pocket. "But what golf course? And where on the fifth hole?"

"Big place, a golf course," Arnie said.

"You play a lot at Lake View, so why not there?" Marion asked. "You two play that course twice a week, don't you? And Jayne's dad taught her to play golf there when she was a little girl, right, Jaynie? Sometime during the Nixon administration?"

"No," Jayne said, biting into a chip with vigor, "I think it was sometime during the Civil War. Abraham Lincoln was our caddy."

"Touchè," Marion giggled. "You can't be that old, darling."

"You never know," Jayne said. "I might have a picture in the attic, like Dorian Gray."

"Who's he?" Ethel asked. "Another Scrabble player?"

"I think he's a character in a book," Nick said. "A man who sold his soul to the devil for eternal beauty."

"Kind of like you, right, Marion?" Noreen was smiling but it did not reach her eyes.

"Pussy cat found her claws?" Marion replied, not smiling. Jayne felt the air crackle with tension.

"You must write down the title for me, Jayne," Ethel said, oblivious of her literary faux pas. "I must look for it in the library."

"Good idea," Fred said. "Let's change the subject."

"Back to the note," Marion demanded. "This is thrilling. Like a scavenger hunt at a party. Golf course clues, menacing warnings—one of us has a hidden secret? Or all of us—don't we, darlings?"

There was a silence as eight faces did a quick scan of each other.

"Well? Don't we?" Marion drained his glass and picked up another egg on the plate and popped it into his mouth.

"I don't know what you mean," Ethel said. "We haven't any secrets, do we, Fred?"

"None at all. What the—?"

A red-faced Marion clutched his throat. "Ahhhh, can't breathe, can't—"

He coughed violently. He staggered across the room, making terrifying gurgling and choking noises. He plowed into one of the tables, causing a waterfall of Scrabble tiles. Crashing into the piano, sheet music flying in the air, Marion sank to the floor, both hands clasping his neck in terror. He scissor-kicked his legs and his body rocked in spasms.

Everyone stared. Time stood still. Lucia jumped out of her dog bed, barking and growling.

"Help him," Noreen shouted, "he's choking!"

Nick and Arnie rushed over, attempting to lift Marion to try the Heimlich maneuver. Nick put his hands under Marion's armpits, Arnie pulled his legs around in an attempt to lift him. Marion's eyes fluttered. He stopped coughing and he lay still.

"Marion!" Nick said. "Wake up!" He nervously patted Marion's cheeks and rubbed his wrists. Arnie leaned over and checked his pulse at the base of his neck. She looked at Jayne meaningfully as she started CPR on Marion's chest. After two minutes, she stopped.

"It's too late," Arnie said quietly. "He's dead."

CHAPTER FOUR

Defibrillator—19 Points

With shaking hands, Jayne dialed 911. "One of my friends has had a heart attack. I think he's dead." She gave her name and address and ended the call.

Within five minutes, her home was crowded with two police officers, two paramedics and three firefighters. Marion's body, lying on the sculpted geometric wool rug, was surrounded by uniformed officers, an oxygen tank, and a defibrillator. Everyone stared at his inert body. Ethel was weeping as Fred cradled her in his arms. Noreen and Nick stood in the kitchen area silently watching the attempt to save Marion's life. Arnie looked hopeful, as if waiting for Marion to utter another wisecrack. Jayne picked up Lucia and tried to calm her down. The paramedics shook their heads. Marion Wayne was truly dead.

Robin sat at the piano staring out the window at the lights across the river. With one hand, he picked out Chopin's Funeral March. He seemed detached from reality. The ponderous melody filled the room. They all turned to stare at him.

Jayne put her hand on his shoulder. "Robin, my dear, will you stop?"

He raised his head and shivered. "What did you say?" His skin had paled to an unhealthy translucency, his light gray eyes were narrowed, like death had stolen some of his sight.

"Can we get some help here," Jayne called out. "I think he's in shock. That's his husband on the…" She couldn't say it, so she just pleaded with her eyes.

A paramedic approached Robin. "Come on, my friend," she said. "Can you walk with me?"

A young police officer was talking into a radio. His partner, an equally young female, stood at attention. "We need to clear the area," he said. "Is there a place where you can sit and wait for a while?"

"Second floor," Jayne said automatically. "Lounge and meeting rooms."

They were escorted out of the condo by one police officer and one paramedic. Jayne, Arnie, and Robin, who was wrapped in a heavy gray blanket and walking like a zombie, rode down in one elevator with the paramedic who said her name was Gwen. Nick, Noreen, Fred, and Ethel and the young cop Melendez rode down in another. The lounge was empty at nine p.m. It was a very comfortable space with a fireplace, large-screen TV, fish tank and tall ficus plants in ceramic pots. A coffee machine with espresso, cappuccino and hot chocolate stood next to a vending machine with snacks and personal items. They spread out on different chairs and waited.

Jayne sat on a swivel chair and slowly turned around and around, holding Lucia in her arms. The little dog growled softly. "She doesn't like strangers very much," she said to the officer. A building custodian checked the conference room door and adjusted the lights and temperature. Jayne stopped spinning and studied the faces of her six fellow Scrabble players.

Robin, wrapped in the blanket and staring into space, was listening to the young paramedic. Her blond ponytail and sweet, pretty face belonged on the cover of a romance novel. She spoke to him gently. He looked shell-shocked and totally unaware of his location. Jayne would have preferred some reaction—tears, disbelief, anger?

Arnie bought them all drinks from the coffee machine. Jayne took a sip of espresso and shuddered. It was black and bitter and even two packets of sugar couldn't make it palatable. Noreen looked uncomfortable and Nick looked sad. Fred kept up a gentle stream of soothing comments to Ethel, who had not stopped crying.

"Was it a heart attack?" Noreen asked the group.

"He looked like he was in good health," Nick said.

"You can never tell by looking," Fred commented. "And he drank a bit."

"He did not drink!" Robin shouted and then sank back into a stupor. He looked wild-eyed and had paled even more noticeably. The paramedic, Eleanor, was talking into her radio. She attempted to give Robin oxygen, but he batted her hand away.

"Fred didn't mean anything by it," Ethel blubbered.

"I hope he doesn't faint," Jayne whispered to Arnie. "Or have a stroke."

"I know," Arnie said. "Come closer."

"What's the matter?" She rolled her chair over to her. "You look strange."

"Jayne," she said very quietly, "when I leaned over Marion to take his pulse, I swear I smelled bitter almonds."

"Bitter almonds? Cyanide? I thought that only happened in books."

"What else could it be? None of the food or drink had almonds in it, did it?"

Jayne thought about it. "No, not at all. I made nothing sweet. But there are the sidecars."

"There are no almonds in that drink. Only lemon juice and the cognac and some orange-flavored triple sec," Arnie said.

"The orange and lemon might have disguised the taste of the cyanide?"

"Maybe. But who could have doused his drink? And when?"

"That's a good question, my dear," Jayne said.

"And why? That's also important." She sipped her coffee.

After what seemed like hours, a man walked into the lounge.

"Take a look at that," Jayne whispered.

"He can't be real," Arnie said.

"He is," Jayne said. "A clone of Columbo," she whispered in awe.

"I am Detective Pericles Schultz," he said. "I am in charge of the investigation." He stuck his hand into a raincoat pocket, pulled out a cigar, put it back, and then pulled out a roll of antacids. As he popped a tablet in his mouth, Jayne's heart plummeted. She hoped to the heavens that Arnie hadn't really smelled cyanide. He looked at the seven people and nodded. He turned to the young cop. "Everything under control here?"

"Yes, sir, upstairs—"

"I've been up there," Schultz said. He cleared his throat. "I know this is not a great time, but I would like to ask you all some questions and then you can go home."

"Home?" Jayne whispered to Arnie. Her eyes briefly filled with tears. "I can see Marion lying there on the floor."

"You can come home with me," Arnie said, "and the pup, of course." Lucia growled.

Detective Schultz glanced at Jayne and Arnie. His face revealed nothing. "Let's start, okay? We can go in here." He nodded at the police officer, whose name was Wilson. "You can come in with me. Melendez, you sit here with these good people. Ma'am"—he nodded at Noreen—"can we start with you?"

Wilson walked into the conference room. The paramedic sat with Robin, talking quietly, and the rest of them looked at each other with part disbelief, part suspicion. Schultz followed Noreen into the room.

The glass walls and door offered some privacy. "Body language can give so much away," Jayne said, looking at the stiff, unsmiling face of Noreen. "I wonder why she's so angry."

"She likes to be in control?"

"She's a very busy woman," Nick said, overhearing them. "And believe it or not, she gets nervous easily."

"That I have a hard time believing," Fred disagreed. "She always looks so capable."

"Even capable people have nerves," Nick said.

Robin seemed to emerge from his shocked reverie. "What's going on?"

"We're each going to answer a few questions and then we can all go home," Jayne said. "Robin, can we call your sister to come and get you?"

He looked at her. "Sister?"

"He has a sister?" Fred asked.

"In the suburbs. I have her number. I'm going to call her." She stood up and took her phone out of her pocket. "May I?" she asked the young officer Melendez who nodded, but Jayne had intended to call regardless of her answer. Jayne moved to a corner of the room and made the call.

Inside the meeting room, Pericles Schultz eyed Noreen Charles. "So, can you tell me anything about what happened tonight to your friend?"

"Happened? How can I tell you anything?" Noreen kept pulling at the cuffs of her crisp white blouse. Neither looked wilted. "We were playing Scrabble and eating food and drinking cocktails, although I would prefer a nice Bordeaux or ale, and then all of a sudden Marion rose up and started choking. He turned red and fell on the floor."

"What did you do when this was happening?"

"Do? We all screamed or said what the…or something… and stood staring."

"No one helped him?"

"Arnie and Fred tried to straighten Marion so they could stop him from choking, but then he lay still. Arnie started chest compressions but he was already dead. I could see that." Noreen grimaced. "It was horrible and happened so quickly."

"What was Mr. Wayne doing prior to his attack?"

"Doing?" She laughed. "Stuffing his face with eggs and slurping cocktails."

"You didn't like him very much, did you?" Schultz murmured, as he unwrapped more antacids.

"He was outrageous, rude at times—most times—and liked to tease people about their looks, age, and anything else that struck his fancy. I didn't dislike him, not really. I hardly knew him except when we played Scrabble, but sometimes he crossed the line."

"I see." Schultz nodded. "So, he won't be missed?"

"His husband will be—is—devastated. Haven't you looked?" She tapped manicured nails on the table impatiently. "Are we done here?"

"Yes, thank you, please wait outside, and then you can leave."

"Wait for what?"

"We need your contact information. And in the case of a sudden death, we ask that you stay available for questioning."

"Sudden? Or do you mean suspicious? What the hell happened?"

"Please, Miss, Ms., Mrs. Charles, we're working on the cause of death."

"Ms. Charles to you." She stood up with a sullen look. "You are being mysterious and obtuse."

"Goes with the job," he shrugged. He walked her to the door and surveyed the faces of the tired people.

Noreen stormed out and threw herself into a chair. "We'll never get out of here," she snapped. They think Marion was murdered!"

Pandemonium followed. Ethel rose and screamed, Fred reached for Ethel, Nick dropped his coffee on the floor, splattering the police officer, Arnie reached for Jayne's hand, and Robin stood up quickly, making a keening sound that raised the hairs on Jayne's neck. Then he fainted dead away. His head hit the tiled floor with a crack.

"Damn it," Nick shouted in disgust. "Can't you keep your mouth shut, Noreen?"

"Is he dead, too?" Ethel wailed and flapped her sparkly hands.

Jayne and Arnie rushed over to Robin. The paramedic was talking into her radio while she cradled his head. His eyes were open but there was blood on his scalp and he was losing consciousness. "I didn't do it," he moaned to Jayne and then passed out.

More radio calls, more paramedics and firefighters, and this time, Robin was put on a stretcher to be taken to the emergency room at Northwest Hospital, six blocks away. Jayne immediately called Robin's sister to give her the new destination. She felt like Alice falling down the rabbit hole in Wonderland. The night was getting worse by the minute, and there seemed to be no end to the madness.

"How come you have Robin's sister's number?" Arnie asked her.

"Robin gave it to me. He thought she might want to play Scrabble with us, but when I called her, she said she wasn't into board games." Jayne shrugged. "I'm glad I kept it."

Schultz came out of the room, surveyed Robin being taken out on a stretcher, oxygen attached to his pale, bloodied face, and looked at them all. "I guess Ms. Charles shared her speculations with you all," he said.

"Why didn't you tell us before?" Nick demanded.

"Tell you what, sir?"

"That Marion was murdered."

"I never said he was. Your friend jumped to an unestablished conclusion."

"Well, can't you get on with this?" Jayne had never seen Nick so emotional. "Before we all get carried out of here?"

"Come in, please," he said, extending his hand to Nick. "Then you can leave with your...friend." Nick stormed into the meeting room.

Schultz shut the door and Wilson took out his notebook. "Name, please?"

"Nick Pappas, 2346 N. Alta Vista Terrace," he said.

"Thank you, Mr. Pappas," Schultz said as Wilson wrote it down. "Nice street. Historic homes as I recall. You are friends with Ms. Charles?"

"We live together," he said.

Schultz nodded and took a peppermint out of his pocket. "How well did you know the deceased?"

"We met him a year ago when Jayne started the Scrabble meet-ups at her place," he said. "We get together usually twice a month to play and eat and drink."

"Wild Scrabble parties?"

"Something like that," Nick said.

"You're a big fan of Scrabble, I guess."

"I actually don't care that much one way or the other, but Noreen thought it would be good for us to have some shared activities, and she thought it would be good for my mind since I don't play bridge or chess."

"And has it been good for your mind?"

He shrugged. "I guess so."

"You need help with your mind?"

"I am a personal trainer and gym owner so everyone assumes I don't know the alphabet," Nick said. "So, Noreen and I decided to try more cerebral pursuits."

"Like Scrabble?" Schultz said.

"Exactly."

"Now, can you tell me what you were doing around the time of the incident?"

"Incident? Who the hell can remember?" Nick's face reddened. "We were eating and drinking and then all of a sudden Marion started to scream and make these horrible noises."

"Where were you?"

"Sitting, I think."

"You didn't get up to get food?" Schultz unwrapped another mint.

"Maybe, probably, I don't remember. Robin was playing the piano, Fred was dancing, the dog was roaming around looking for treats…that's all I remember."

"Anything else happen that was different or unusual from other nights?"

Nick frowned in thought. "Nothing really. Oh yeah, there was that strange poem Jayne read to us."

"Poem?" Schultz sat up straighter. "What poem?"

"Some strange thing she got in the mail, she said. It was about Scrabble and golf and a team killer. I forget exactly what it said."

"And what did everyone do after the poem was read?"

"Ethel screamed as usual, Robin asked to see it, Marion made some jokes about secret lovers or something equally stupid. I can't remember exactly."

Schultz and Wilson exchanged a glance. "Was Ms. Charles in the room when the poem was read?"

"We all were." Nick shrugged. "Some of us eating and drinking and just hanging out."

Schultz looked at the young man intently. "Okay, that's it for now. Thank you. We'll come around tomorrow to see if you and Miss—Ms.—Charles—remember anything more."

"We both have to work tomorrow."

Schultz smiled. "We'll find you, no worries."

"The long arm of the law?" Nick wasn't smiling.

"Something like that."

Nick left and Schultz turned to Wilson. "This is going to be a long week with these people. Very touchy, they are, and I don't think they liked the deceased very much. And I have two years to retirement." He ran his hands through his shaggy, brown hair.

"Do you think it was a heart attack?"

"Maybe." Schultz shrugged. "But he did look funny. His skin was a strange color. Maybe one of this group slipped something into his drink. We have his glass and his plate of food. It will be tested. The toxicology report will confirm if he was poisoned. Or not." He sighed. "He did have the look of a man surprised by the kiss of death. I wonder why Ms. Charles didn't mention the poem."

"She forgot?"

"That dame doesn't look like she would forget anything," Schultz said, shaking his head. "Okay. On to the next one."

Fred and Ethel sat huddled together, chairs pushed close together. Tears were flowing in her eyes. "It's all right, Ethel dear," Fred said, and rubbed her back. "Here, let me wipe your face." He dabbed at the blue streaks of mascara running over her rosy rouged cheeks. "Can we get on with this, please?"

"Did you notice anything odd tonight before Mr. Wayne started to cough in distress?" Schultz asked.

Fred looked at Ethel. She shook her head no and blew her nose. "I can't tell you anything, Detective," he said. "We played, we ate and drank, made small talk, nothing out of the ordinary."

"How did the deceased act?"

Fred opened his mouth, but Ethel cut in vehemently, "He was terrible as always! Saying the most outrageous things to us all." She burst into tears. "He could be so mean!"

"Now, Ethel dear, he wasn't that bad."

"He was awful," she wailed. "Always making jokes about my clothes and pies and the way we talked. Like we were hillbillies. And then he would make those nasty comments about you being a mortician and your tap dancing." She looked at Wilson. "You getting this all down?"

"Yes, ma'am," he said, choking back a laugh.

"He would pick on Noreen and Nick because she's older than he is and has more money. He would joke about Jayne and her name and being *friends* with Arnie. And he made fun of Arnie being a private detective. Would call her Sherlock in the most odious way." She pulled another lace hanky out of her pocket and wiped her face.

"Thank you, ma'am, for a very complete character sketch." Schultz sucked on a mint and tapped his fingers on the table. "Besides all the smart remarks, can you think of any reason why someone would want to hurt Mr. Wayne? Money problems? Love affair gone wrong?"

"Oh no," Ethel said, "they were happily married."

"More or less," Fred put in.

"Yes, there was a bandage on his hand," Schultz said. "What happened?"

They both sat there silently.

"Robin stabbed Marion in the hand with a pencil last time at Scrabble," Ethel said, "but he didn't mean it! Marion was acting so mean and talking crazy to Robin."

"So, he stabbed him?" Schultz asked.

"He couldn't spell rutabaga. I think he spelled it wrong on purpose so they would lose the game. And he stuck out his tongue at Robin and Robin tapped him with the pencil." Ethel said.

"Tapped? He was still wearing a bandage," Schultz said.

"Marion has very delicate skin," Ethel explained.

"Robin is a very nice man, don't get us wrong," Fred said. "He did our taxes this year for practically nothing. Remember, Ethel?" She nodded, still wiping away tears. "But he could get mad playing Scrabble. Not furious, but a slow burn, like a hot plate warming up. And so, a week ago—"

"No, two," Ethel sniffled.

"What?" Fred looked at his wife.

"It was two weeks ago, Fred, we play every two weeks."

"Okay, okay, it was two weeks ago," he said, throwing up his hands. "Two weeks ago, we were playing at Jayne's and Robin got mad at Marion. And I don't blame him."

"Jayne Marple?" Schultz rearranged his coat. "You always play at her home?"

"Always," Fred said. "She's very nice to offer to host as she's in a central location. Nick and Noreen live on the north side in Lake View, Robin and Marion live in the south loop, I mean they used to live, I mean, Robin lives there now—"

"I understand," Schultz said. Ethel sniffled. Wilson kept writing.

"And we live in Beverly."

"Far south side of the city," Schultz cued Wilson. "Nice area."

"We love it," Fred said. "We both grew up on the south side. Ethel near the lake in South Shore and me near Gage Park, Fifty-fifth street."

"I grew up in Bridgeport," Schultz said. "Mayor Daley and all that." Three south siders smiled. "So, you play at Ms. Marple's place twice a month."

"Yes, and every time someone brings snacks and wine for the group," Ethel said.

"Who made the food this week?"

"Jayne did," Fred said. "And Arnie made the cocktails. It was a fifties theme."

"Fifties? Like T-birds and poodle skirts?" Wilson looked interested. "My grandma—"

"Yes, thank you, Wilson," Schultz cut in. "What kind of drinks did Ms. Palmer make?"

"Sidecars," Ethel said. "Something with oranges and lemons, isn't that right, Fred?"

"Cognac and triple sec and fruit juice." He shuddered. "But everyone liked them and Marion—"

"Marion, what?" Schultz asked and leaned closer.

"Can I have a mint?" Ethel asked. She had stopped crying.

"Of course." He pulled a handful of mints from his coat pocket and put them on the table. "Marion, what?"

"Tell him, Fred, everybody knows, it's no secret! Marion drank like a fish," Ethel said defiantly.

"He was guzzling faster than usual tonight," Fred agreed. "Arnie had to make another batch of drinks."

"She did? In the cocktail shaker that was on the bar?"

"Yes, she made one batch when we arrived and then made another after an hour when it wasn't her turn," Fred said. "You don't think there was anything wrong with the drinks?"

"Drinks?" Ethel gasped. "We all had some!"

"Except me," Fred said. "I only drink beer."

"Then, was there something in the cocktail shaker?" Ethel sucked on a mint and dabbed her moist eyelids.

"Not so, my pet. If someone had put something in the cocktail shaker, then you all would be sick or dead, not just Marion."

Ethel broke into a fresh torrent of tears. "Oh, Fred, don't talk like that! It's so horrible when you put it like that. Marion had a heart attack. And that stupid poem Jayne read didn't help at all."

"What poem?" Schultz and Wilson exchanged glances.

"Jayne got a poem in the mail today. Something about Scrabble team killers and a golf course. It was very strange," Fred said.

"How did everyone react?" Schultz asked.

"We talked about it being weird, and no one knew anything about it, and then she put it away. Marion made some funny remarks about it, at least he thought it was funny," Fred said. "And then we moved on. Then Marion had his seizure."

"It probably caused Marion to have a heart attack!" Ethel blew her nose violently and stood up, a shimmering, rhinestone wearing, outraged senior citizen. "I watch crime shows. They can't keep us here all night, Fred! I want to go home!"

CHAPTER FIVE

Subterfuge—16 Points

The residents' lounge was cleared except for Arnie and Jayne. The paramedics had left, the extra cop had gone back upstairs, and the firefighters had disappeared with no puff of smoke. Jayne watched Nick and Noreen stomp off. She had tried to be supportive as Fred escorted a dazed Ethel down the stairs to the lobby, and she hoped Robin was at the hospital getting treatment. She looked at Arnie, Arnie looked at her.

"Jayne," Arnie said, "what are you going to tell the police about the poem?"

Her eyes widened. "Arnie, my love, I've got a great idea. Let's tell them nothing."

"Nothing? How can we not?"

"Let's you and me solve the crime! Think about all the good publicity the detective agency would get. We could make the news and the newspapers. It would be fantastic."

"Jayne, this is a real murder investigation, not some irate husband trying to scare his wife like last night. We have to tell them. And how do we know that one of the others didn't mention the poem?"

She frowned and thought. Lucia stirred in her lap. She patted the little dog's head. "We don't know that they did or didn't. Let's say nothing and see what happens."

"Withholding evidence?"

"Evidence of what? It came to us in the mail, not to Marion. I'm not going to mention it."

"I admire your nerve and stubbornness," Arnie said. "But I feel I got you into this mess and we should be honest with the detective."

"How so? What mess?"

"I got the private investigator's license. I encouraged you to join me. And I talked nonstop about the agency to anyone who would listen. Someone is challenging us."

"English teachers think too much," Jayne said. "But I appreciate your protection. Let's hope I don't need it."

Schultz opened the conference room door. "Okay, you two, could you please come in here?" They stretched a bit, walked in, and sat down. Jayne arranged the little dog in her lap. Lucia sniffed, growled once and went to sleep. "Nice to meet you, finally," Schultz said, unwrapping another mint. "I heard quite a lot about you from Vanessa Harding."

"You know her?" Jayne asked.

"Yes, I was assigned to her case last night, when she said someone broke in and tried to kill her. She thinks it was one of her ex-husbands. We're trying to track them all down. She told me she'd hired her own private detective. She was quite proud of it. I've been meaning to call you, Ms. Palmer, but I got tied up with other things."

"Nice to meet you," Arnie said. "We seem to have a few things in common."

"Yes, attempted murder and a possible real murder."

"So, you think he was murdered?" Jayne demanded.

"Doesn't look like a natural death, but don't quote me," Schultz said. "I want to wait for the autopsy before I share it with your friends." He put his hand in his pocket, took out the cigar, looked at it with regret, put it back in his pocket and pulled out a roll of LifeSavers. "I'm trying to quit smoking," he said, "and it's killing me." He looked at Arnie. "So how did it go with your client today?"

"She was very upset, naturally, after her ex invaded her home, if it really was her ex," Arnie said. "We upgraded and redid her home security system."

"Good idea," Schultz agreed.

"Did you find the husband?" Jayne asked.

Schultz sucked on a mint. "I am not at liberty to say."

"Really? You're kidding me." Jayne ran her hands through her platinum spikes in frustration.

Arnie squeezed her arm. "He really can't tell us."

"Then, we aren't going to tell you either," Jayne retorted. "Whether we found David Harding or not."

"Now that we've got that settled," Schultz sighed, "can we please get on with this? I don't want to be here all night."

Jayne opened her mouth to protest. "Jayne," Arnie stopped her.

"Okay, ask away," she said, slumping down in the club chair. Lucia opened an eye and then went back to sleep.

"You were friends with Marion Wayne?" Wilson had his pen poised over his notepad. Jayne choked a laugh into a cough. "Something funny?"

"Just the absurdity of this situation," she said. "I love your raincoat."

"Thanks. Were you friends with Marion Wayne?"

"Yes," said Arnie.

"No," said Jayne.

"Which is it?" Schultz asked. He looked tired. A streak of gray in his hair caught the light.

"We were only Scrabble-playing friends," Jayne said. "We did not socialize outside of our bimonthly games."

"Yes, that's right," Arnie agreed. "That's what I meant by friends. We played Scrabble together. And I only met him six months ago."

"Oh? I thought this group met up a year ago."

"I am the newest member," Arnie said. "I found this group on a social media page. Jayne posted a message looking for Scrabble players."

"Really into Scrabble, huh?"

"My daughter, who lives in California, thought it would be a good way for me to make some new friends," Arnie said. "I lost my wife five years ago to cancer and Tina, my daughter, thought it would be good for me to get out more." She looked at Jayne and smiled. Jayne squeezed her hand.

"I see," Schultz said. "Sorry about your wife."

"Thank you," Arnie said.

"So, you played Scrabble with Marion Wayne twice a month. You didn't know him outside of the games and what else? Did you know his husband outside of Scrabble?"

"Robin does my taxes," Jayne said. "He offered a discount for new clients last year and I thought, why not? He was so efficient and reasonable, I used him this year, too."

"Don't forget, Jayne, that Marion redecorated your living room," Arnie said.

"He did, did he? Spent a lot of time in your home?" Schultz asked. Wilson kept writing.

"I forgot about that." Jayne frowned. "Not a lot of time. He came over a few times to measure and show me paint samples, fabric swatches for the chairs and sofa, some pictures of rugs, and the art deco liquor cabinet. Then he contracted the painters for me."

"He didn't have a shop?"

"No, he made home visits and everything else was online. Less overhead, he used to say." Jayne shrugged. "It worked out for him."

"You were pleased with his work?"

"I know you heard he could be outrageous at times, but Marion was an excellent interior designer and most intuitive about discerning what his clients liked and needed. We got along fine."

"That's good to know," Schultz said. He stared at Jayne just a fraction longer than she liked.

"Are you implying that I killed him because I didn't like the color of my walls?" Her usually low, alto voice rose an octave in exasperation.

Schultz chuckled. "I knew you must have good lungs from being an ex-rock star," he said.

"You know that about me?"

"I saw the photographs on the walls," he said. "Must've been fun times. I would've liked to see you play with your band."

"As you're about twenty years younger than me, that would have been impossible," she said. "Unless your Boy Scout troop took you out to hear punk bands."

"He can see your band on YouTube," Arnie suggested.

Schultz's eyes lit up. "I'm going to check you out real soon."

"Can we go now?" Jayne said. "I'm tired and crabby and I don't want to say things I'll regret later."

"Almost done," Schultz said. "Did any of your Scrabble friends have a relationship with Marion or his husband outside of game night?"

"I don't know them that well," Arnie said. "Jayne? Do you know?"

"I know Robin did Fred's and Ethel's taxes this year," Jayne said. "You can check on that. I don't think Nick and Noreen saw either one of them outside of our games."

"Marion did work out with Nick a few times," Arnie added. "Remember Marion demonstrating leg lifts and squats for us?"

"Yes, he did. Most dramatically," she agreed.

"All right," Schultz said, "I have to mention this. It's kind of off the record, but your friends have some interesting names."

"How so?" Jayne asked, not making it easy for him.

"Fred and Ethel? You got to be kidding me."

"An amusing coincidence," Arnie agreed. "Fred and Ethel, friends and neighbors of Lucy and Desi."

"Amazing," Schultz said. "And Nick and Noreen Charles?"

"From *The Thin Man*," Arnie said happily. "But she was Nora Charles. And he's Nick Pappas."

"Close enough," Schultz said. "You understand any of this, Wilson?" The young officer shook his head emphatically no.

"And you two—"

"What about us two?" Jayne's dark eyes narrowed.

"Jayne Marple and Arnie Palmer, famous sleuth and famous golfer. It's too good to be made up."

"Truth is stranger than fiction," Jayne said. "Our parents had a sense of humor."

"You're telling me," Schultz agreed.

"Will there be a postmortem?" Arnie asked.

"Postmortem," Jayne mused. "I wonder if he was poisoned?"

"Sudden death, yes, there will be a postmortem," Schultz said. "Interesting that you mention poison, Ms. Marple. You were the one who made the snacks tonight, right? All by yourself?"

"Are you accusing me of putting poison in the food?" Jayne straightened up. Lucia growled.

"You mentioned it first," Schultz said, popping another mint. "If we find something in the food and drink that's being analyzed, you'll be the first to know."

Jayne opened her mouth. Arnie squeezed her hand. "Jayne," Arnie warned.

"I'm sure you'll run right over here," she fumed, feeling her face grow warm. "With handcuffs. I'm getting tired of these questions. Am I allowed back in my home?"

"I don't see why not," Schultz said as Jayne stood. "But first, don't you want to tell me about the poem you got in the mail that you read to everyone?"

Jayne sat down with a thump, avoiding Arnie's gaze. "What poem?" Jayne asked, looking down at Lucia in her arms.

"The one about murder and Scrabble and the golf course," Schultz said.

"Oh, that one," Jayne said. "It was really a haiku."

"Splitting hairs," Schultz murmured.

"Being precise," Jayne told her sleeping dog.

"How do you spell that?" Wilson asked.

"H-A-I-K-U," Schultz answered. "Good Scrabble word, isn't it? Japanese form of poetry, three lines, five syllables, then seven, then five. Did yours fit the bill?"

"Detective Schultz, you are a veritable wealth of information," Jayne said.

"I try," he said, and unwrapped another mint. "Not all cops are illiterate, as some might think. So, to reiterate, you received a poem, a haiku in the mail today?" She nodded. "Good timing. Then you read it and then told who—Arnie?"

"Yes." She nodded again.

"No, hon, you told me about it, and then I read it to us as you chopped onions, remember?" Arnie's sweet face was starting to get moist.

"Yes, that's right, you read it to us and then later Robin read it to everybody. And nobody admitted to knowing anything about it," she said.

"So, then what?" Schultz asked.

"What do you mean, then what?" Jayne asked.

"Jayne, don't be purposely obtuse," Arnie muttered.

"*Moi*? Obtuse?"

Schultz exhaled. "Let's try this again. What happened when you took the note out to read it?"

"It was in your knitting basket, remember?" Arnie asked.

"You knit?" Schultz said.

"Yes, since I was a little girl." She paused and chewed her lip. "Now I remember what happened. I talked about it, Robin read it to us, Noreen took it from him to look at it, Ethel looked unhappy, Fred was eating, Nick looked thoughtful, and Marion made some wild remarks. He was enjoying the drama of the moment. Marion always enjoyed drama."

"You have a very good memory, Ms. Marple," Schultz said.

"Yes, just like my namesake," she retorted.

"Robin York read it. Any reaction from him?"

"No, none. He just looked it over. Then he handed it to Noreen, as I recall."

"What were you doing during this haiku discussion?" Schultz asked Arnie.

"I think I was pouring more drinks," Arnie said. "Yes, that's right. I had just fixed up another batch of sidecars."

"Sidecars? Haven't heard of that drink in a long time," Schultz mused. "Like a martini or a Tom Collins."

"Yes, we had a fifties theme," Arnie said. "It changes every time we meet up. This time Jayne made salmon mousse and dips and deviled eggs and marinated bacon-wrapped water chestnuts."

"Rumaki, I believe that's called," Schultz said.

"Detective, you absolutely astound me with your wealth of knowledge," Jayne said.

"My grandparents liked to go to Trader Vic's back in the fifties. Polynesian food and drink." He shuddered, and his raincoat rustled. "Rum and fresh coconut cocktails, oh boy."

"Don't drink rum cocktails?" Jayne asked.

"Don't drink at all," Schultz said. "Gets in the way of the job."

"Very admirable," Arnie said.

Jayne sniffed and Lucia picked up her sleepy head and yipped twice.

"Where is the note now?" Schultz asked, suddenly still and rigid as a Jack Russell terrier at a mouse hole.

Jayne looked at Arnie and raised her eyebrows. Arnie looked at Jayne and wiped her brow with the kerchief.

"We can go upstairs with you and help you look if that helps," Schultz offered.

Jayne looked at her watch. "It's getting late," she said.

"Yes, it is," Schultz agreed. "So, are you going to give me the note or what?"

Jayne sighed and fumbled in her pocket. She produced the note and tossed it on the table. "Here, take it."

"Thank you." He put on latex gloves, picked it up, unfolded it and read aloud. "'Scrabble team killer. Check out the fifth hole Friday. No one is safe here.' Succinct and to the point." He pulled an ear and looked at Jayne. "What fifth hole?"

"No idea," she said.

"You're a pro golfer?"

"I am."

"So, shouldn't you know what golf course the note is referring to?"

"I have no idea," she said, frowning.

"Neither do I," added Arnie. "But since we play a lot at Lake View...ow!"

"Problem?" Schultz asked, staring at Jayne's too-innocent face.

Arnie leaned over and rubbed her ankle. "None at all," she said.

"Lake View? You play often at Lake View? Nice course by the lake. You can hear the Cubs fans cheering on a windy day. So, what's with this fifth hole?"

"We have no idea," Jayne said.

"And are you going to be on the fifth hole tomorrow looking for clues?"

"Detective, I am going to be giving a golf lesson tomorrow and helping Arnie with her paperwork," she said. "Aren't I, Arnie?"

Arnie scrunched the bandana in her hands. "Oh yes, of course, we have a lot of paperwork to sort out with my new business."

Schultz eyed them both. "So, you say." He put the note in a plastic bag and handed it to Wilson.

"Hey, that's mine!" Jayne said, sticking out her hand.

"Not anymore," Schultz said. "It's the property of the Chicago Police Department."

Jayne glowered but Arnie nodded. "It's evidence, Jayne."

"Of what?"

"Being difficult?" Schultz was not amused. "Don't you two think it's suspicious that the day you get a strange note in the mail a friend of yours dies at the Scrabble table?"

"A strange coincidence," Jayne said. "Accidents can always happen. May I go back to my home now?"

Schultz looked them over. "Wilson, go radio upstairs and see if it's all clear."

"Yes, sir," said the young officer as he left the room.

Jayne, Arnie, and Schultz sat silently. Schultz blew out a breath. "Who would have thought it? Us all being involved with Vanessa Harding. Small world."

"Indeed," said Arnie.

"Indubitably," said Jayne. Lucia growled.

Schultz rubbed his chin. "Believe me, I like you guys, you know a lot of trivia, and you're a lot of laughs."

"Even in the middle of two ongoing investigations?" Jayne asked. "One the attempted murder of the femme fatale, Vanessa

Harding, and the other, the unexplained death of our Scrabble colleague?"

"I appreciate a little humor with my work," Schultz said. "How's the Elsinore Detective Agency coming along, Arnie?"

"Slow but sure. Perhaps one day I could pick your brain about how to find clients?"

Jayne expected a swift put-down. She was wrong. "Anytime, Arnie, call me. You've got my card."

Wilson poked his head in the room. "All clear," he said, nodding at Jayne and Arnie. "They're waiting for them to come back up."

"Thank goodness," Jayne said.

Arnie stuck out her hand. "Thanks for being so helpful." They exchanged a brisk handshake.

"I'll be in touch," Schultz said. "Don't go anywhere for a while, okay?"

Jayne did not offer her hand. "Are we under suspicion?"

"What do you think?"

Jayne and Arnie walked to the elevators, Lucia sleeping peacefully in her arms. "What do you mean, helpful?" she chided. "When was he helpful? He practically accused us all of murdering Marion and having deep, dark secrets in our lives. And he knows I made the food tonight."

"That's what the police do, act suspicious of everyone. He knows I made the cocktails. I think acting suspicious is part of police procedure."

Jayne sniffed in derision as they stepped into the elevator. She twisted her torso. "I am so stiff from sitting. Need yoga. And, Arnie, you have such a nice way of putting things. Police procedure, my eye."

Outside her door, an officer waited. "May we go in?" Jayne asked.

"All clear, ma'am," he said. He opened the door for them. "Good night. We're done here now."

"Thank goodness!" Jayne placed Lucia in her dog bed and sank down on the sofa. She exhaled. "What a night!"

"Would you like a cup of tea? And would you like me to stay over or would you like to come to my house?" Arnie asked.

Jayne made herself look at the Scrabble tables shoved to the side of the room. The tiles that had fallen to the floor during Marion's episode along with the fallen sheet music were stacked neatly on one of the tables, no sign that anything shocking had occurred this evening. Or deadly.

She sighed again. "No thanks, my dear, no tea. Let's turn in now. If you don't mind staying over. And I will set the alarm for four a.m."

"Why so early?"

"Arnie, dearest, if we are going to get to the golf course at five a.m., before it opens to look for clues, we're going to have to get up before the birds."

"So, we're going to the golf course?"

"How could we not go?"

Arnie stared at the other Scrabble table. She froze.

"What's up, Arnie?"

She pointed silently to the undisturbed board, tiles intact.

"Someone has a macabre sense of humor," Jayne said, looking at the board. "That word wasn't there before."

M-U-R-D-E-R.

"But it is now," Arnie said. "Jayne what have we gotten ourselves in for?"

CHAPTER SIX

Kale—8 Points

Five a.m.

Nick Pappas sat up in bed and stretched. He cracked his neck and spine. The sound ricocheted around the room. Behind the bamboo shades, the sun was peeping through. He poked his partner in the ribs. "Noreen, wake up, we've got to talk."

She groaned and rolled over. She pushed the ivory, down comforter away from her toned body. "What now, Nick? And no good morning?"

"Good morning." He jumped out of bed. "We've got to talk."

"Okay, I hear you. I'm up now."

"We're in a fine fix, my love," he said.

"Jeez, Nick, can't you wait until I'm awake?" She stomped off to the bathroom. He stumbled down the steps from the sleeping loft into their gourmet kitchen and pushed a button on the expensive coffee maker. Espresso for Noreen, chai tea with soy milk for him. He sat on a white leather and chrome stool at the granite kitchen island and held his head. "Coffee is almost ready," he called up to her.

Noreen came down wearing a short scarlet silk robe adorned with gold dragonflies that exposed shapely, tanned legs.

"What's the matter with you this morning? Why so grouchy?" He opened the refrigerator and took out a pitcher of dark green slime. "Want some?"

"How you can drink that slop before coffee is beyond me."

"Kale is good for you. Are you sick?"

"Nick…that awful food and those drinks last night. I have a food and drink hangover," she moaned. "And what do you mean, what's the matter with me this morning? Don't you remember Marion dying last night, right in front of us?"

"Of course, I remember, but what can we do about it? He's gone now. Why, did you have something to do with it?"

"What are you talking about? I didn't have anything to do with it. He had a heart attack."

"If you say so, darling."

"I think he ate and drank with wild abandon," she said, taking a sip of espresso.

"Maybe he had too many of those nasty drinks, and what the hell was in those cocktails?"

"Cognac and fruit juices and something orange flavored. I thought they were a bit sweet."

"You must have a cast-iron stomach. I'm glad I don't drink anymore," Nick said.

"I don't drink cocktails often." Nora grimaced, taking another sip of espresso. "But last night was a terrible exception. So, what's up? What do you have to talk to me about at this hour?"

"Thank you, darling." He squeezed her hand.

"For what?"

He sighed. "For being you, for believing in me and my business—and for not telling the police about our past run-ins with Marion."

She laughed, and in that moment, he saw the ruthless streak that had cut out some of her competitors. "Yes, who would've thought he would recognize you from your days as a male stripper? And how he would use it for free personal training sessions and massages."

"Damn YouTube and Instagram." He slammed his coffee mug down. "If word got out—"

"Do you think it would hurt your business? I think all those ladies who admire your muscles might be titillated to know that you used to accept money in your G-string."

Nick scowled. "It was humiliating. I don't want anyone to know. If I didn't have loans to pay off, I never would have done it."

"If you didn't owe, what was his name? Sharky Madrazzo. If you didn't owe on a gambling debt, you wouldn't have had to bust your buns."

"Are you sorry for me or what, Noreen?"

"I'm not sorry. It's a bit amusing, and now that he's dead—"

"Now that he's dead, I don't have to worry about him anymore? How about this?" He pulled out a note from his gym bag and tossed it to her.

"What's this, more poetry?"

"Not funny, Nor."

She put on her reading glasses and recited.

> I'M A DANCING QUEEN
> YOU ARE WHAT YOU EAT, RIGHT NICK?
> YOU WILL PAY UP SOON

"Pay up? Pay up, what? Did you get a note demanding money?"

"This is all I got so far," he said. "I wonder if Marion mailed it before he died?"

"Maybe Marion didn't mail this at all."

"Then somebody else knows about me. I wonder if he told Robin." He took a gulp of kale smoothie.

"Does it matter?" She yawned and stretched.

"You could show more concern."

"Why? This is just another prank letter like the one Jayne received."

"Marion died after Jayne got the note!" He slammed his glass down, a spray of green splattering the counter. "I don't want to be next!"

Noreen sighed. "I love the way your freckles stand out when you get upset." She held up graceful hands to stop another outburst. "If you're so upset about this note, why don't you call that police detective we met last night? Schwartz? Schultz? I've got his card somewhere in my purse."

"I can't call the police! Then they'll start asking questions that I don't want to answer."

"What are you going to do, darling?"

"Nothing right now." Nick crumpled up the note and threw it down in disgust. "I will wait this out. I refuse to be intimidated. I will stay calm."

"Good for you," she said. "I've got to get to the brewery soon. And don't you have to get to work?"

Nick grabbed Noreen and held her close. "We're going to get through this, babe," he groaned, kissing her neck.

"What do you mean, *we*?" She slid out of his arms. "Time to get your big boy pants on and deal with this. Mama can't take care of all your business for you, darling."

He watched her sensual body until the last silk dragonfly was out of sight.

"Bitch," he whispered. "Wait until *your* secret gets out."

CHAPTER SEVEN

Sapphire—15 Points

5:15 a.m.

"Only you, Jayne, would make me come out here on a wild goose chase so early in the morning," Arnie grumbled, as she sidestepped a pile of goose droppings.

"Arnie, I promised you a big omelet at Eggy's when this is all over," she whispered, looking to the right and left as she scrutinized the fifth fairway.

"Yes, that's all good," she answered, "but what are we looking for?" She sneezed. "Darn! This early morning dew is rough on my allergies. And why are you whispering? There's nobody around, although I think us sneaking in before the course opens is pushing it. What if we're spotted?"

"Sorry, honey," Jayne said. "I am whispering because you're making enough noise to rouse the dead. And I used to work here, remember? So, what trouble could we get into?"

"With you anything is possible. And what possible clue could be here?" Arnie tripped over a tree branch laying on the fairway.

"I don't know, but that's what the note said. If you were a clue, where would you be? I mean where's the best place to hide a secret?"

Arnie removed the bandana from her windbreaker and wiped her nose. "If I were hiding a clue, I would not fool around and I would put it in an obvious place."

"Like where?"

"Like right in the cup on the green."

Jayne looked down the fairway and focused on the flag, waving gently in the breeze. "Really? But that's so easy."

"Want to bet on it?"

"You're on. Winner buys breakfast."

Arnie took off for the green while Jayne looked under bushes and around tree trunks. She watched Arnie's bobbing Cubs cap as she approached the hole. She leaned over, removed the flag from the cup and reached in. She pulled out something and waved it overhead.

"Got it!" she yelled, and did a little victory dance around the hole.

"Damn it, she's right." Jayne jogged down the wet fairway to meet her.

In her hand, Arnie held an egg-shaped object with a note tied around it. "I know it's my detective agency but it was your murder," she said, bowing slightly.

"My murder?"

"Yep, and here's your clue."

She took out plastic gloves from her pocket and put them on.

"Good thinking, Jayne." Arnie looked embarrassed. "I should have thought of that."

She took the ball from Arnie's hand. It rattled suspiciously. She carefully removed the paper and looked at the ball. It was actually a plastic egg, the kind that splits open easily and can be filled with candy for a party.

"Strange, it's not a golf ball at all," she said. She carefully opened the paper.

"What does it say?"

"OMG, another haiku. Our murderer is a poet."

SCRABBLE A FUN GAME
SAPPHIRES A GIRL'S BEST FRIEND
MURDER IS QUICKER

"This is getting out of hand, Jayne," Arnie said. "We must go straight to the police."

She opened the egg, and something bright and glittery blue glowed in the morning dawn.

Arnie's blue eyes widened in shock. "Wow, it's a sapphire. Vanessa Harding said she was missing a sapphire stone. How could this stone…How can this stone—"

"Did she even tell the police what was missing? Is Marion's murder related to Vanessa? What is going on here?" Jayne held the stone to the light. "Your eyes are a prettier color, Arnie, and this sure is a mystery. Who are these people we play Scrabble with? We really don't know much about them."

"And I don't know anything about my client." Arnie chewed her lip. "Is she a tremendous liar?"

"She's a tremendous pain in the—"

"Our first real client, Jayne. We have to give her a chance. Perhaps she's not as untrustworthy as she appears."

"You're a very good detective, Arnie—and a wonderful lady. I would have given her the air the minute I saw those cigarettes and marabou feathers. And those skinny eyes when she squints at us. Blind as a bat." Jayne placed the sapphire back in the egg. "I guess we should go talk to Detective Schultz." She looked at the golf course and sighed.

"Do you think he's up? It's so early." Arnie checked her watch. "It's only 5:40."

"We're going to have breakfast first," Jayne said. "I owe you an omelet."

CHAPTER EIGHT

Coffin—14 Points

Ethel Woods sat at the retro '50s Formica kitchen table and clipped coupons. Neat little stacks of paper covered the bright, fruit-patterned vinyl tablecloth. "More coffee, Fred?"

"No thanks, Eth," he said, dunking biscotti into his cup.

"Are you still reading the obituaries?"

"Yes, you know I like to see what the business is up to these days." He folded the *Tribune* and opened the *Sun-Times*. "How are you feeling? You look pale, doll."

"I didn't sleep a wink last night," Ethel said, shaking her head. "The shock of watching Marion die—"

"It was terrible and we have to put it out of our minds," Fred said. "He had a heart attack or something and was taken suddenly."

"Do you think so? That policeman asked a lot of questions."

"Policemen always ask a lot of questions," he said. "They have to justify their pensions. Just routine. Ah, honey, listen to this," he mumbled through a mouth full of crumbs. "Joey DeVecchio passed. He was eighty-nine. I used to caddy for him when I was a kid."

"Where did he live?" Ethel arranged the stacks of paper. One for meats, one for produce, one for paper goods, and another for toiletries.

"South side, not far from where we grew up. He never left the old neighborhood."

"Who did his funeral?"

"Sullivan and Sons," he sniffed. "Not a bad outfit but—"

"Are they still cutting corners?" Ethel peered over her pink rhinestone encrusted reading glasses and looked at her spouse.

"Yes, and it makes me crazy! When we went to Bob Martin's wake, I could tell they were using the cheaper coffins."

"Something you never did, dear," Ethel said, patting his hand. "But there's nothing you can do about that, so try and stay calm. Not good for the heart."

"No, you're right, Eth," he said. "I'm out of the business now. Got to forget about it and work on my golf game."

"When is your next lesson with Jayne?"

"I hope this weekend, if the weather's good," he said. "I want to get in as much practice as possible before the snow flies and we take off for Florida."

"Florida," she mused. "It will be good to get away from here, won't it?"

"Yes, after last night it will be very good to get away. We need to forget. Give me the golf course and the pool—wonderful."

"I guess you're right," she said. "And I'm looking forward to Patricia and her family coming to visit. I never see them enough, now that they moved to Milwaukee. And Mother loves seeing the ocean."

"I know you miss them, but it was a good job offer for them, you know that." Fred stood up and stretched. "I'm going to water the geraniums outside and get the mail."

"Okay, dear," Ethel said, clipping away in coupon heaven. She threw away some outdated coupons, not used, but not forgotten. She looked up as Fred returned, watering can in one hand, a stack of mail in the other. He had a funny look on his face.

"What's the matter, Fred? Is something wrong?"

He dropped the can on the kitchen floor and pulled a cream-colored envelope out of the mail. "Here, read this," he said. "I shouldn't even show you this, Ethel, but we've never had secrets from each other."

"Fred, what are you talking about?" Ethel pushed her glasses up on her nose and opened the letter.

WHO IS IN THE GRAVE?
GRANDMA GOT LOST ON HER WAY
FRED NEEDS NEW GLASSES

"What? That was five years ago, that mix-up. Who would know about it now?" Her big baby-blue eyes widened in shock.

Fred sat down with a thump. "My reputation and good name could be ruined."

"But it was the coroner's fault. Everyone knows that. Mixing up..." Her voice dropped to a whisper. "...the bodies?"

"I can see that day like it was yesterday."

"One elderly lady resembles another," Ethel said.

"Still, when the family came in that morning to preview the body and saw it was the wrong woman..." He shuddered. "I'm shocked I wasn't ruined then."

"But you weren't," Ethel said. "The coroner took full responsibility and you didn't charge the family for your services, so it turned out all right."

"I think my heart trouble started that day," Fred said, not for the first time. "You don't get over something like that. And now, this." He took the poem and stuck it in his pocket. He looked at his strong hands that had tended to so many dead people with respect and care. "I wonder when it will start?"

"When what will start?"

"The blackmail, the demand for money."

"Money? We're not going to pay anybody money for a threat, are we? You did nothing wrong, Fred. It was all a big mistake!"

"I have to think about this."

"You should show that policeman, the one with the raincoat and the Tums."

"The police? Heck no, I don't want them to know my business."

"After Marion's death, my dear, and Jayne's letter, they are going to ask more questions."

"Not if I can help it," he said. "I think I'm going to call up Arnie. She's a licensed detective. Let's see what she thinks."

Fred picked up his cell and speed-dialed Arnie. "Arnie, do you have time to talk today? Where are you? Eggy's in the park? If I leave now, I can be there in twenty-five minutes. Wait for me? Sure, coffee would be great." He turned off the phone. "They're both having breakfast, so I'm going to meet them there."

"If you think that's wise." Ethel swept all the coupons into one big pile and sighed.

"Not going shopping?" Fred looked amazed.

"I'm not in the mood anymore."

"Want to come with me to visit Arnie and Jayne?"

"No, that's all right," she said. "I think I'll go join the ladies at Zumba today. And Mother is coming with me. It's her day for mahjong." Ethel stood, shook out her paisley caftan, and gave Fred a hug. "Don't worry, Fred. It's going to be all right. That's old news and who really cares anymore?"

"Somebody does," he said grimly. "I'll be back in a few hours, Ethel." He kissed the top of her head. "You be careful."

"Always," she said.

She watched him drive away. Then she cleared the table, putting the coffee cups in the dishwasher and brushing toast crumbs into the trash. The raspberry jam and low-fat margarine were placed into the immaculate refrigerator. She wiped down the table and hung up the dish towels on the chrome rack before walking into the living room and sitting down on one of the matching his and hers tan leather recliners. She sighed. From the pocket of her caftan, she pulled out a letter.

WHERE IS THAT BABY?
GOOD CATHOLIC GIRL, REALLY?
PRAYERS WON'T SAVE YOU NOW

Ethel began to weep.

CHAPTER NINE

Blackmail—19 Points

Arnie and Jayne talked over the remains of veggie omelets, blueberry pancakes and fried potatoes smothered in hot sauce. "I wonder what Fred has to tell us?" Jayne said.

"We're going to find out," Arnie said as Fred walked up to the table. "Good to see you, Fred." Arnie rose and shook his hand. "Coffee? Want to order some food?"

"Hey, Fred, how you doing?" Jayne peered up at him under her Illini cap, her alma mater and where her daughter had earned her master's in social work. "What brings you downtown so fast?"

Fred sat down, poured himself a cup of coffee and avoided her question. Jayne waited patiently while he opened three sugar substitute packets and carefully poured the contents into his brew. He looked at the cream pitcher. "I'm not supposed to have a lot of fat," he said. He looked crushed. "And after overindulging last night, black coffee it is."

Their server came over to the table. "Any food today, sir?"

"French toast." He closed the menu with a sigh. "That's light, right? I would love biscuits and gravy, but if Ethel found out, she'd kill me."

"Wise choice," Arnie said.

"Any news about Robin?" Fred asked.

"I spoke with his sister this morning. He's being released today from the hospital. He's got a slight concussion but nothing too serious," Jayne said.

"Thank goodness for that," Fred said. "Two deaths in one night would be unbelievable."

"I agree," said Arnie. "We're going to visit him today at the hospital."

"That's very kind of you." Fred took a sip of coffee. "He went through hell last night."

"How's Ethel doing?" Jayne asked. "I was worried about her. You left so quickly; I didn't get a chance to say goodbye."

"She'll make it, still a bit shook up as you can imagine, but she's going to Zumba today at the senior center. She likes to dance. It makes her happy," he said. "She's amazing."

"Got to work off all those amazing pies," Arnie said, smiling.

"Tell me about it," Fred said, patting his stomach. "I'm supposed to lose twenty pounds. Torture."

The server came with his food and again they waited while he put one pat of margarine and two teaspoons of syrup over his French toast. "I'm trying to be good," he explained.

"You're doing better than us," Jayne said, looking at the high-calorie leftovers on their plates.

"You two are in great shape," Fred said. "Jayne, you're an athlete and I doubt, Arnie, you were ever overweight."

"The Palmers were always a bit on the thin side," Arnie said. "So, what can we do for you, Fred?"

Jayne looked at Arnie with a smile. It was *we*, not *I*.

He coughed and looked embarrassed. "I got one."

"Got one?" Jayne asked. "Got what, Fred?"

"I got one of those crazy poem notes like you did last night, Jayne."

"You did?" Arnie put down her coffee cup with a clunk. "When?"

"This morning. It must have been in the mail last night, but I forgot to check it because we were busy getting ready for your Scrabble game. I went out to water the flowers, remembered the mail, and there it was."

"Do you have it with you?" Jayne asked.

"Yeah, I do. I don't really want to show it to you. It's a big mistake I made in the past, but it seems it's going to haunt me. I showed it to Ethel. She's not worried but I am." He dropped his head and covered his mouth with one hand. "Blackmail," he whispered.

"Can we see the note?" Arnie said.

Fred looked around him. The restaurant was half empty and no one was paying any attention to them. "All right," he said, and pulled out the envelope from his jacket pocket.

He handed it to Arnie, who opened it and then passed it to Jayne.

"What does this refer to, Fred?" Jayne asked. "Did something happen at your funeral home?"

Fred exploded, bits of French toast spewing the air. "It wasn't my fault! The damn coroner sent the wrong body!"

"It's okay, Fred, stay calm," Arnie said. "So, there was a mix-up at your place of business?"

"Five years ago. There was an accident. I was sent Mrs. Browne with an 'e' at the end of her last name instead of Mrs. Brown, no 'e'. I missed it completely. I was worried about my mother, who was declining from Alzheimer's. I totally screwed up. When the family came to view the body before the wake, the daughter fainted and the husband tried to punch me in the nose. It was the worst day of my life."

"I'm sure it wasn't all your fault, was it?" Jayne poured more coffee and watched him grip the cup with tense hands.

"The coroner's office took all the blame, but still...I should've caught it. I knew it was time to retire. I shouldn't have missed that error. I made reparations to the family as best I could, but I had to get out of the business." He took a sip of coffee, made a face, and put the cup down. "Needs cream." He opened a little cup of cream and then another and then another.

He stirred, and the black brew became beige. "Ah, that's better. Screw being healthy when my life is going down the drain."

"Fred, let's not get ahead of ourselves," Jayne admonished him. "Who do you think has any knowledge of this…mistake… and who would try to contact you about it in this strange way?"

"That's why I'm here," he said. "You got a note, and what does it mean and what are you doing about it?"

CHAPTER TEN

Boudoir—10 Points

Jayne, Arnie, and Lucia the pup, were all huddled together on the dove-colored leather sofa in her home. The sun was shining, the sparrows were happily eating seed from the feeders on the balcony, and all was right with the world. NOT.

"What are we going to do, Jayne?" Arnie wiped her face with a fresh handkerchief.

"Do? Don't ask me Arnie, I'm in a trance, induced by all those lovely carbs we had at breakfast."

"Now, Jayne, snap out of it!"

"All right, all right, I'm going to focus," she sighed. "It's a lovely day to play golf."

"Now, none of that," Arnie said. "What are we going to do with the note and the sapphire?"

"I thought you would get to that," she said, scratching her little dog's head.

"We should go see Detective Schultz."

"We should, we really should," she said. "Or, we could go see the Black Widow Spider and show her the sapphire."

Arnie looked doubtful. "Did she even report the missing jewelry?"

"I don't know. Schultz wouldn't say. He was being mysterious, like all coppers." She ran her fingers through her spiky hair in frustration. "And Madame Harding was being very vague and myopic. Can that woman even see across the room? She kept squinting at me."

"Dazzled by your beauty, I'm sure," Arnie said.

"Bull—"

"Now, now, let's be nice," she said.

"Why? It's boring to be nice," Jayne sniffed, and put her nose into Lucia's soft black fur. "Vanessa Harding isn't nice."

"No, she's not," Arnie agreed. "But I am sure she has some finer points."

"Maybe," she conceded, "but she's no Mother Teresa."

"No, she's not. But looks can be deceiving. Do you think going to see her is a good idea? Maybe I should just call her with an update."

"We need to look at her and listen to her," Jayne said. "We need to find out how Vanessa is related to any of our Scrabble playing friends. How did this sapphire get into the hole on the fifth green?" She held it up to the light. It glowed and the blue stone shimmered a rainbow across the floor-to-ceiling windows. "This rock has got to be the real thing. It's magnificent."

"It is pretty," Arnie agreed. "I'd like to get you a sapphire."

"Why, Arnie, you old sweetie." Jayne nudged her in the side. "How romantic."

"I would like to give you a token of my affection after all this…murder is resolved," she said, smiling. "You would look lovely with sapphires in your ears. The deep blue would make a beautiful contrast between your hair and your lovely complexion."

"Stop! You're embarrassing me! I'm not used to such admiration."

"You should be. You're a truly beautiful woman, Jayne, inside and out."

Jayne exhaled and continued scratching Lucia on the head. She leaned over and kissed Arnie square on the lips. "So, call her."

"Who?"

"Do my kisses drive all rational thought out of your head? The antique femme fatale, Vanessa Harding."

"Oh, her." Arnie smiled. "Okay, I'll call her."

"Good, and I'm coming with you."

When they rang the bell at the Astor Street townhouse, a petite woman with auburn, upswept hair and startling green eyes opened the door. She was wearing an expensive-looking silk dress with a full swishy skirt that rustled seductively when she moved.

"Yes? Can I help you?" She spoke in a soft, silvery voice with an exotic accent that Jayne could not place.

"Good morning," Arnie said. "We have an appointment with Mrs. Harding."

The woman looked them up and down. "Names, please?"

"Arnie Palmer and Jayne Marple."

The woman did not blink. "I am Tanya, Mrs. Harding's personal assistant. Step inside, please."

She ushered them into the hallway and had them wait next to the armoire, the one where Jayne had seen the pink gun. She wanted to see if the gun was still there and started opening drawers.

"What are you doing? Stop that!"

"I'm looking for something. Hold your horses," Jayne said, and kept pulling out drawers. "Got it!" She pulled out the pink .38 Special with a triumphant flourish.

"Put that back!" Arnie hissed in horror.

They smelled the assistant's perfume and heard her skirt before they spotted her. Jayne stuffed the gun in her backpack and assumed an innocent look.

"Come this way, please," Tanya said, and they followed, enveloped in a waft of musky perfume. Jayne her head held high and ignored Arnie, although she was totally aware of the gun stuck in her backpack. It felt as heavy as a brick.

They arrived at the boudoir door. Tanya rapped softly. "Mrs. Harding, your guests are here." She tapped again. "Mrs. Harding?"

"All right, okay, I'm ready, bring them in," said the husky voice, followed by a bout of coughing.

When they walked in, Jayne blinked at the pinkness of the woman and the room. Pink satin walls, pink rococo lamps with gilded cupids, pink silk bedspread and curtains and a pink negligee dripping with hot pink marabou feathers. Wasn't that an endangered species? Jayne made a mental note to look that up. She was sure she saw Vanessa stuffing a pair of pink eyeglasses behind her heart-shaped satin pillow. Didn't the woman ever get out of bed?

"Arnie, how nice to see you again," she cooed, ignoring Jayne. Her full lips were painted hot pink and her cheekbones sparkled with pink glitter. Long pink diamond earrings dangled from her ears, almost colliding with her feathered-encircled neck. The diamond pendant lay between her breasts, sparkling. "Will you have some tea?"

Jayne rolled her eyes. *Oh brother, tea? Was she the Queen?*

Vanessa gave her a foul look. "And, Judy, how interesting to see you again. I know Arnie needs a good secretary."

Jayne opened her mouth to blast her but Arnie intervened. "Good to see you, Vanessa. No thank you, we won't have tea, we don't want to intrude on your…rest."

They stared at the bed covered in boxes of chocolate, packs of menthol cigarettes, silk pashminas, and underneath it all, Tutu the Pomeranian.

"No tea," Vanessa snapped at Tanya. "You can leave us."

"How are you feeling after your ordeal, dear lady?" Arnie asked.

She unbent a little and smiled—crocodile teeth, Jayne thought.

"I was a bit put out that you didn't come and see me earlier, Arnie, but I read that Jayne had an incident at her home last night."

"What incident?" Jayne said. "Nothing was in the papers."

"I follow that neighborhood website for downtown crime and news," she said. "I read that a strange death occurred in your building, Jayne, and I assumed it had to be you."

"How do you know it was my building?" Jayne asked.

She pulled out a gold tablet from under a mound of scarves. "I white-paged you and Arnie to see where you lived—and if you lived together." She raised her eyebrows at them and smirked. "I see that you don't." Jayne opened her mouth to speak but Vanessa continued, "You see, Janet dear, you are not the only one with detective skills." She broke into a wheezy laugh. "So, Arnie darling, you are unattached." She leaned forward in bed, her diaphanous ruffled negligee falling open, exposing a large expanse of white bosom. Arnie blushed.

"I'm confused, Mrs. Harding," Jayne blurted out, "are you gay, bi, or what?"

Arnie gasped; Vanessa chuckled. "I have been known to swing both ways," she said, "So, you see, Jill dear, I am most attracted to Arnie." She smiled again, her fake white veneers gleaming. "Don't look so upset, Arnie, I am most amused by Joan's jealously."

Jayne opened her mouth to blast the diva, but Arnie spoke first. "Mrs. Harding, we must focus on the matter at hand," Arnie said, wiping her brow. She shot Jayne a warning look. "I'm afraid your personal safety is being threatened."

The diva pouted and put down a box of candy. "If you say so, but you must call me Vanessa."

"Vanessa," Arnie said, "did you find the list of your jewelry?"

She spat out a chocolate into a tissue. "Ooh, yuk, cherry." She shrieked, "TANYA!"

The chic assistant appeared at the door. "Yes, Mrs. Harding? Did you need something?"

Jayne could not place the accent. Russian? Swedish? Italy with a layover in Brooklyn?

"Did you find that list of jewelry that I was supposed to give to the police?"

"Yes, Mrs. Harding." Tanya walked over to the white desk and pulled out a long envelope. "Here it is. The list was here all the time."

"Give it to Ms. Palmer," she cooed. "I'm bored with this already. And mix up a shaker of martinis, will you?"

Tanya handed the envelope to Arnie. "Yes, Mrs. Harding," she said and exited the room.

How does she do that silent thing, Jayne wondered, while wearing stiletto heels? A feat Jayne, at six feet tall, had never mastered. She always wore flats, mostly for balance and because she got tired of being taller than most people she met.

Arnie looked at the list of jewelry. "So, you reached out to the insurance company today?"

"Oh, Arnie," Vanessa sighed, lighting up another cigarette. "I forgot. Could you pwease do it for wittle ole me?"

"I will," she said. "What insurance company?"

She blew a smoke ring up to the crystal chandelier. Jayne felt nauseated; she hated cigarette smoke. She started to cough ominously. Arnie shot her a *be careful* glance. Jayne gave her back a *hell no* look.

"You know, Arnie dear, I'm not sure I ever got that insurance policy. I think my ex-husband was supposed to do that a long time ago."

Jayne couldn't believe this drivel. "Which ex-husband?"

"Why, Judy dear, how can I remember? One of them was supposed to. It wasn't Edwin, my first, he was an attorney, or Theodore, my second—he owned a nightclub, oh he was a bastard, let me tell you, he cut up all my credit cards. I suppose it was my husband David…or was it Donald?"

"You really can't remember which twin was your last husband?" Jayne was ready to slug her.

"Well, they looked alike and their names were so close. David or Donald, does it matter? One of them was supposed to take care of my business. They both had a good head for figures."

"Literally and figuratively," Arnie said, with a smile.

"Why, Arnie, you bad girl!" Vanessa preened and smirked. Jayne wanted to barf and glared at Arnie. Arnie took a step away from Jayne.

"So, there is no insurance on your jewelry and you never gave the police a list," Arnie said. She looked worried, Jayne thought. Serves her right.

"That is correct," Vanessa sighed. "Too many details. And look"—she pushed away her hair from her neck—"I still have marks from where he tried to strangle me, that monster, whoever he was."

"He didn't try hard enough," Jayne muttered.

"What did you say, Janet?"

"I said it's a shame he was so rough."

"Yes, well," Arnie cut in, "we have some news for you, Vanessa. Guess where we were this morning? The golf course! And you will never guess what we found." She opened the briefcase but Jayne stepped in and grabbed the bag.

"Your work phone is ringing, Arnie!"

"I don't hear anything," she said. She hung onto the bag, but Jayne wouldn't let go. "Are you crazy?" she hissed at her.

"Can't you hear your cell phone? It must be the police. I'll take it!" The tug of war continued until Jayne yanked the bag, opened it, and stood in the doorway, texting.

"What a strange woman she is," Vanessa mused. "Do you always let her answer your phone and take over?"

"She's been very helpful to me," Arnie said. "And very enthusiastic."

"Very bossy," Vanessa sniffed. "That's because she's a giant, I suppose. Tall women are rather pushy. Now me, I'm a perfect *five-foot-two, eyes of blue! Oh, what those five feet can do. Has anybody seen my gal!*" she sang with a raspy alto.

"You have a lovely voice," Arnie said. "We came here to see you, Vanessa, because we wanted to see how you were doing and ask if the police had been back."

"An assistant of the detective who was here the other night stopped by, but they had nothing new to report and neither do I. They can't find any traces of David or Donald for that matter. Both of those guys seem to have fallen off the face of the earth," she said, and pawed through another box of candy. Tutu sniffed, stood up, and buried himself under a pile of velvet blankets.

It was warm in the room, and the aroma of smoke, chocolates, perfume, and dog filled the air. Arnie tapped her foot until Jayne reentered the room. "Are we finished here, Arnie? The police want to talk to us again."

"About what?" Vanessa asked.

"Another case," Jayne answered, giving Arnie the "Let's go" signal with her eyes.

"My, you are such a busy bee, Jill, helping Arnie," Vanessa said with a look of distaste. "And what were you going to tell me? What did you find on the golf course?"

"A pink-footed goose," Jayne improvised. "And since we—"

"Since I know how fond you are of pink, Vanessa, I thought of you," Arnie said, mopping her forehead again.

"How sweet." She blew another smoke ring at Jayne. "That's adorable. Maybe I could get one as a pet. Tutu would love a playmate, wouldn't you, snookums?" She shook the little fluff ball under the blanket. Tutu growled.

Right on, Tutu! Jayne tried not to smirk and Vanessa shot her another filthy glance.

"Arnie, next time you come to see me, please come alone. I'm very susceptible to auras and Judy's here is not doing me any good." She picked up a crystal bell. "I'll ring for Tanya to let you out."

"Don't bother," Jayne said, grabbing Arnie by the arm. "Our auras can find their own way out."

Jayne pulled Arnie down the front steps with vigor. "What a bitch! Can you believe her? Calling me Judy and Jill and referring to me as your secretary? And looking up where we live? What nerve! And me a busy bee?"

"A very attractive bee, I assure you," Arnie said, as they got into her car. "You know she's jealous because you're so young looking and fit and she's confined to that bed. I wonder if she can even walk."

"Hmmm, that's an idea."

"What is?" Arnie looked in the mirror, pulled away from the curb and headed south.

"Maybe she is the murderer. Maybe she's sending the notes. Maybe lying in bed like an invalid is just a ruse." Jayne chewed her lip.

"But what is her connection to Marion? And why should her sapphire be connected to the poems and to his death? And then be hidden on a golf course? What if we hadn't found it? Someone else surely would have discovered the stone in the hole. And I can't see Vanessa creeping around a golf course at five a.m." Jayne handed Arnie a fresh bandana as she was getting moist.

"Watch it, Arnie, there's a bus!"

She put her foot down on the brake with vigor while Jayne grabbed her seatbelt.

"I saw it," Arnie said and accelerated. "Jayne, the murderer must have been there watching us. On the golf course. If we hadn't picked up the note and the stone, he surely would have come out to get it, wouldn't he? We could've hidden and waited." She turned to her in consternation. "Wouldn't he? Or she?"

"You've got something there," Jayne admitted. "But I never thought about setting a trap."

"Me either." Arnie shook her head. "I am too new at this detecting business."

"This is an amazing case and those are excellent questions, my dear Watson, that demand more investigation. Good points. What started out as two different cases now appear to be one. Vanessa, her ex-husbands, the stolen jewels, Marion's death, those darn haikus threatening everyone."

"Not everyone yet," Arnie reminded her. "Not everyone has gotten a poem in the mail."

"Not everyone has admitted it, you mean," she said. "When I think back to last night, everyone seemed on edge, much more than usual. I mean there was always a little snarky undercurrent at times, but last night was right off the charts."

"I still don't see the connection between Vanessa Harding and any of our Scrabble friends. It seems farfetched." Arnie pulled onto Lake Shore Drive. The waters of Lake Michigan were a placid, aquamarine today and the brilliant sky was streaked with feathery clouds.

"She could be connected to any of the men in this case—Marion, Nick, Robin, Fred. She looks like she could devour anything in pants."

"Marion and Robin are gay. And too young." Arnie slowed for a school bus.

"That wouldn't stop Vanessa from seduction. She would call it an experiment." Jayne shuddered. "It might've happened if she'd gotten them drunk or high on drugs. I could see her slipping a roofie into their drinks."

"Rohypnol? You think she's capable of that?"

"I think she's capable of anything. I wouldn't trust her and her little powder-puff pooch as far as I could throw them. Sleeping with Vanessa would be like bedding Dracula's mother, but strange things do happen. Perhaps there's a secret from her past. A love affair from many years ago that went wrong."

"Robin and Marion are too young," Arnie repeated, "and Nick is out of the question. He would've been in high school twenty years ago. No, they're all too young for a dalliance with Vanessa Harding, in my opinion, except Fred."

Jayne cast Arnie a sly look. "And you, dear Arnie, and you. You're the right age."

CHAPTER ELEVEN

Suspect—11 Points

"You can start talking to me any time now," Jayne said as they walked down the pristine, white hallways of Northwest Hospital.

"What do you mean?" Arnie asked, looking straight ahead. A Cubs cap sat atop her auburn hair, pulled back in a ponytail. She clutched a visitor's pass.

"You're still mad at me for making that crack about being the right age for a fling with Vanessa, back in the day."

"I'm not mad at you for your ill-advised joke," she said stiffly. "Although it was not in very good taste and not especially funny. I am more concerned with my car getting towed." She dropped her voice to a murmur and added, "With a stolen and probably illegal gun hidden under the seat. Jayne, what were you thinking?"

"I couldn't bring it in here, could I? That would be illegal."

Arnie looked at her in astonishment. "That's your reasoning? It's okay to leave it in my car but not bring it in here?"

"There are hidden metal detectors when we walked in," she argued. "We wouldn't want to get arrested."

"Jayne, I don't think I really know you. You're much more a daredevil than I ever guessed you to be."

"You knew I was in a rock band once," she offered.

"Yes, but that was over thirty years ago."

"I guess I haven't changed that much."

Arnie knocked on the hospital room door. "We're going to talk later today."

"I feel like a chastised child," Jayne said. "This relationship was going so well. I didn't know you were so sensitive, Arnie."

"*She jests at scars that never felt a wound,*" Arnie paraphrased ponderously.

"Spare me the *Romeo and Juliet*," Jayne groaned. "Once an English teacher always—"

Arnie ignored her and knocked again.

"Come in," called a voice.

Inside the bright private room was Robin, lying in bed, propped up with pillows, studying a stamp catalog. He looked serene, all things considered, Jayne thought.

"Hey, Robin, how you doing? You must be okay if you're looking at a stamp catalog. Another George Washington on your list?" Jayne made her voice sound very cheery.

"Jayne! And Arnie, how good of you to come see me during this stressful time," Robin said, extending a hand to them both. "Actually, I yearn for a Benjamin Franklin, 1888." First Jayne, then Arnie grabbed his hand and pressed it warmly. Jayne wondered if she should give him a hug, but with his head wrapped in a bandage, she decided against it. "Can you believe that Marion's gone? I can't, I just can't believe it! Who could do such a thing? The police think it might be poison!"

"They're still waiting for results," Arnie said. "It will take a few days, Robin. Try not to worry yourself over it. You've got to heal."

"I know, but it's so hard not to think about it, see it, smell it and hear him. Poor Marion lying on the floor gurgling and choking. It's a nightmare."

Jayne patted his hand. "I know you can't get it out of your mind. I'm so sorry it happened in my home. I can't stop thinking about it. Was I responsible for not calling the police immediately when I got the note? I thought it was a crank and forgot about it."

Robin's cool gray eyes assessed her. "How could you know what was going to happen? You don't have a crystal ball. I can't believe anyone had a grudge against Marion enough to kill him. I'm sure it was a heart attack. He lived life to the fullest."

"He certainly did," Arnie said. "He loved to laugh and dance, and he enjoyed himself everywhere he went."

"He could be a bit bitchy at times," Robin said, "but he really had a good heart."

"Yes, he did," Jayne agreed. "He wanted us all to be happy and beautiful and colorful."

They paused to honor Marion.

"How are you feeling?" Jayne asked.

"Better, except for a headache. I should be mad at Noreen for yelling about murder last night, but I forgive her. She was upset and mad and was blurting out anything that came into her head."

"That's very good of you," Arnie said.

"Good? I don't know about that. But I can appreciate we were all in a state of shock." He scratched the bandage on his head. "I can't wait to get this off. I'm going home tonight after the doctor signs me out and my sister comes to get me. She spent the night here and she must be exhausted." He raised a tissue to his moist eyes. "She's been a lifesaver. Although she was never overly fond of Marion and his sense of humor, she's been so sympathetic to my loss."

Jayne picked up a photograph on the nightstand. Robin and a woman, about the same age and coloring, were staring into the sunshine on a bright summer day, holding drinks with little paper umbrellas on top, at a racetrack. There was no strong family resemblance except for the shape of the face, diamond-shaped and slim. "This is your sister?"

"Yes, that's Sarah last summer. We were having a rare, fun day together. She brought it here to cheer me up."

There were no pictures of Marion. "What can we do for you, Robin? Both Arnie and I are happy to help you in any way we can."

"That's very kind of you, Jayne, but when I get home and get my strength back, Sarah and I are going to plan a small, intimate celebration of life for Marion. As soon as I can get him back to me." Robin picked up the box of tissues again and wiped his eyes.

Arnie and Jayne stood by silently, watching him weep. A nurse came in and broke the moment of sadness. "It's time for your scan, Mr. York," he said. "I'm sorry, but your friends have to leave now."

"We'll check on you later, Robin," Jayne said, "when you get home."

"I hope everything goes well for you, Robin. Have your sister text us later. We're available for anything you need," Arnie said.

"Thank you, dear friends," Robin sniffled. "And I hope someday, down the road, when all these memories are behind us, never gone but behind us, we can have another game of Scrabble? In memory of Marion."

"Absolutely," Jayne said. "In honor of Marion."

"Very, very sad," Arnie said, as they got into the car. "His grief is tangible."

"I didn't know Robin could be so emotional. He was usually so cool and quiet during our Scrabble games."

"Still waters...and they seemed to be very attached to one another."

"I know," said Jayne. "They weren't together very long but their love seemed real and deep."

"He wasn't an easy person, though, was he?" Arnie skirted around a bus. "Sometimes Marion's comments bordered on the abusive."

"I guess Robin was used to him and could deal with his mouth," Jayne mused. "We should all be so lucky."

"Yes, we should," Arnie said and cleared her throat.

"Are you still angry at me about the joke I made?"

"You included me in the list of suspects."

"It was only a joke," Jayne protested.

"Was it? I felt some serious consideration in your tone."

"Arnie, Arnie, stop it! We're on edge. We've been running on adrenaline since last night. It's been a marathon of golf, marabou feathers, death, police, and enough food to choke a pig. Aren't you tired?"

"I'm exhausted," she admitted. "Ready to drop, if you must know." She pulled into a parking space at the condo and put the visitor's card on the dashboard.

"Then let's go take a nap and rest our eyes for a while," Jayne said, touching her hand. "Let's try and shake off some of this negative energy. Let's relax."

"Lucia isn't too sure about me," Arnie said. "Whenever I get near you, she either licks my hand or tries to bite me."

"She'll behave, I promise," Jayne said.

"Thank you. I could use a hug and some affection."

"Plenty upstairs." They looked at one another and smiled, then jumped when someone tapped the window.

"Sorry to scare you," said Detective Schultz. "Can I talk to you two for a minute?"

They took the staircase down to the Riverwalk and sat at a table facing the Chicago River. The afternoon sun was brilliant, the fall air cool and invigorating, and lingering white roses on the shrubbery perfumed the joggers' path. It was idyllic and peaceful. Tourists on the Skyline boat cruise floated by, listening to the guide talk about Chicago architecture and the history of the river. The aromas of coffee, beer, and Chicago-style hot dogs smothered in onions, floated around them. Detective Schultz sniffed.

"Want a coffee?"

They shook their heads no.

"Mind if I get a coffee?"

They shook their heads no.

He ambled off to the counter and they snapped to attention.

"What does he want now?" Arnie asked, taking off her cap and dabbing her head with the bandana.

"To pick our brains, I expect. If it's definitely murder, we are suspects."

"And what about that gun in your bag," Arnie said, "are you going to give it to him?"

"How can I? I stole it from Vanessa's house. That makes me a thief and a liar."

"You could say you took it to protect her and wanted to give it to the police."

"Maybe she has a permit for it," Jayne said, "and that would make me a thief."

"Better than an unprofessional detective," Arnie said, frowning.

"Really, I thought I was helping you! You didn't even put on gloves this morning."

"We need to give him the sapphire right now, Jayne."

"Why should we? I thought we were going to solve this case on our own and get your agency tons of publicity."

"When did we say that? My dear, you have a vivid imagination. Life is not an Agatha Christie mystery!"

"You are diminishing my involvement in this case," Jayne sniffed.

"I am not. I'm trying to be law-abiding and prudent. You've got a stolen gun in your bag and I'm holding a stolen gemstone in mine. This is getting out of hand."

"What's getting out of hand?" They jumped. Jayne stared at the river; Arnie looked down at her briefcase nervously. "Hey, you two, what's going on? You were really going at it." Schultz arranged his raincoat, sat down and took the lid off his coffee. Unlike Fred, he wasn't worried as he poured four creams and three sugars into his brew. "You having a fight about something?"

Jayne regally stood to her full six-foot splendor, grabbed her backpack, and slung it over her shoulder. "Ms. Palmer will be happy to explain it to you," she said. "I've got to go feed my dog.

See you, guys. You know where to find me if you need me." She stomped off, hips swinging, platinum head held high.

"She sure is an attractive woman," Schultz said, sipping his coffee.

"She certainly is," Arnie agreed, "but very, very stubborn."

"The interesting ones always are. Sorry you two had a scuffle. Was it about last night?"

"Sort of…not really…maybe." Arnie said, with a shrug.

"Tell me about it?"

"Last night was a disaster, as you know."

"That's an understatement."

"I should backtrack a bit. You know my client is Vanessa Harding."

"I do. Who could forget her and her pink bedroom?"

"I was hired to look for her ex-husband, David Harding, who was threatening her. He was going to steal her jewelry and rough her up, so she said.

"You mean you and your lady friend were hired." Schultz eyed her over his coffee cup. "I heard all about it from Mrs. Harding. Jayne Marple help you a lot with your cases?"

"She is my unofficial partner, more or less. She still teaches golf but wanted to help me make the agency a success. This was the first time we made a client call together. I met her six months ago, about the time I was starting the agency."

"Big year for you, huh? Starting a detective agency and meeting Jayne Marple?"

"Yes, very big." Arnie felt miserable, but Schultz was studying her face, so she tried to look tough.

"So, you're investigating Vanessa Harding's ex-husbands?"

"Yes, but she didn't tell us her ex, David, still had a key to her house. Very unprofessional of us, not to ask," Arnie said, clutching her case with white-knuckled fingers.

"I don't know about that. You're only as good as the information your clients give you. Although I agree you should have asked about the locks." He finished his coffee with a sigh. "Could use more coffee, but my stomach won't thank me for it."

Arnie nodded. "I know. I have to watch the caffeine. Keeps me up at night."

"Although for our line of work, not a bad idea, right? Gotta stay awake." Schultz eyed Arnie and the briefcase. "You going to tell me about the sapphire, or what?"

CHAPTER TWELVE

Subterfuge—17 Points

Arnie gulped, an unprofessional sound. "Sapphire? What sapphire?" Schultz unwrapped a Tums slowly, ignoring her. "Okay, so you were watching us this morning."

"Yup, two of our people were camped out on the golf course. They didn't see who put the rock in the hole, but they sure as heck saw you two take it out of the cup and jump around yelling at one another."

Arnie groaned. "We didn't see anyone on the course this morning."

"Of course not," Schultz snapped. "We're professionals."

"Why didn't you stop us?"

"I wanted to see what you two were going to do. And I wanted to see what you were going to tell Mrs. Harding."

"We didn't tell her anything."

"I know," Schultz said, looking down into his empty cup.

"How do you know?"

"I was there a minute after you left."

"You've been following us?" Arnie wiped her brow.

"Bingo."

"What did Vanessa, I mean Mrs. Harding, tell you?"

"I asked her if you had found any of her stolen jewelry and she said no. Now I wonder why you did that?" Schultz carefully brushed a fly off his jacket. "Got plans of your own, huh? You and Ms. Marple? Great name for an amateur sleuth. Her parents must have had a sense of humor. Well? Nothing to tell me? Okay, we'll get back to that. Tell me about Marion Wayne."

Arnie stood. "Now I need coffee. Can I get you another one?" Schultz nodded. Arnie went to the snack shop. *What the hell am I going to tell him about the sapphire? Should I say we wanted to show Vanessa first? To make my agency look good? I'm in deep shit. I wish Jayne was here.* She came back with two coffees and a couple of hot pretzels. "Didn't have lunch," she explained.

"No, you were busy today, golf course, breakfast with Mr. Woods, Mrs. Harding, visiting Robin York at the hospital—"

"You really do know our business."

"It's my business too. You know, until we get a conclusive autopsy report, everyone is a suspect." He popped a couple of antacids in his mouth and then started adding cream and sugar to his coffee. "Thanks for the coffee and pretzel."

"You're welcome." Arnie mopped her forehead. "And then," she reflected, "if it's poison, then everyone is still a suspect." Schultz said nothing. "Hot in the sun," Arnie said, replacing her cap, pulling it low.

"Suspects always think a hat will hide their emotions," Schultz chuckled.

"You really suspect me?"

"No, I don't. I can't see any connection between you and the deceased. But I got to keep my options open."

"It's usually the spouse, isn't it?" Arnie asked.

"In your mystery novels, it is. In real life, it can be anyone. Do you think Robin York is responsible for his husband's death?"

"I'm not sure," Arnie said. "Now that the notes have started coming, it widens the field."

"Notes? Who else got a note?" Schultz put down the pretzel and straightened up. "What else are you holding out on me?"

"When we met Fred for breakfast, he gave us this." Arnie took the note out of her briefcase. "I'm not really sure I should share this with you, as he was very concerned about his reputation and the past scandal."

Schultz read it aloud.

WHO IS IN THE GRAVE?
GRANDMA GOT LOST ON HER WAY
FRED NEEDS NEW GLASSES

"This is referring to the body mix-up at the funeral home?"

Arnie shook her head in disbelief. "Do you know everything about us?"

"Just the important facts," he said. "Had to do a background check on all the Scrabble players last night."

"Find anything else interesting?"

"Maybe, but I can't share it with you, sorry."

"No, I guess you can't," Arnie said. "Too bad."

"Tell me about Marion Wayne."

Arnie exhaled. "He was flamboyant, a show-off, a brilliant decorator, according to Jayne and Noreen, and liked to stir things up with his comments and bitchy remarks."

"Did you like him?"

"Not very much. He could be funny but usually at someone else's expense."

"He was observant?"

"Like a hawk. He knew everyone's weak points and foibles. He could make even Ethel's pies sound nasty. And he wouldn't let up about Noreen being older than Nick, or Jayne being in a rock band. He teased me and Jayne about our relationship. He just wouldn't stop with the jokes."

Schultz stirred his coffee. "How did he and Robin get along?"

"I never really saw the attraction between them. I couldn't see how they were a couple. Robin is so quiet and conservative and Marion was so outrageous."

"Opposites attract," Schultz murmured.

"You mean like me and Jayne?"

"Well…yes," Schultz said. "Pro golfer and English teacher, one very daring and the other more prudent. Yes, opposites do attract."

Another boat floated down the river, happy people on the top deck enjoying the late afternoon sun. "I thought life would be more relaxing now that I'm retired," Arnie admitted.

"And yet, you started a detective agency and began dating a lady golf pro who's a former rock star?"

"I'm not sure if I will be dating her anymore," Arnie said. She opened the bag and took out the plastic egg. "The sapphire is in there. Jayne thought we should hang on to it and see what we could find out."

Schultz pulled gloves out of his pocket, opened the egg and studied the stone. "Looks real," he said. "But you can never tell by looking. I'll take it to the lab. The question is, how did Jayne get a note about the sapphire on the golf course? How is it related to Vanessa Harding? Someone at your Scrabble party must know her."

"No one has mentioned her," Arnie said. "We, I mean I, should ask everyone about that."

"I would hold off on that question," Schultz said. "Wait until the autopsy is done. If Marion had a heart attack, case closed on his end. We can surmise that someone at that party knows Vanessa Harding and was trying to play a joke on you and Jayne by getting you to the golf course. If he was poisoned, then this adds a whole new layer to his death. The theft of her jewels, assuming this stone is real, and if the ex-husband, she had four, take your pick, was the one who broke in, he did a lousy job of trying to strangle her. Then it will all become relevant."

"You think it was someone else who tried to kill her?"

"She can't see worth a damn. How does she know who it was in the dark, in her boudoir, as she calls it? We only have her word that it was her ex-husband, David Harding. Could be any one of them. Or someone in her circle who knows about her jewels and is aware of her sloppy bedroom. And why only take a few of her jewels? Why not swipe them all?" Schultz broke off a piece of pretzel, scattering salt grains.

"Maybe he only had enough time to grab what he did before she started screaming."

"Did he start to steal and then strangle or start to strangle and then steal?"

"That is the question," Arnie said with a smile.

"Glad you still have your sense of humor."

"Always. Life is too short."

"As Marion Wayne found out." Schultz threw pretzel crumbs to the sparrows, waiting by their table.

"Yes, he did. His laughs didn't keep him alive."

"Perhaps he knew too much about somebody in the Scrabble game."

"And had to be silenced?" Arnie finished her pretzel and brushed salt off her pants.

"Something like that," Schultz said. "There is more to this than—"

"Meets the you know what," Arnie said. "I should be getting home. I've got some reports to write. I do have some other clients."

"Sure, you do. Thanks for talking. Are you going to check on Jayne?"

"I think we're both tired and can use some time apart. Although…" Arnie stood up, sat back down, pulled off her cap and started twisting it in her hands.

Schultz stared at her with suspicion. "What now? Your face is getting as red as your hair. What else haven't you told me? You guys seem to get into a lot of trouble in a short amount of time."

"I know Jayne is impulsive and means well and is trying to help me but—"

"But what?"

"This has been bothering me all day, and I have to tell you. It's too dangerous."

Schultz stood up, straightened his raincoat, pulled a cigar out of his pocket, sniffed it in sorrow, and looked down his long Greek-Germanic nose at Arnie. "Okay, give, what's up?"

CHAPTER THIRTEEN

Heartbroken—20 Points

Jayne was upset. She and Lucia walked along the side of her building, dragging their paws and feet. She kept looking around her. Where was Arnie? Still with the detective? Had she given the sapphire to Schultz? Had she told him about Fred's note?

Lucia sniffed the grass and bushes, growling at a Yorkipoo and a Pit Bull. She was an equal opportunity growler. Big or small, any breed, any color, Lucia the Chihuahua was ready to mix it up—much like her owner, if truth be told. But at this moment in time, Jayne was not ready to mix. She was more in the mood for reconciliation. She was longing to call Arnie to see how she was doing with Schultz and maybe work in a small apology for stealing the gun and not showing Vanessa the sapphire. The gun was a big error on her part, but she felt in her bones that keeping the gemstone from Vanessa was a good idea. She didn't trust that painted pink floozy as far as she could smell her.

Arnie's car was still in the parking spot. Not that she was checking or anything. She was a big girl and could come and go as she pleased. Jayne took the long way around the park, enjoying the fresh autumn air, the gold and scarlet leaves on the maple and oak trees, and the happy chatter of little children with their parents and nannies in the playground. She sighed. She had booked a ticket for London at Christmas to see her daughter and family and had hoped she could convince Arnie to travel with her. But now she wasn't sure if that was a good idea. After six months of nonstop companionship, she wondered if they had seen too much of each other. Was she getting on Arnie's nerves? Maybe she was too bossy about telling her how to run her agency?

"Lucia, my little love, what's a woman to do? Time to start giving golf clinics and forget about Scrabble? Time to forget a cute red-haired doll who is sweet and a great kisser?" Lucia looked at Jayne with big brown eyes filled with love. "At least you like me," she told her little love and walked back to the condo. She poked her head into the parking lot. Arnie's car was gone. Her heart felt as empty as the parking space.

Deciding to walk up to the twenty-fourth floor for exercise and some soul searching, Jayne picked up her pooch and started up the stairs. With ten pounds of adorable fur under her arm it was both an aerobic and upper-body workout. She climbed slowly, singing to herself, and striving for inner peace. When she opened the staircase door, she jumped. Standing in front of her door was Detective Schultz.

"Good afternoon, Ms. Marple, I hope I didn't scare you."

"I'm all right," she said. "Just surprised to see you. And you can call me Jayne." Lucia growled in her arms. "Quiet, sweetie. Detective Schultz is our friend—sort of. Two days in a row we've met. To what do I owe this pleasure?"

She unlocked the door and entered her sunny condo, Schultz close behind her. She deposited Lucia on her cashmere doggie bed and sprinkled a few treats around her. Lucia growled at Schultz and then settled down to scarfing her treats with her remaining five teeth. Schultz looked around her sleek, modern home.

"Sit down," she said. "Relax a bit."

"Thanks," he said, and sat in the reclining chair. "Nice place. Lived here long?"

"About five years. I moved downtown after I sold my house on the north side. I didn't need a big house after my daughter moved to London."

"Are you divorced?"

"Yes, I am. For a long time now. I learned quickly how to be a single parent and keep my home after my husband left."

"Where did he go? If I'm not being too inquisitive."

"He ran off with our savings and ended up living in Peru in a commune. He needed to express his artistic side. I scrambled and worked two jobs, got loans and kept the house."

"Quite an achievement for a woman."

"Quite an achievement for any single parent," she said, frowning. "I'm not special. I've had my ups and downs. I came out later in life, and it was the best thing that ever happened to me. Finding my true self at fifty."

"I think you are special. Very unique." He popped a mint into his mouth and waited. "And I think you have something to tell me."

Jayne examined her hands. She pulled at her hair. "Something to tell you?" She blew out a long stream of air, whistling softly. "You mean about the sapphire on the golf course?"

"We already know about that."

"Arnie told you?"

"No, we had officers on the golf course this morning. We have a video of you taking the stone out of the fifth hole cup."

"Why, Detective, what big eyes you have," Jayne said, but felt her hairs rising on the back of her neck. "And what are you going to do about it?"

"Ms. Palmer surrendered the stone to me this afternoon," he told her.

"She did? What else did she…surrender?"

"She gave me the note Mr. Woods received."

"So, you know about the funeral home mishap."

"We knew about that before we received the note." Schultz shrugged.

"Sure, you did. You know all our deep, dark secrets." Jayne jumped up and walked into the kitchen. She opened the refrigerator. "Beer? Water? Coke Zero?"

"Nothing, thanks."

"So, we're all suspects?" Jayne pulled out a beer and popped it open. "You don't mind?"

"Go right ahead, don't let me stop you. It's a lovely day for a snooze and a beer. Wish I was off duty. I would go take a nap in the sun."

She put the untouched beer down on the coffee table and plopped down on the couch.

"What can I tell you now, Detective? What else do you want to know?"

He leaned forward, a sorrowful look on his face. "Now, Ms. Marple—Jayne—suppose you tell me about the gun."

"Damn it," she said softly, and ran her hands through her hair. "I suppose Arnie told you about that, too? Or are there security cameras in Madame Harding's house?"

"Does it matter?"

"Arnie told you. Damn."

"She was worried about you. Stolen gun, who knows who would be looking for it? Why do you think she told me? She cares about you and you're in danger. You're also breaking the law and have a lot of nerve." His voice rose as he pulled a roll of Tums out of his pocket. Lucia growled, circled in her bed and went back to sleep.

She looked at the detective, picked up the beer, put it back down again, stood up, sat down and then stood up again. "Okay, you win."

"This is not a game."

She picked up her backpack, opened the straps, stuck her hand inside and pulled out the gun. Schultz stood at attention, like a beagle at a fox hunt, ready to pounce.

"May I have that, please?" he asked.

Jayne frowned, turned the barrel around and thrust the gun at Schultz. "Sure, here it is. Going to arrest me now?"

He reached inside his coat and extracted latex gloves and a bag. He took the gun, examined it, sniffed it, removed the bullets, and placed the pink .38 Special into the evidence bag. Then he exhaled.

"You've been carrying that around all day?"

She nodded.

"Didn't you know it was loaded?"

She made a face. "I didn't think about it."

"Save me from amateurs," he groaned, and sat back down. "There is no safety on a .38."

"I'm sorry. I'm really sorry. I saw the gun twice and had to take it the second time."

"Second time? When was the first time?"

"When we went to interview her after the break-in yesterday. I saw the gun in the armoire. And then today, when I looked again, it was still there and on impulse I took it."

"You realize," he said, "that if this gun is licensed and registered, you can be arrested for theft."

"And if it's not?" Jayne challenged him.

"I'll get back to you on that. Don't go anywhere. Don't play Scrabble. Stay out of Vanessa Harding's house and behave yourself."

Jayne felt relief and an overwhelming urge to hug the detective. "I'll try," she said. "I'm way too impulsive, always have been."

"That didn't stop you from winning the Junior Ladies Pro Golf Association tournament in—"

"That was a million years ago. Do you know everything about us?"

"Just the interesting things," he said. "Well, I'm off. Things to do, people to see, autopsies to check."

"Thanks for not getting me in trouble."

"You're not in trouble—yet." He stood and Lucia growled. "I'll get back to you, Jayne Marple. Try to lay low for twenty-four hours, will you?"

CHAPTER FOURTEEN

Autopsy—12 Points

"Keep your head down, Fred," Jayne said. "Try to keep your eyes focused on the ball."

He tapped the ball and it missed the cup by two feet. "I thought I was focused," he said.

They stood on the practice putting green at the Lake View course, not far from where Arnie and Jayne had discovered the stolen sapphire.

"Your head moved a tiny bit," she said. "It really makes a difference, staying still and concentrating."

"Hard to do, but I appreciate the lesson," he said. "It's good to get out on a great day like today. It's good to have something else to think about."

It had been only two days since Marion Wayne's untimely death at Jayne's condo. Jayne was giving Fred a golf lesson at his request. The afternoon autumn sun warmed their faces and felt life-affirming. Still, Jayne felt a cool breeze and pulled her jacket collar up.

"I'm glad we could get out here today, too," she said, neatly sinking a ten-foot putt. "We all had a very rough week."

"Did you hear from that detective about the autopsy?"

"No, he hasn't called me yet."

"How about Arnie?"

"No, she hasn't heard anything either," she lied.

Not one call or text from Arnie since yesterday. Totally unlike her. She usually greeted Jayne in the morning by text and if they weren't spending the night together, she would call to wish her a good night. She knew Arnie was upset. But how long would the silent treatment last?

She did get one message from Schultz this morning while she was out walking Lucia.

"Hey, Jayne, just wanted you to know that the sapphire is a fake. A very good fake, but a fake, nevertheless. Just as fake as the rest of Ms. Harding." He laughed. "So, someone is playing a joke on you. The question is—who? Catch you later." Jayne had listened to the message twice. She had not called Arnie, expecting she'd gotten the same information. She longed to compare notes with her.

Fred took out another putter with a bigger head from his bag. "How long do autopsies take?"

"Days? If they're testing for poison, could be longer."

Fred stumbled on the green and whacked the ball way too hard. It sailed over the grass and landed in a nearby sand trap. "Poison? Do you really think it could be poison?"

Jayne shrugged. "He died quickly. I've never seen anything like it. And he had no history of heart trouble."

"Who said so?"

Jayne shrugged again. "You're right, we don't know that for a fact. Maybe he was on heart meds. And the way he was choking down those eggs and drinks—"

"Could finish anybody off. And he never stopped talking. Biggest mouth I ever heard. He never let up on Ethel. And making fun of my dancing and everyone's name. He had a lot of nerve." He took the club back and gave the ball a tap. The ball slowly but surely rolled into the hole. "There, that's a good one."

Jayne watched Fred's face. She knew he was protective of Ethel. Would he poison Marion to stop his insults? "Good putt, Fred. And how is Ethel doing?"

"Better today. She was very upset about the other night. The Zumba helped. She's very sensitive. She's baking today for our church group."

"Pies?"

"Red velvet cake," he said. "Keeps her busy and keeps me fat." He patted his girth. "But as long as she's happy."

"That's all that counts," Jayne agreed. "Let's try working on the sand wedge, Fred. What do you say?"

"Sounds good to me."

They walked in the direction of the sand trap. Jayne again wondered how much she knew about her Scrabble friends. Fred had been a mortician and was used to working with chemicals. He had received a threatening haiku. And Ethel, for all her sweetness, was a master baker. Who else could better disguise arsenic or some other poison in frosting or filling for a cake? Could they have poisoned Marion Wayne to stop Fred's past mistake from getting out if it had been Marion sending the notes? She again wished she could talk to Arnie about this but she was going to give her some space.

A few miles away at the Universal Brewery, Noreen Charles was inspecting a kettle of brewing ale with her brew master. The heady aroma of hops, malt, and fruity yeast filled her nose. The added chocolate flavor sensuously filled the moist air. The steam rising from the enormous stainless steel 150-gallon kettle drenched her face and hair. She was pink-faced from the steam, the exertion of work, and the contents of the letter in her pocket.

She gave her approval to the brew master, climbed down the steps from the kettle, and went to her office. She turned the AC on full blast and sat down at her desk. She looked at the photographs in silver frames—one of her parents, younger and smiling, one of her at her graduation from college, and another one of Nick and her after they had moved in together. They were grinning at the camera, delirious in their new love, and his arm was wrapped protectively around her shoulders. Had that only been a year ago? Now she was riddled with doubts. Nick was very close to some of his clients, too close for his own good. She wondered if his ladies would really be shocked by his stripping days. Probably not. But they might be shocked by his hooker days, when he worked as a high-priced male escort. He thought she didn't know about that, but she had him thoroughly investigated before she loaned him the money for his gym.

She rolled that nasty piece of information around in her mind. It was filed for future use and ready to be exposed at any time. She would have confronted Nick about that disgraceful tidbit from his past but now…She felt the note in her pocket. How did they find out?

LITTLE CHILD KILLER
PSYCHIATRIC HOSPITAL
ARE YOU REALLY CURED?

It had been a long time ago. She had been in foster care as a child. She'd hardly known her real mother, who had been in and out of rehab before a fatal overdose. And her father was unknown. When she was eight years old, she'd stabbed another foster kid in a home. It hadn't really been her fault. She'd been bullied, everyone knew that, and the girl she stabbed had been trying to choke her and steal her food. But the kitchen knife Noreen had grabbed to defend herself punctured a lung and the girl died six weeks later. Noreen had been sent to a state psychiatric facility for three years. They worked on her anger issues and feelings of abandonment. She emerged into a beautiful teenager with an angelic face that moved an older couple to take her into their home and then adopt her. They had her name changed to erase the past and she had no trouble with that.

She had received every advantage. Good schools, travel, her own horse, summers in France, and most of all, unconditional love. She tried to love her parents back as best she could, but she always felt like there was a hole in her heart and she was playing a role.

Until she met Nick. She really felt something with him. So now, to think of him cheating on her, if he was cheating on her, made her want to do terrible things. But first she had to find out who sent this note and how she was going to deal with them. She picked up the silver letter opener on her desk and stabbed it into the wood. She felt satisfaction.

The weekend passed quietly for Jayne. She golfed, walked Lucia, talked to her daughter in London, and had lunch with friends who lived in her building. She waited for Arnie to call but a call never came. She knew she should call her. She had made the joke about Arnie being a suspect because of her age. And she had stolen the gun, which was totally wrong, as Arnie had pointed out, but something held her back. Pride? Stupidity? She had plenty of both.

Monday morning, she woke up very early as usual. She looked at Lake Michigan from her windows and watched the sunrise. Like a Turner painting, the sky was a parfait of rose and gold, tinged with mauve and violet—breathtaking. She felt a lump in her throat and blinked away tears. Such beauty for her to appreciate on this new morning. What was she going to do for the world today? She was going to text Arnie.

She picked up the phone but her gal had beaten her to it. *Good morning. How are you feeling, dear one? Did you receive an invitation, hand-delivered by messenger? Call me.*

She dressed in comfy workout clothes, fed Lucia, and got her ready for a walk. At the front desk, there was indeed an envelope for her. "This came in five minutes ago," Brandon, the concierge, told her. "I was just going to call you."

"Thanks, Brandon," she said. "I hope your family is doing well and that the kids are enjoying school."

"We're all good. Thanks, Jayne. You doing okay after the other night?"

The whole building knew about Marion's passing; it was inevitable. Sad news traveled fast.

"I'm fine, thanks. We're coping. It was a huge shock."

"Let me know if you need anything," he said.

She smiled as she left. She loved living here. Her neighbors and staff were like family and they kept an eye out for each other.

She and Lucia walked out into the bright morning. It was six a.m., quiet and peaceful, except for a few runners, delivery trucks and people walking their dogs. She tossed birdseed to the waiting sparrows, who dive-bombed the building when they saw her. They knew she fed them every morning. Although she lived downtown in a high-density area, early mornings on the river were like being out in the country.

She sat down on a park bench and opened the brown delivery package, hand-delivered by ACE Messenger Services. Lucia sat by her feet, tongue out, watching for squirrels. Inside was a pale lilac envelope. She carefully opened it. There was an invitation, also in lilac. She held the note to her nose. No sandalwood or sage but definitely a spray of something flowery. Roses? Lily of the Valley?

IN HONOR OF MARION ANTHONY WAYNE
MEMORIAL SERVICE
FRIDAY 1:00 P.M.
DRAKE HOTEL
LUNCHEON TO FOLLOW
RSVP Sarah York

So soon? The body must have been released. That was quick. Death on a Thursday, service a week later. Did Marion have any family besides Robin? She picked up the phone and dialed.

"Hello, Jayne."

"Hi, Arnie, how you doing?"

"I'm okay," she said. "Did you get the invitation?"

"Yes, I did. Delivered by messenger at six a.m."

"Mine came to the house very early, too. Dropped in the mailbox. Strange."

They both paused.

"Listen, dear heart—"

"Arnie, I'm really sorry I screwed up—" Two voices rose as one.

"I shouldn't have gotten so annoyed with you," Arnie said, in a low voice that warmed Jayne's heart.

"I was in a terrible state! Making jokes at your expense, stealing the gun, acting crazy, what was wrong with me?"

"As a retired teacher, Jayne, I must admit you seemed a bit hyper, like some hidden ADHD was coming out. You were not quite yourself."

"Last week was a nightmare," she said. "I apologize. I don't know what came over me. Vanessa Harding in all her splendor, giving you the eye, Marion dying, the fake sapphire on the golf course—"

"Schultz called you about that?"

"Yup, yesterday."

"Me, too, and he told me about the body being released."

"*That*, he didn't tell me," Jayne admitted. "I guess I'm in disgrace after stealing the gun."

"That was reckless of you, Jayne. I'm glad Schultz didn't arrest you for that."

"I know, I know, I know! I lost my marbles there for a minute. But that woman and her pink feathers really makes me crazy. I wouldn't be surprised if she's the murderer and faked her own attack. And by the way, Arnie, was it cyanide? Was Marion poisoned? Or was it a heart attack? Can you tell me? Or didn't Schultz share that with you?"

A long silence on the phone. "Jayne, you have to promise—"

"I knew it! He was poisoned! I was sure it wasn't a heart attack!"

"Did I say he was poisoned?" Arnie asked.

She groaned. "Come on, Arnie, spill it! I won't say a word. You know me."

A chuckle. "Indeed, I do. Yes, he was poisoned. Powdered strychnine in his drink and deviled eggs. Someone moved around like lightning."

"So, no cyanide?"

Arnie cleared her throat. "I was totally wrong there," she said quietly. "I thought I smelled almonds."

"Maybe it was his cologne or Ethel's vintage perfume."

"I shouldn't have spoken out of turn."

"You were half right, Arnie, about the poison. My, my, in my own home. Poison."

"Shocking," Arnie agreed. "How are you holding up, Jayne?"

For once, she kept her big, independent mouth closed. "I'm still a bit shook up, Arnie, and I'm not sleeping well."

"Maybe I can come over tonight and massage your neck?"

"That would be amazing," Jayne said, softly. "I'll order salad and the everything-on-it pizza."

Lucia barked. She approved. She liked olives.

CHAPTER FIFTEEN

Memorial—12 Points

The Drake Hotel, a vintage Beaux-Arts jewel on the Magnificent Mile in Chicago, was ready. The classy hotel was prepared for the memorial service of Marion Anthony Wayne, in a small ballroom tucked away on the third floor. The original 1930s décor had been restored and subtly refurbished. The walls were covered in silk wallpaper decorated with butterflies and pagodas. Statues of goddesses and archers rested atop marble columns. There were Chinese deco rugs with more butterflies and pagodas in brilliant shades of magenta and emerald green at the entrance and in front of the bar and buffet. The tables were set with pristine white linen tablecloths, sparkling glassware, and polished silver. The reception table was draped in lilac satin, and a retrospective of the life of Marion Anthony Wayne was displayed for the guests. There were more pictures of his triumphant work as an interior decorator than of his life, although there were a few grainy shots of Marion in a cap and gown, hugging Robin at their wedding, and in a bathing suit on a cruise ship off the Greek island of Santorini. Marion had magnificent legs.

Robin was standing alone in front of the reception table, wearing a pale gray suit with a lilac rose in his lapel. His sister Sarah, was sitting behind him, asking friends to sign the guest book. She was petite, her graying hair styled in a severe bob. Perched on her head was a black fascinator hat with a tulle veil that partially obscured her face and thick glasses. With the veil and the glasses, it was hard to determine her age.

On the table were remembrance cards with Marion's smiling face, his amazing (so it said) bio, and the Twenty-third Psalm. In the photograph, Marion was wearing a silver jacket and holding up a champagne flute. With his raised eyebrows, brilliant white teeth and long shiny hair, he resembled a hipster Dracula.

Arnie and Jayne arrived together. The neck massage had soothed away the friction of the weekend and they had made up. They had spent every night together, rising early to go their separate ways, but still hugging as the dawn broke over the river. The week had passed quietly, Arnie working on minor cases, Jayne teaching a few golf lessons and ushering at the morning service at her church. Five years ago, when she had moved downtown and wondered what life would bring, she had joined a new church and had discovered new friends, new beliefs, and a desire to feel peace in her life. She often ushered and helped out on Sundays.

Arnie wore a navy-blue blazer with a subdued green paisley blouse and khaki trousers. Jayne, who rarely wore dresses but was in a reckless mood, managed to unearth a Diane Von Furstenberg wrap dress from the back of her closet, that she had worn to her daughter's wedding. It was also navy blue and sported tiny white polka dots. It wrapped around her tall, slim figure elegantly. Black flats and diamond-studded earrings finished the look. Arnie gazed at her in admiration. Jayne felt she looked good. At her age, why not flaunt it once in a while, even though this was a somber occasion.

"Not many tears are being shed," Arnie said, echoing her thoughts.

"I think everybody came for the meal," she whispered.

They waited their turn to come to the front of the line.

"Robin, I am so sorry," Jayne said, clasping his hand and looking down into his eyes. Today, his palette was gray—graying hair, gray eyes, pale complexion, to go with the gray clothing. He could easily be overlooked in a crowd. He made a dignified appearance, slim and dapper in his subtle but expensive suit, handmade Italian shoes and silk lilac tie. Understated but elegant. Jayne had never noticed the expensive gold watch on his wrist. He was not wearing his wedding ring.

"It's a great loss to me, to his friends, and to humanity," Robin said quietly. "Thank you for coming."

"Robin, if there's anything we can do," Arnie offered. "Please let us know."

"Thank you," Robin said. "I appreciate your concern." He snapped into host mode. "I have place cards at each table, so look for your names. I wanted friends to sit together. I am going to say a few words and then we'll have lunch. Marion would have wanted us all to break bread together."

They stopped to sign the guestbook.

"You must be Sarah, Robin's sister," Jayne said to the silent woman. "I'm Jayne Marple, and this is Arnie Palmer, we're friends of Robin and Marion." She held out her hand which was ignored. Sarah pushed the veil up from her face. Gray eyes, like her brother's, but ringed with long, luxurious lashes, behind the heavy glasses, surveyed them.

"I know who you are," she said. "You're practically responsible for killing my brother's husband at your Scrabble game."

"Sarah!" Robin had heard and moved in quickly. "Don't say that. They had nothing to do with poor Marion's accident."

"Accident? Are you sure about that? I thought he was poisoned."

"Lower your voice," he whispered. That is not conclusive."

"You're in denial. You never want to believe the truth. If he died of natural causes, then why is that policeman here?" She jerked her head toward the door and pulled the veil back down over her angry face. They all turned and looked at Detective Schultz who had entered the ballroom. He nodded at them and got in line.

"I'm sure we'll all find out," he said, glaring at her. "Please don't say any more about it."

She sniffed. "You can stick your head in the sand, Robin—"

"We'll go sit down," Jayne said. "We can talk later."

"Wow, is she hostile," Arnie said, blinking at the crystal chandelier that dangled over their heads. "This is quite a fancy room for a funeral."

"She looks like Robin. Two shades of gray. And yes, this room is quite worthy of Marion. He liked glamor."

They entered the ballroom. About twenty tables were placed near floor-to-ceiling windows that had exquisite views of the lakefront and the Oak Street beach. In the center of the room, dominating the long table covered in lilac satin, was an ice sculpture in a huge silver bowl.

Arnie gulped and squeezed Jayne's hand. "Don't tell me," she said in shock.

"It is," she answered, equally in awe. "It sure is. That had to be Marion's idea. I can see him leaving vivid instructions in his will."

The head of Marion Wayne had been carved most expertly into a bust of ice. It was an amazing likeness of the dead designer. Flowing locks, huge eyes and an enormous toothy grin stared at them. Behind Marion there was a large fountain of pink champagne gurgling and splashing. A waiter in a white jacket was handing out champagne flutes to all the arrivals. Jayne took a glass for both of them as Arnie was staring just long enough to be impolite.

"You're staring," she said and handed her a glass.

"I am? That is the most astounding thing I have ever seen in my life," Arnie said.

"And you a schoolteacher," she retorted. "Fancy that." She took her arm. "I spy a table that I bet we're sitting at," she said. They moved in the direction of Fred and Ethel, sitting next to Nick and Noreen. The two couples weren't speaking to each other. Their silent discomfort was tangible.

"Hi, everyone," Jayne said, picking up her place card. A sigh broke out at the table.

"Jayne, Arnie, at last," Fred said. "Finally. Come sit down."

"Thank goodness you're here," Ethel said, fanning herself with a photo of Marion.

"Hello," Noreen said, fingering her gold bracelets. She looked bored.

Nick got up and held the chair for Jayne. "Thank you, Nick. You are too kind," Jayne murmured with a wicked glance at Arnie. "It's good to see everyone looking so well after—"

"Last week's tragedy?" Noreen did not look upset. She took a sip of the pink champagne and made a face.

"I hope there's beer later," Fred said, looking at his untouched glass.

Nick looked anxious. "Did the police ever give a report on the autopsy?"

Jayne and Arnie exchanged glances. "I'm not sure," Arnie said. "We should ask Robin."

"Not today." Ethel was horrified. "Today is a sad day. We can't ask Robin if Marion was poisoned."

"Why not?" Fred asked. "We're all thinking it. Maybe we should ask that policeman."

Nick jumped in his seat and almost knocked over his water glass. He caught it between strong hands. "Why is he here? Why is a cop at a funeral lunch?"

"Can't you imagine why, darling? He probably wants to trap one of us into an indiscretion," Noreen said.

Ethel frowned. "Indiscretion? Whatever do you mean?"

"Don't worry about it, Eth," Fred said, patting her hand. "Noreen is talking out of turn. We have no idea why Detective Schultz is here."

"Collecting more haiku? What do you think, Jayne?" Noreen said.

"I think Robin is about to speak," she answered. She was not going to rise to anyone's bait today.

Robin and his sister, along with their attorney, sat down at a small table in front of the room and appeared to be having a heated discussion. He cut her off and picked up a glass of water and took a long swallow. He stood and reached for a small microphone. With his other hand, he raised his hand for silence and the room quieted.

"My dear friends," he began as a horrible squeak emitted from the microphone. Ethel shrieked and the guests erupted into quiet laughter. Robin, red-faced, turned and fiddled with the dials on the amp. The buzzing subsided. "My dear friends," he began again, "on behalf of myself and my sister, Sarah, we thank you for coming to the celebration of life for Marion Wayne, my husband, my friend, my love." He cleared his throat and tugged at his tie as if being strangled by emotion. "I hope you enjoy your lunch and please partake of the open bar."

"Hear, hear," muttered Fred.

"Marion, as you know, was a great lover of life. He lived it to the fullest. He was known for his outstanding design work, his kindness to his friends, and his affection for his mother, before she was so tragically taken from us, last year at the age of ninety."

Jayne and Arnie looked at each other.

"He never mentioned a mother passing away last year," Jayne whispered. "Is this significant?"

"As you might know, Marion was the talker of the family." *Quiet laughter.* "I'm the shy, boring, financial guy." *More chuckles.* "Although we hadn't been together very long, our life together was amazing. Marion was taken away from us too soon." A pause, a little sob, a hiccup. "I've put together a video of his amazing life. Please watch with me."

The room darkened and above the champagne fountain, a screen appeared. Music filled the room, dramatic and showy, if a bit inappropriate, Jayne thought. *Really? "Don't Cry for me, Argentina?"*

"I guess Marion envisioned himself as a modern Evita," Noreen said. "What nerve."

"Evita, Evita?" Ethel whispered. "Wasn't she related to Jackie Kennedy?"

Fred smiled and patted her hand. Nick had a coughing fit into his napkin. Jayne and Arnie stifled laughs and tried not to look at the others. The video played. Marion as a young man, Marion as a model on the runway, Marion fondling bolts of fabric at the Merchandise Mart for his clients. There were numerous shots of Marion on a variety of beaches—Miami Beach, Fire Island, Key West, the French Riviera, and Santorini, the Greek sun almost as wide as his smile.

A minute was devoted to Robin and Marion, their condo, their travels, and standing in front of a wedding cake, location undetermined. Jayne felt a momentary pang. Marion was dead, probably poisoned by one of the people sitting at this table, and she should feel more remorse for a fellow human being who had met an untimely end. Instead, she felt excitement and impatience. She was plunged straight in the middle of a mystery that she wanted to solve, with the collaboration of Arnie, naturally. Arnie, sitting next to her, was watching the room instead of the screen. She was studying the faces of their Scrabble friends and the other guests. Detective Schultz sat two tables away, doing much the same. Looking, studying and waiting.

Jayne listened to the lyrics, "*my mad existence, I kept my promise,*" and watched Robin wipe away a tear. Sarah sat stone-faced, watching her brother. Yes, Marion had a mad existence. He had a big life and a big mouth. What was he really like behind the flashy exterior and wisecracks? Perhaps that was all he was, lots of show without much depth. They wouldn't know now. The song ended, "*that every word is true.*" The film ended. There was a silence. A polite smattering of applause was stalled by a raucous voice in the doorway.

"Well, bless my soul, what is this? A funeral or a party? Bartender, pour me a drink."

"OMG," Jayne and Arnie said at the same time.

Vanessa Harding, dressed in a short, tight, pink Chanel suit, with enormous diamond brooches on each shoulder, tottered in on silver stiletto heels. In one arm she held Tutu. In the other, she dangled an unlit cigarette. She paused in the doorway for maximum dramatic effect. It worked.

CHAPTER SIXTEEN

Lobster—9 Points

There is a certain type of person who attracts attention wherever they go, both consciously and unconsciously, Jayne thought, watching Vanessa undulate into the room. She was a parody of every screen sex symbol from the past, a composite of Marilyn Monroe, Jayne Mansfield, and Mae West. The bleached-blond hair, the deep, bosom-baring cleavage, the excessive display of diamonds and the outrageous little dog, dyed pink today and adorned in a sparkling rhinestone collar, stopped the room cold. She was such a show of outrageous sexuality for a woman over sixty, or maybe seventy, if one could find her birth certificate. And yet, many of the men straightened up just a little bit to get a better look at the femme fatale as she sauntered up to the head table.

"Robin," she said, speaking in a loud, throaty voice so the whole room could hear, "I am so sorry for your loss. Let me introduce myself. I am Vanessa Harding. I was one of dear Marion's first clients when he took up decorating. My patronage helped establish his name." She extended her hand royally, as if expecting it to be kissed. Robin stood, blinked several times and took her hand. He appeared dazzled by the vision in pink. Sarah scowled, the attorney stared, and the guests waited. Tutu, the Pomeranian gave a little squeak.

"Thank you for coming. I wasn't expecting you," he said, looking around the room for the headwaiter. "Let me find you a seat."

"That's okay, darling." She plopped herself down in the seat next to Robin. "This chair will suit me just fine."

Robin, with a smile frozen on his face, looked at the microphone in his hand. "Friends, please get a drink at the bar and the buffet luncheon will be served momentarily. Today, we will be enjoying all of dear Marion's favorite foods. Please, everyone, eat, drink…" He wiped away a bead of sweat from his forehead with a lilac handkerchief.

"He's going to say it!" Arnie said under her breath.

"He is not," Jayne whispered.

"And please enjoy," Robin finished with a smile.

Jayne choked back a laugh. "Told you." Arnie looked crushed and made a face. Jayne laughed out loud.

"What a floozy she is," Noreen said with a sneer. "Who dresses like that these days? I'm going to get a proper drink." Noreen stood. "Coming, Nick?"

"All right, Noreen." He looked at Jayne. Can I get you something?"

"Thanks, Nick, but I'm going to get up soon and stretch my legs."

Nick and Noreen moved away in the direction of the bar.

"She's got him trained," Fred observed. "She says jump and he says, 'How high?'"

"I think his devotion is sweet," said Ethel. "I hope he's not tempted by all the alcohol at the bar."

"I'm sure after ten years of sobriety, he can handle it," Jayne said, fighting down a moment of annoyance. Couldn't Ethel leave that alone?

"He never seemed upset by the cocktails at our Scrabble games," Arnie said.

Ethel was getting pink in the face. "I didn't mean anything by that. I really didn't."

"Of course, you didn't," Fred said, patting her hand.

Ethel looked over at Vanessa with a frown. "She certainly likes her pink and sparkle, doesn't she?"

"She can't hold a candle to your beauty," Fred said.

"She is a bit overdone for a funeral luncheon." Ethel smiled.

Jayne stood. "I think I will get a glass of wine. Can I get anyone a drink?"

"I'll come with you, Jayne," Arnie said.

"I will too," said Ethel. "I need to walk a bit and I want to take a closer look at her diamonds."

"I want to start on the food," Fred said and looked at the full buffet table. "Ethel, can you get me a Bud? And how about another glass of champagne?"

"I haven't finished this one yet, but I'll get you your Bud," she said. She kept looking at Detective Schultz and then at Vanessa. Her little rosebud mouth was puckered.

"Let's go, Arnie," Jayne said. Suddenly, she was sick of everybody.

At the head table, a nervous hotel supervisor was attempting to explain hotel policy to Vanessa Harding.

"I'm sorry, madam, but dogs are not allowed in the dining rooms unless they are service animals."

"Of course, Tutu is a service animal," she said, burying her nose in the fluffy pink fur. "I can't go anywhere without him. He is my comfort animal. I'd be lost."

The man looked very uncomfortable. "There are rules," he pleaded.

"I won't put Tutu down for a second," she assured him. "He'll be with me the whole time. I promise."

"Very good, madam," he said, looking miserable. "Please keep the animal on the leash."

"Animal?" Vanessa picked up a glass of champagne from the table. It didn't matter whose glass it was, as long as it was full. "He's not an animal. He's my little love, aren't you, snookums?"

Jayne, standing at the bar, had to laugh, as did Detective Schultz, who had ambled over to talk to her. He had shed the raincoat and was wearing a very respectable brown suit. "She's really something, isn't she?" He sipped iced tea and nodded in the diva's direction. "Almost too good to be true. Is she really like that without trying, or is she just a big phony?"

"That's something I've been trying to figure out since I met her," Arnie said. She had ordered two pinot grigios and handed one to Jayne. She surveyed the head table, watching Vanessa talk to Robin, while Sarah hovered and listened intently.

"She's as real as she wants you to think she is," Jayne said.

"Explain that," Arnie said.

"She's been a phony so long she believes she's gorgeous, fascinating, and that every man and woman wants her. She's kind of grotesque when you take a good look at her. The makeup, false eyelashes and the hair extensions…How long does it take her to get put together before she goes out, I wonder?"

"Fake eyelashes and hair?" Arnie looked crushed.

"I believe the rest of her is real," Schultz said.

"Why, Detective Schultz, you bad boy," Jayne said. "Silicone can do wonders, you know?"

"Call me Perry," he said. "I feel like we're old friends by now."

"Okay, Perry," Jayne said. "Like Perry Como, the singer?"

"Like Pericles, the Greek general."

"Great name," Jayne said. "Pericles Schultz sounds like a boxer or a poet—"

"Or a gangster," Arnie chimed in.

"I've been accused of all of those," Schultz said. "But back to bosoms. So you think half is real? Which half? The top or the bottom?"

"Look, the buffet is open," Arnie interrupted. "As much as Ms. Harding's chest is fascinating, I could use some food. Let's go see what Marion's favorite foods are, shall we?"

Jayne, about to speak on the history of fake breasts, allowed Arnie to take her arm and lead her over to the buffet. It was quite an eclectic feast. There were steaming silver trays of Lobster Newburg, cream of celery soup, fish tacos, guacamole and chips, baked brie cheese covered in almonds, toasted slices of French bread, Caesar salad, and mini burgers, smothered in onions, affectionately known as sliders, imported from the White Castle, a Chicago fast food institution. A lavish sweets table was laden with little pots of chocolate mousse, crème brûlée, chocolate chip cookies, and slices of cheesecake. An enormous tray of chocolates arranged to spell out *Marion*, amused and attracted Jayne, who did not usually have a sweet tooth. The array of carbs from the ridiculous to the sublime was very tempting.

"This luncheon is very heavy on cream sauce and fats," Arnie sighed. "It'll be hard to digest."

"Eat light," Jayne suggested, "so we can work the room after lunch. I'm sure there are a lot of clues here." Jayne eyed their table, where Fred had just sat down with two full plates. She spotted Noreen at the bar, holding a martini glass. The blond took a healthy swallow and bit into an olive, sliding it off the swizzle stick with a display of firm white teeth.

"I am sure there are a lot of clues—over there. Jayne, you realize that Marion was poisoned by one of us? There is no way out of that one. And that's why Schultz is here watching us, without appearing to watch us. I'm going bring this drink to Fred. Will you put a few things on a plate for me, please?"

She strolled off, still surveying the room. What was she looking for? Jayne watched her, feeling like she had been dismissed. She put her wineglass down untouched on the bar and got in line at the buffet table. She started filling two plates, one for her and one for Arnie.

With a little smile, she put a little of everything on the plates—the gooey lobster dish swimming in flamingo pink cream sauce, a hunk of almond-studded baked brie cheese, a couple of tacos and burgers and a few nachos with a dollop of guacamole. *Let Arnie digest that.* She filled another plate for herself. To hell with being healthy today.

Jayne, Ethel, and Arnie came back at the same time. Fred had already tucked into the food. Ethel handed Fred his beer.

Jayne put the calorie-laden plate in front of Arnie. "Thanks, Jaynie," she said, and started eating without an examination of the plate.

"Aw," Fred groaned, sampling a little bit of lobster. "This is to die for."

"Aren't you eating?" Jayne asked Ethel.

"I'm going up there now," she said. "I was a bit upset but I've finally worked up some appetite."

"Enjoy, my love," Fred said.

Ethel, wrapped in a black tulle stole, emitting wafts of Midnight in Paris, blew him a kiss and went to do battle with carbs and trans fats.

Nick came back with two plates. Noreen followed, looking bored. "Here, Nor, better eat something."

She looked at the plate with distaste. "What is this slop?"

"Come on, Noreen, don't be like that. Eat something. You need to soak up the booze."

"Don't tell me what to do," she hissed. "I'll eat what I want." She glared at Arnie. "What are you looking at, Mizz Detective? Haven't you ever seen anyone having a meltdown? I don't know why Nick made us come here today."

"I hope you don't mind me saying this," Arnie said, "but it's not good for your health, Noreen, to get upset. You must stay calm. We're all under a lot of stress right now, with Marion's death and the police watching our every move."

Noreen put the martini glass down with a thump. "They are?" She looked around and then picked up a big chunk of brie cheese. She ate it and then scooped up some Lobster Newburg, making a face. "This stuff tastes so oily. What's in this sauce?" she grimaced.

"Back to oatmeal tomorrow, my love," Nick said.

Nick, a vegetarian, had filled his plate with veggie sticks, cheese and salad. He picked an anchovy out of the salad and laid it carefully on the far end of his plate. He started crunching on the nachos and used the guacamole for dipping celery sticks. "Not bad grub," he commented.

Detective Schultz walked up holding a very full plate.

"Care to sit down?" Nick asked. There were two empty places at the table.

"I don't mind if I do," he said. He sat down next to Noreen, who ignored him.

They ate silently for a minute. Jayne wondered what could they say to each other with Schultz sitting there? The food, although very rich, was delicious. Robin walked up and went around the table, checking on the comfort of his guests.

"How's the meal?" He put one hand on Nick's shoulder and the other on Schultz's.

"Very yummy," Ethel assured him.

"Marion had eclectic taste in food," Arnie said. "But it's very tasty."

"It's very good, Robin, thank you," Jayne said, studying her host. He seemed less gray than earlier, more animated, and there was color in his cheeks. Was he enjoying himself? Maybe now that Marion wasn't stealing all the attention, Robin could relax and be himself. "I didn't know Marion liked White Castle burgers. Surprising but fun."

"Marion was a lot of surprises," Robin said. "He enjoyed everything in life—as he would say—from the ridiculous to the sublime. I will miss his wild exaggerations and poetic utterings." He walked over to Ethel and Fred. "Can I get you another drink?" They shook their heads no.

He walked over to Arnie and Jayne and patted their backs. "You won't forget the dessert table, will you?"

"Looking forward to it," Arnie said.

Jayne could feel her hands already swelling from the salty food. "It looks amazing," she said. "I love cheesecake."

"And I love chocolate," Arnie said. "Can't wait to try the chocolate mousse."

"Splendid." Robin beamed. "And please have another cocktail. This is a day for indulgence and memories."

"He seems chipper," Fred said, washing down a fish taco with a swig of beer. "Not in too bad of shape, considering."

"He does seem happy," Ethel said. "But I wouldn't want him to bring me a drink."

"Why? Do you think he would add something to it?" Schultz asked.

Dead silence from the table.

"Anyone would be happy without Marion on their back twenty-four-seven," Noreen said and stood. "I'm going to get another drink."

"Noreen seems to be in a bit of a mood today," Ethel said to Nick. "Is she doing okay? She seems so edgy. She's a bit young for menopause, but these things happen."

The entire table stared at Ethel, silenced by her presumptions.

"That's a thought," Nick said, "but I don't think so. She's just sensitive." He stood. "I'm going to get more veggies."

Jayne and Detective Schultz locked eyes. She rose and looked at the table. "I'm going to get some desserts for us to sample."

"Get chocolate," Arnie said.

"A little bit of everything, please," said Ethel. "I wish there were some pies. Like I made for the last Scrabble party."

"Ethel, nobody, even the Drake Hotel, could match the excellence of your pies," Fred said. Ethel beamed, again saved from her indiscretion by her spouse's praise.

Jayne took a detour from the desserts and boldly walked up to the head table. Robin was still making the rounds of his guests. His sister was sitting at one end of the table, eating silently. At the other end, Vanessa Harding was feeding little bits of taco to Tutu. She had a plate of food in front of her that looked like a tornado had hit it and another plate loaded with desserts.

"Hello, Vanessa," Jayne said, taking a seat. "Enjoying your lunch?"

"Why, Jill, fancy meeting you here." She squinted and looked her up and down. "You look good in that dress. You got good legs. No wonder Arnie goes for you." She took a cigarette out of her purse, inserted it in a jeweled cigarette holder and then watched in amusement as two staff members hurried over to her.

"Ma'am, there's no smoking here," one said.

"There's an outdoor smoking lounge on the fourteenth floor," said the other man.

She chuckled, her bosom rising with the humor. "Gentlemen, relax! I'm just going to suck on this for a while." She waved the jeweled holder in their direction while they stood silent.

Jayne wanted to barf. *Suck on this? Really?*

Vanessa put down the cigarette holder and picked up a spoon. She scooped up a huge hunk of chocolate mousse and topped it with a chocolate. "Chocolate, hmmmm, delicious. Almost as good as sex, right, Jayne?" She winked. Her outrageously long eyelash extensions reminded Jayne of a toothbrush. "How is Arnie?" She smirked.

"We were so surprised to see you here today, Vanessa," she replied, ignoring an impulse to push her painted face into the mousse. "We didn't know you knew Marion."

"Yes, I was his client about ten years ago. Before he met Robin. We were very close. He helped me find all the beautiful décor for my home."

Jayne thought of the rosy cocoon that Vanessa lived in and suppressed a shudder. "He did find some very…pink things for you," she agreed.

"He was an amazing, intuitive decorator," Vanessa said. "After my last divorce to Donald—or was it David—I always get them mixed up. No, now I remember, it was David, the quiet one. When we spooned at night, his chin dug into my back. And he drooled." Jayne gawped at this nauseating revelation. "After that disastrous marriage, I needed to surround myself with luxury, beauty, and positive energy. I'm a Scorpio, born in the year of the dragon, and I need to be in control of my environment. And soothed. Constantly."

Jayne nodded, like she knew what the heck Vanessa was talking about. "Vanessa, did the police ever recover your stolen jewelry? The stuff your ex-husband stole, supposedly?"

"Supposedly? Of course, he stole my jewels. And the police are so very incompetent." She pouted. "Look at that police detective over there, stuffing himself on food when he should be working. And on our tax dollars. Disgusting."

Detective Schultz was shoveling in cheesecake with a satisfied expression. Jayne looked over at him with amusement.

"Oh, he's working, Vanessa, he's really working. He's keeping an eye on all of us. He's trying to figure out who killed Marion."

Vanessa dropped her spoon. "What are you talking about? Marion's death was an accident." She gripped Tutu tightly and the little dog squirmed and squeaked.

"Was it?" Jayne stood. "Then, why is Detective Schultz here?"

Vanessa stuffed the cigarette holder in her magenta mouth. She puffed on air.

"Maybe he wanted to pay his respects."

"Seriously, Vanessa? Don't be so naïve."

Vanessa squinted and focused on Schultz and Arnie talking. "Perhaps I should ask Arnie to investigate Marion's death."

"Why? Do you feel there's some connection between your jewelry theft and Marion's death?"

Vanessa narrowed her heavily made-up lids.

"I don't know," she said. "Probably not, but since Arnie is working for me, I might as well have her look into it. Maybe she and I can solve the mystery before the police and you do. Wouldn't that be thrilling?" She gave Jayne a look of speculation and challenge.

"Thrilling," Jayne said. She suspected Vanessa wanted to get Arnie into her bed, in that overheated rhinestone-encrusted boudoir. She felt sick and stood. "You'd better be careful, Vanessa, if you start investigating. You don't want your ex to come back and try to strangle you again."

Vanessa smirked. "I'm not worried," she said, tossing a lock of blond hair over her shoulder. "I've got a .38 Special at home and I'm going to start sleeping with it under my pillow."

Jayne felt her stomach plummet. The gun, she thought, was with Schultz. Or had he returned it to her? And if so, how did he explain it being gone? "Be careful, Vanessa, that you don't shoot yourself—or your little dog. Put your glasses on first."

"I don't wear glasses," Vanessa said with a snarl. She dropped her cigarette holder on the floor, bent down, brushed her fingers under the chair, and then shrugged. "Garçon!" she called to a waiter, "I need your help, pwease."

"Sure, you don't wear glasses," Jayne muttered. She stood, making sure Vanessa could squint at her most excellent legs. Jayne caught Arnie's eye. *Get me out of here.* Arnie nodded. *Let's go.* She raised her brows. Arnie stood but then sat down again. She winced in pain. Jayne rushed to her side. "What's up, honey? You don't look good."

She clutched her stomach. "I don't feel so well." Her face matched her green blouse.

"Oh, heavens, no," said Noreen. She was sweating and holding her sides.

Across the room there was a commotion. Both Vanessa and Robin were making noises of distress.

"What the hell is going on?" Schultz shouted, as Noreen passed out, knocking over her martini, creating a river of shaken not stirred vodka and olives, across the table.

Jayne watched in shock as Noreen almost fell out of her chair, Nick saving her just in time. Arnie clutched her stomach and looked gray. Schultz pulled out a radio and started barking orders. He checked Noreen's pulse, put a hand on Arnie's forehead and then hurried over to the head table where Vanessa was laid across two chairs, moaning. Tutu kept licking her face between barks and yips. Robin, sitting hunched over, looked miserable. His sister Sarah, was fanning his face with a linen napkin.

Within ten minutes, paramedics arrived. Noreen, still out cold, was placed on a stretcher, with an oxygen mask attached to her pale face. Arnie stood, tried to walk and then doubled over in pain. She was placed in a wheelchair and strapped in by a young paramedic. Jayne was standing by in confusion and fear as Robin bravely took up the microphone.

"Dear guests, I'm sorry but I'm going to have to leave you. Please have a drink and don't rush away." He was strapped into a wheelchair. Vanessa Harding sat up and started to shriek. Tutu barked happily. They were both placed on a gurney and escorted out of the ballroom. The guests watched silently and then the confusion began. Almost as one, everyone grabbed their belongings and rushed to the door. There were tears, scared laughter, and indignation among the guests.

"What's going on?" a woman screamed at Jayne as she rushed to the exit. "Are we all going to get sick?"

"I don't know," Jayne yelled back. "I sure hope not."

Schultz strode up. "I need a list of all the guests," he said to Jayne.

"I imagine Robin's sister can give you one. Should everyone be rushing off like this? They might need medical attention. This might be a case of mass poisoning."

"If they get sick, I hope they have enough sense to go to the emergency room," Schultz said. "Listen, I got to go. I'll be in touch."

"Poison? Not like Marion?" Ethel looked like she was about to pass out.

"Too early to tell, my dear," Fred replied. He looked at Jayne. "Aren't you going with Arnie to the hospital?"

She snapped to. "Yes, I am," she said, and ran to catch up with her as the paramedics waited for an elevator. "Arnie, sweetie, how you doing?"

"Like a locomotive is running through my insides," she said and promptly vomited on Jayne's shoes.

At Northwest Hospital, the four people were carried into the emergency room. Vanessa was still clutching her little dog. She saw Jayne and thrust Tutu at her. "Jayne, please take Tutu, I don't want him to get lost or be with the police. Please," she begged.

Although not a fan of Vanessa, Jayne certainly had a soft spot for dogs. She took the pup. "Don't worry, Vanessa, I'll look after him." Tutu looked forlorn and cuddled up to Jayne, as Vanessa was wheeled away. Arnie was next. "I can't come in with you, sweetie, I'm so sorry."

"It's all right, babe, I'm going to be fine. I'm sorry I puked on your shoes."

"No worries." She leaned over and placed a kiss on her sweaty brow. "I'll keep in touch on your condition and come get you when you're ready to leave. I'll call your daughter in California too." Arnie gave her a weak smile. Tutu growled. "What am I going to do with this little mutt?"

"Feed him caviar," Arnie said and then promptly passed out.

Noreen and Robin were already inside. Jayne walked to the waiting room. Nick leapt up when he saw her. "Jayne, this is terrible! What happened?"

"Food poisoning? I don't know." She saw Sarah staring out a window. The veiled hat was gone. She walked over to her. "I'm sorry Sarah, I hope Robin is going to be okay soon."

The woman looked up. Unlike Vanessa, her amazing lashes were real. "Thank you," she said stiffly. "I hope so. I don't know what happened." In her hands, she was twisting Robin's lilac silk handkerchief.

CHAPTER SEVENTEEN

Lavage—10 Points

"Aren't we cozy? All of us together again, comrades in tragedy," sighed Vanessa Harding from her bed. It was early Monday morning, at least early for Vanessa, as it was before noon, and three days after the memorial luncheon. Vanessa was wearing a ruffled magenta negligee, and her bed, as usual, was littered with chocolate boxes, silk scarves, and cigarette cartons. A scarlet-lacquered box filled with letters and photographs was near her elbow. Underneath the mess, Tutu squeaked and growled.

Jayne, Arnie, and Schultz were cloistered in her boudoir. Tanya, the assistant, had let them in, her large green eyes showing no emotion as she escorted them to Vanessa's lair. Jayne again had been impressed with the Chanel-style suit, the stilettos, and the assistant's amazing red hair. Now, Tanya stood silently awaiting instructions.

"You may go now," Vanessa commanded her. "Bring us some drinks later, when I ring for you."

"Very good, Mrs. Harding," she murmured and exited.

"First of all," said Schultz, pulling a plastic bag out of his raincoat pocket, "I would like to return your stone to you, Mrs. Harding."

"My sapphire! Where did you find it?"

"On the fifth hole at the Lake View golf course," Schultz said.

"What? On a golf course? How did it get there?" Her eyes bulged with curiosity. Jayne thought she looked like a goldfish.

"We are still investigating that," Schultz said, handing her the bag. She pulled it open and shook out the blue rock.

"It's so beautiful, isn't it?" She held the stone up to the light. "I love blue, almost as much as pink."

Jayne held up a hand to her mouth and made a gagging noise. Arnie gave her a look.

"I am obliged to tell you, Mrs. Harding, that the stone isn't a real sapphire, but a very good imitation."

"What? What are you saying? Of course, my sapphire is real! My husband Donald gave it to me and he was very, very wealthy—at times."

"I'm sorry but it's cubic zirconia," he insisted.

"The bastard! I should have never trusted him! Oh, what is the world coming to?" She rose up among her pillows like a ruffled pink sea monster and promptly passed out. Jayne groaned, Arnie and Schultz leapt up, and Tutu emerged, barking his little brains out. Minutes later, after smelling salts, cold compresses, and eau de cologne had been administered, she woke up. After a shot of whiskey and two Tylenol had been swallowed, she calmed down.

"I can't believe it. I just can't believe it," she said, sipping Irish whiskey and holding a lace handkerchief doused in Chanel to her brow. "I can't believe the stone is fake."

"It's an excellent imitation, Mrs. Harding," said Schultz. "The untrained eye could never tell. Whoever gave it to you spent a lot on a fake."

She sniffed. "As if that makes it all right. What a louse. Then why did David or was it Donald, dammit, try and steal it?"

"That's a very good question that we will be pursuing," Schultz said. "When we find David and/or Donald. Kind of slippery, your exes." He raised his brows at Jayne and Arnie. "How are you feeling now, Mrs. Harding? May we talk about the incident at the memorial lunch?"

"Of course," she cooed.

She looked remarkably fresh for a woman who had just fainted, Jayne thought, if she had indeed really passed out.

"I am here for you." She batted her dragonfly eyelashes. "We escaped the jaws of death, didn't we, Arnie?"

"Not exactly death, Vanessa," she said. "But it sure was a scare."

"A scare? I was never so scared or sick in my life!" She broke off into a wheezing cough and Jayne sat way back in her chair, trying to escape germs that were probably heading straight for her immune system.

"It was unexpected," Arnie agreed.

"Very," Jayne said. "You four getting poisoned with rat poison, total shock."

"Brodifacoum," Arnie said. "That's the real name of the chemical. Used in pesticides. Causing anticoagulant reactions. We were lucky to get to the hospital so quickly."

"Lucky? Getting an IV of whatever? And then having to have a tube put down my throat with that horrible, horrible stuff?" Vanessa was furious.

"It was vitamin K in the IV and charcoal in the lavage," Arnie told her. "It was necessary, dear lady, or we might have bled out and died."

Vanessa shrieked. "Don't say that! I am not ready for death."

"Someone thought you were," Jayne murmured. "The question is, why you?"

Vanessa looked at Jayne, opened her mouth, shut it, and then opened it again. "Judy dear, I cannot tell you how much I appreciated your welcoming dear, dear, Tutu into your home for a night. That was so kind and I want to make it up to you, but I'm not sure you know what you're talking about." She appealed to Schultz. "It was food poisoning, wasn't it?"

"Traces of the chemical were found on your plates and in your drinks," Schultz said. "Only you four."

"How did you find out?" Vanessa asked, wide-eyed with wonder.

"Our officers bagged up your plates and glasses after the incident and the food was sent to the lab. It didn't take long to find chemical traces, and another day to determine exactly what was in your food."

"Yes, but why those four? And did they all eat the same food? What was it in? How can this make sense?" Jayne was indignant.

"Rat poison was found in the chocolate mousse and in the lobster dish that were on all your plates, Arnie's, Robin's, Noreen's and Mrs. Harding's. The poison was also in the wine glasses that you had been drinking from."

"Rat poison, how disgusting." Vanessa frowned and clutched her heart. "The thought gives me palpitations."

Jayne wondered if she had a heart hidden somewhere under her fuchsia chiffon negligee, with pushup cups filled to the max, displaying a scientifically engineered bosom. Arnie was ogling her and Jayne managed a swift kick to her ankle.

"Ouch," she muttered.

"Quit staring," she whispered.

"What did you say, Janet?" Vanessa demanded.

"How daring! To put rat poison in the chocolate mousse and Lobster Newburg," Jayne improvised. "And the drinks." She had eaten neither of those dishes and had left her wine on the bar. "And how did it get there?"

"That's a good question," Schultz agreed. "It would stand to reason that someone spiked your dishes and drinks with the powdered substance. You were all walking around at some point, so it could have been anybody who sprinkled the poison. But, why you four? We don't know yet. And it's very lucky one of you didn't die."

He opened a fresh package of antacids and popped pink and green tablets in his mouth. Goes with the décor, Jayne thought. She wanted to kick him, too.

Vanessa shrieked again and grabbed Arnie's arm. As she moved, she knocked the lacquered box of photographs and letters off the bed, scattering mementos of her life on the floor.

"Oh, damn," Vanessa said, "I'm so upset I don't know what I'm doing."

"I'll get them," Jayne said, wanting to snoop. "No worries."

"That's so kind of you," Vanessa cooed, sticking another cigarette into the holder. She unearthed a lighter from the silken shambles of her bed.

Jayne knelt next to Arnie and picked up yellowed papers and vintage photos.

"Would you mind not smoking?" Arnie asked. "It's very stuffy in here and I've got allergies."

"Why, Arnie, of course not, sweetie. You should have said something before. I don't want to make you feel bad." She pouted. "I would never do that, honey."

"Thank you," she said. "So, Perry, let's get back to the administration of the poison."

"Yes, right, well I think we can eliminate Mrs. Harding as she didn't walk around the room after she sat down at the head table."

"Eliminate me? Why would you want to eliminate me? Did you think I poisoned myself?" She was livid and sat up with a jerk, knocking a box of nougat candies off the bed onto the other side of the room.

"I'm not picking those up, girlfriend," Jayne muttered, as she looked through Vanessa's mail and personal notes.

"No, but it's good to know you didn't have the opportunity to do so, right? You didn't walk over to Arnie and Jayne's table. So, how could you put the poison in their food?" Schultz asked.

"So, you're saying someone had to walk over and poison Noreen and me?" Arnie asked. Jayne was busy reading Vanessa's mail. She picked up a beige note, read it, then stuffed it in her jacket.

"How else?" Schultz asked.

"Then the same person had to walk over to Vanessa and Robin's table," Arnie said.

"Seems like it," Schultz said. "Who brought you your food, Mrs. Harding?"

"I'm not sure. Was it a waiter? Maybe it was that sister of Robin's? I can't remember. What are you doing down there?" Vanessa leaned over the bed, glaring at Jayne.

Jayne, even on her knees, at six feet, made an impressive figure. "Picking up your mail, Vanessa, and all your photos and love letters."

Vanessa chuckled. "Yes, I get plenty of those."

"Look, there's even one from Robin," Jayne said, standing up to her full height, holding the box crammed full of letters and a lilac-colored paper in her hand.

Vanessa snatched the letter away. "Give that to me! Yes, he wrote to me after our terrible ordeal in the hospital. So kind of him."

"What did he say?" Schultz asked. "Can I get a cup of tea? I've got heartburn. This case is giving me indigestion."

"He just wanted to say he was so sorry I'd taken ill at the luncheon and was there anything he could do for me, and..." She smiled in delight. "Would I be his Scrabble partner at your next game." She picked up the crystal bell and rang it with vigor.

Jayne's mouth dropped open and Arnie's forehead started to gleam with sweat. There was a silence. The door opened and Tanya appeared. "Yes, Mrs. Harding?"

"We want some tea," she ordered. "The good stuff."

"Yes, right away." Her fiery red hair was done up in an elaborate chignon. Jayne wondered if that was her natural color or enhanced at the salon. Of course, with those green eyes...

"What do you think, Jayne?" Arnie cut into her reverie. "Should we set a night for another Scrabble game?"

Jayne looked at her, dumbfounded. Had she lost her mind? "So soon? Do you think we should have another game right away? We don't even know if Nick and Noreen or Fred and Ethel are interested in playing. Noreen was pretty sick and Ethel said she never was going out in public again."

"I think that was an overstatement," Arnie said.

"Ms. Charles is feeling better. I saw her this morning at the brewery," said Schultz. "She seemed to have the worst case and was in bed all weekend after she was released from the hospital.

But she's better now. Has to watch what she eats and her throat is sore."

"So is mine," Arnie said, massaging her neck.

"Mine too." Vanessa pouted. "I need a massage."

She leered at Arnie. Jayne longed to wring her neck.

"Whoever did the deed knew enough to put just enough in your food to make you sick, not kill you," Schultz said.

"Kill? I hate that word!" Vanessa shrieked again and fell back against her pillows. Her eyes closed and her eyelashes made zigzag shadows against her rosy cheeks.

"It's a good thing you have your gun, Mrs. Harding," Tanya said, walking into the room, holding a full tray with teapot, cups and saucers and plates of tea biscuits and scones.

Vanessa's eyes lit up at the sight of food. "Gun? What gun? Pour Detective Schultz some tea immediately, Tanya," she ordered.

"The gun that you told Arnie and Jayne about at the luncheon," Schultz answered. "The gun that you keep in your hall bureau downstairs," he lied with a straight face. Jayne was impressed, although she felt her face heating up with anxiety. Would he expose her theft? Arnie paused, teacup in hand, waiting.

"How do you know about that?" Vanessa said.

"The night your house was broken into, you gave us permission to look around your house, remember? We found it then. We checked it out. It's registered to you and you have a license for it." Schultz looked over at Jayne, who grabbed a handful of biscuits and sat down with a bland look on her face. Arnie raised her eyebrows at Jayne.

"Yes, I did tell your boys in blue to look around," she said. "They were so impressed with my beautiful home and the rest of the décor." She looked down at her expansive chest and smiled.

"Unbelievable," Jayne murmured.

"What did you say, Jesse?"

"I said, 'Your home is unbelievable—such unusual furnishings.'"

"Yes, it is special, my little haven of love," she sighed. "But lately, I've been so lonely," she purred at them. "Detective Schultz, are you married?"

He gulped his tea. "Yes, happily married for twenty-five years this coming January."

She frowned. "Then you're not available."

"Hardly," Jayne said.

Jayne opened her mouth but Schultz spoke first. "I don't think it's a good idea, Mrs. Harding, to keep a loaded gun downstairs where anyone who comes in can take it and maybe use it against you. You should keep it locked up."

"Yes, that's an idea," she said, yawning. She ate a cookie, spit out half of it and took another. "I hate hazelnut," she said to Tutu, who gobbled up the remains.

"You should get it now," Schultz said.

"All right," Vanessa sighed. She rang the bell.

Within seconds Tanya appeared. Was she hanging out in the hall, Jayne wondered?

"Tanya, bring me the gun that's in the hall drawer," she ordered.

If Tanya was surprised by the request, she gave no sign of it. She left the room and they waited. Schultz and Arnie sat drinking tea. Jayne fiddled with biscuit crumbs on her plate, and tried not to be nauseated by the sight of Vanessa feeding Tutu bits of scone as she kissed the little furball's head repeatedly. Jayne loved animals but this was way too much.

Within a minute, Tanya returned, empty-handed. "I'm sorry, Mrs. Harding, but there is no gun in the front hall armoire."

"What do you mean, there's no gun? I never moved it. Are you sure? Did you check all the drawers?" Vanessa sat up, scattering cookie crumbs, candy wrappers and an ashtray over the bed.

"Yes, Mrs. Harding, I did."

"Well, go back and look again," she ordered. "Check all the drawers and go into the salon and look there too. Maybe I moved it in my distress after almost being strangled and I forgot."

"Yes, Mrs. Harding." The assistant sighed and left the room.

Schultz looked at Jayne. She shook her head. *I didn't take it again.*

"I'm going to go give your assistant a hand," Schultz said and left the boudoir.

Jayne, Arnie, and Vanessa sat silently. An ornate rococo wall clock ticked like gunshots. Jayne looked down at Robin's letter on the bed.

"When did you get Robin's letter, Vanessa? He must have mailed it the minute he got out of the hospital Friday night for you to get it so soon."

"It arrived this morning in the mailbox." Vanessa shrugged. "Who cares when he mailed it?"

"Can I see the envelope?" Jayne asked.

"Why?" She squinted at Jayne. "Is it any of your business?"

"Just part of our detective business, dear lady," Arnie said. She smiled at the diva and she thawed.

"Of course, dear Arnie," she said, handing her the box of letters. "If you think it will help you."

Arnie carefully examined each letter, card, and envelope, arranging them neatly when she was done. "Here it is," she said. The lilac envelope was addressed to Mrs. V. Harding in purple ink.

"May I see it?" Jayne asked.

She studied the envelope. There was no postmark, and the stamp was untouched.

Schultz returned.

"Did you find it? Did you find my gun?"

He shook his head. "Nowhere to be found downstairs. Are you sure you don't have it up here?"

"No, absolutely not. I wouldn't want dear Tutu to get hurt. It's never been up here."

Jayne and Arnie exchanged glances. Schultz frowned. "I think, Mrs. Harding, you and I need to have a serious talk."

"Yes, there's a lot to discuss," Jayne said.

"Not you," Schultz said. "You and Arnie can go and I'll get in touch with you later."

"But we can help," Jayne protested.

"Jayne," Arnie cut in, "let's go. We can talk to Perry later."

"Perry?" Vanessa was all agog. "What a sexy name. Perry."

Jayne rolled her eyes and Arnie took her by the arm. "See you later," she said, bowing to Vanessa. "Mrs. Harding, I hope you have a very good rest of the day."

"Now don't forget about that Scrabble game," she said. "I really, really want to pway Scwabble with you, Arnie dear," she lisped.

"I won't," Arnie promised.

"Over my dead body," Jayne said, as they headed downstairs.

"Don't say that!" Arnie shushed her. "It could happen, the way things are going."

At the front door, Tanya stood with Arnie's Cubs cap and Jayne's jacket.

"Thank you, Tanya," Jayne said. "You have such beautiful hair. Does red hair run in your family?"

The woman looked at Jayne with wide eyes, green as a shamrock. Long lashes that Jayne would have given her right arm for, blinked once. "I don't know," Tanya said. "I was adopted."

CHAPTER EIGHTEEN

Brewery—15 Points

"I should know better," Jayne said, as they stood outside, inhaling fresh air.

"How so?" Arnie tugged on her Cubs cap and looked at the sky. The maple leaves had turned scarlet and amber-colored. Fall was here. "Pretty this time of year, isn't it? The air is crisp."

"Any air is crisp after being in that overheated hot house," Jayne said, scuffing her toes in the fallen leaves.

"And why should you know better? About what?"

"I shouldn't have asked if red hair ran in her family. That was thoughtless. I hardly know her. But it's so red, I wondered if it's dyed."

"I'm sure she wasn't offended, Jayne. It was just an offhand remark, wasn't it? You didn't mean anything offensive by it, did you?"

"No, I did not." They walked to the car. "Arnie, what do you think happened to the gun?"

"A true mystery," Arnie said, starting up the engine. "If Schultz replaced the gun this morning, as he said he would, then where did it go?"

"How do you know he returned the gun?"

"He told me."

"He didn't tell me." Jayne scowled. "He's got a lot of nerve."

"My dear, I am a licensed professional detective. I think Schultz was affording me some professional courtesy by telling me about the gun." Jayne sniffed. "And he was most certainly affording professional courtesy by not arresting you for tampering with evidence and stealing her property!"

Jayne sat up and grabbed Arnie's arm. "Is it evidence? Was it used in a crime?"

"I'm driving," she said calmly. "And no, it's not evidence—yet. But now that it's missing—"

"Who could have taken it? I bet it was that slinky, silent, red-haired, green-eyed purple people eater."

"You're dating yourself with that old song," Arnie said, smiling.

"I don't care." She burst into song. "*It was a one-eyed, one-horned, flyin' purple people eater, sure looks strange to me!*"

"Well done," Arnie said.

"It should be a big-boobed, big-haired, flyin' pink man eater."

"You really don't like Vanessa at all, do you?"

"She's ridiculous! All that pink and painted face and baby talk blub! And she thinks she's irresistible! How outrageous! The nerve of her."

"I suppose after four husbands and scores of lovers—"

"How many lovers?" Jayne pinched her arm. "Four score and seven years ago—"

"As I was saying, after four husbands and being the Queen of the Saint Patrick's Day Parade—"

"Circa 1492—"

"Let me finish!" Arnie roared, and Jayne chuckled. "After all that attention, she thinks she's hot stuff and that every man is after her. And with the way she dresses and acts, she probably gets a fifty percent return on her audacious ways."

"Marrying twins, can you believe that?" Jayne asked.

"Why not? She's rather ridiculous. She probably thought that was a feather in her sexual cap to marry twin brothers. And not be able to tell them apart, after the fact."

"Ridiculous and bodacious," Jayne added. "She's as blind as a bat. If she can't tell them apart by their faces, maybe she can by the size of their—"

"Please, spare me," Arnie groaned. "Let's not go there. I have a weak stomach, my love."

"Am I, your love?" Jayne asked lightly.

"You know I've fallen very hard for you," Arnie said, stopping at a red light. She turned to Jayne. "I hope you feel the same way about me, too."

"I thought you were getting ready to go out on the town with Vanessa."

"Why, I do believe the little woman is jealous."

"I'm six feet tall. I am no *little* woman."

"No, you're not, but you're my woman."

Jayne exhaled softly. "And you're mine." They beamed at each other and were about to lock lips, when a cacophony of car horns sounded behind them.

"Drat, green light." Arnie stepped on the gas.

"You owe me one," Jayne said.

"I owe you many," Arnie said tenderly. Jayne felt herself blushing. *At my age?* Why not, her inner diva said and did a little tap dance around her heart.

They pulled up along the north branch of the Chicago River, to their first stop—The Universal Brewery, where Noreen was back at work. Jayne had bought a small fruit basket for Noreen and one for Robin. She was also taking care of Arnie, cooking her bland meals and making sure she got to bed early. However, Vanessa Harding was not included in Jayne's care, although she had taken charge of Tutu, and what a nightmare that had been. Lucia did *not* care for Tutu, not at all.

Getting out of the car, Jayne looked at her shoes. "I don't think I got all the poo off my shoes after Tutu let it go all over the kitchen floor. Poor animal. I shudder to think of his daily diet—martinis, onions, and chocolate nougats. And all the cigarette smoke can't be good for the little thing."

"You were extremely kind to take the dog overnight, Jayne. It would have gone to the police animal shelter and that would have been traumatic for it."

"It was traumatic for me. Lucia hated Tutu and the feeling was mutual. They sat on opposite sides of the room growling at each other all night. I couldn't sleep a wink. And, I was worried sick about you, Arnie. I was so happy when I could get you out of the hospital in the morning and we could deliver Vanessa her dog. What a twenty-four-hour shitshow that was."

"I hope we never have to repeat that day," Arnie agreed. "I didn't want to stay overnight for observation but the nice young doctor was so insistent about it."

"I'm glad you stayed," Jayne said. "Possible internal bleeding is no joke."

The brewery was just about to open for lunch. As it was Monday, the place was deserted, except for a bartender and a few servers getting the tables ready as they walked up to the bar.

"Hi, we're here to see Noreen," Jayne said, holding the wrapped basket of fruit. "Could you tell her Arnie and Jayne are here, please."

The bartender, a young woman with purple hair and a wide smile, pointed to the back. "Noreen is expecting you. I'll take you there. Come right through." She picked up the end of the heavy cherry wood bar and they entered the heart of the brewery. Large vats of brewing ale and lager were lined up against the back wall. The smell of hops, yeast, and oranges filled the air. The brew master, with two attendants, was measuring the beer in each vat with a hydrometer, checking its strength. The woman, whose nametag read Trixie, knocked on a huge oak door. "Noreen, your friends are here."

"Come in," she answered.

Jayne and Arnie walked into a cluttered office stacked with boxes of invoices, delivery receipts, payroll printouts, and bills of lading. Jayne was amazed to see Noreen working in an old-fashioned, paper-driven office.

"Yes, it's a mess here, isn't it? My brother, bless his heart, was the most unorganized person in the world. When he passed away eighteen months ago and left me the brewery, which was so unexpected, and I must admit, a bit exciting, he also left a lot of disorder. I've been so busy trying to learn the mechanics of becoming a great brew master that I haven't found the time to sort out his papers."

"All in good time," Arnie said.

"No rush," Jayne agreed. *Platitudes 'r' us. Can't we think of anything more original to say?*

"And to tell you the truth…" She pointed to the stacks of wooden boxes and antique-looking cabinets which gave a sort of Harry Potter vibe to the office. "…I hate to dispose of all this. It reminds me of Jay, who was taken away from us too soon." She fought back tears.

Jayne was astonished and rendered into silence for once. Arnie stood by, cap in hand. Who would have thought Noreen, cool, calm, blond Noreen, would display so much emotion and sentiment about her brother? It gave a whole new dimension to her, Jayne thought.

"We know how busy you are, and we don't want to keep you, but we wanted to bring you this." Jayne handed the fruit basket to Noreen. "And to see how you're feeling."

"That's very kind of you," Noreen said, setting the colorful basket down on her desk. Through the plastic wrap she saw fruit, biscuits, candy and herbal teas. "Very thoughtful. After a rough weekend with stomach cramps, I'm now feeling much better."

"I—we—felt terrible that you fell ill at the luncheon. I—we—feel that somehow you four getting sick is all related to Marion's passing."

Noreen looked Jayne up and down. "I should say it is. If Marion hadn't been poisoned at your home during your Scrabble game—"

"It wasn't Jayne's fault," Arnie protested. "How could she know that would happen?"

Noreen played with the ribbon on the fruit basket. "Indeed, how would she? Except for that crazy poetry note she received. Wasn't that a warning? And why didn't you do anything about it?" She looked at Jayne, all signs of sentimentality gone.

"I thought the note was a joke," Jayne said. "As I told the police several times."

Noreen made a face. "Some joke. Marion's dead. And what did you find on the golf course? I'm sure you went there, you two bloodhounds."

Jayne opened her mouth to blast her, but Arnie cut in, "We didn't find anything. We went to follow the clues and it was a false lead. The note must have been a prank."

Jayne watched Noreen's hands tie the ribbon in little frenzied knots. "Did you get a note, Noreen?"

"Certainly not, why would I?"

"Fred got one that he shared with us. If you did, we would be happy to take a look," Jayne pressed.

Noreen's pale complexion reddened. "I did not get a note, neither did Nick," she said. "Thank you for the fruit, but I have to get back to work."

"Of course, we don't want to interrupt your day any longer," Arnie said. "We just wanted to say how sorry we were that you fell ill and see how you're feeling."

"Thank you for your concern," Noreen said. "I appreciate you coming."

They started for the door. Then Jayne paused. "Noreen, one quick question. Robin wrote Vanessa Harding and invited her to be his Scrabble partner for the next game. Would you and Nick be up for that?"

"Certainly not! I am in no mood for Scrabble. How can you ask?"

"Okay, just checking," Jayne said and scooted out the door.

They were driving to their next destination, Robin's house, and Arnie asked, "Do you think that was wise, asking her about the note?"

"It sure got a rise out of her," Jayne said. "I bet she got one, too, and won't admit it. In fact, I think before we go see Robin, we should make an unannounced visit to Nick at his gym."

"Do you think that's a good idea?"

"We can try it. Maybe Lady Macbeth hasn't called her boyfriend to tell on us."

"Why Lady Macbeth?"

"Something about her makes me think she would be a great instigator of murder. She's very cool and calculating. I don't trust her."

"Perhaps so," Arnie said. "But can we trust anybody?"

"I guess not. I thought I knew these people, at least a little, but now I'm not sure."

"Dear heart, where's the gym?"

Jayne gave directions.

"Where do you think the gun went?" Arnie asked, as she carefully turned around in an alley and headed in the opposite direction.

"I think the assistant took it or Vanessa hid it and won't admit it," Jayne said.

"Why would she hide it?"

"Just to be mysterious and draw attention to herself and get you and Schultz to dance around her and spend time with her."

"Jayne, you said the letter from Robin had no postmark on the envelope. So maybe it wasn't mailed. Maybe he or someone else dropped off the note."

"And snuck in and stole the gun? How would they know about it? And how would they get in unobserved?"

Arnie exhaled. "Perhaps the person who stole the gun had been there before and knew where to look, maybe even has a spare key."

"You know, that narrows the field of suspects down very significantly," Jayne said.

"Yes, I know," she replied with a small smile. "And you and I are included on that list."

"Touché, Sherlock. You got me there."

The Power Gym was located in River North about a mile from Jayne's condo. They found street parking, fed the meter, and went inside. A very attractive blond woman, willowy yet buffed, was sitting at the desk.

"Can I help you?" Her nametag read Melanie. "Are you here for a session?"

"No, we're here to see Nick Pappas, if he's available. We're friends of his," Jayne said.

"Let me check." She picked up a phone and hit a button. "Nick, there's two people here to see you." She paused.

"Jayne and Arnie," Arnie told her.

"Jayne and Arnie," she repeated. "Okay, I'll tell them. He's just finishing a session with a client and he'll be out in five minutes. Can I get you a tea or a juice?"

"No thanks," said Arnie.

"I'm fine, thanks," said Jayne. They sat down on white swivel chairs in front of a large window that faced Hubbard Street. Nestled under the "L" tracks, the noise of the trains occasionally rattled overhead.

"This is a trendy sort of place," Arnie said, looking around the room filled with treadmills, bikes, ellipticals, and weights. At the far end of the room, punching bags hung from the ceiling.

"Boxing is in these days," Jayne said. She looked down at her hands. "I wonder if boxing would strengthen my grip for golf?"

"It might," Arnie said, "but if you get any stronger, I won't have a chance." She winked.

"Why, Arnie, you little devil," Jayne said.

Nick Pappas walked out of the back room. By his side was a very attractive woman, in her forties, wearing the tightest purple Lycra pants and bra Jayne had ever seen.

"See you next time, Annette," he said to her, patting her shoulder.

"Absolutely, Nick," she said, squeezing his bicep.

Hmm, Jayne thought.

"Hi, Jayne, Arnie, how come you're here?" Not one to beat around the bush, Nick stood, hands on hips, dressed in shorts and a T-shirt. He had a towel around his neck and looked sweaty. "Everything okay?"

"We just paid a visit to Noreen. We brought her some fruit. We're so sorry she was ill all weekend, and we wanted to stop by and see how you're doing," Jayne said, watching his reaction.

"I'm okay, thanks," he said. "Noreen had a rough couple of days. She couldn't keep anything down except some soup and ginger ale. I told her to stay home this morning, but she wouldn't hear of it. She's tough."

"She looked good," Arnie agreed. "I'm glad she's feeling better. I'm so sorry she got sick like I did."

Nick laughed. "Sick?" He dropped his voice. "Poisoned, you mean. By some nutjob who wanted to get us like he got Marion."

"What do you know about that?" Jayne said.

"Know? I don't *know* anything," Nick retorted, "but it stands to reason that someone is out to get the Scrabble players."

"Robin contacted Vanessa Harding and asked if she would be his partner next Scrabble game," Jayne said.

"You're kidding! What a lot of nerve, wanting to play again and asking that old lady to be his partner. When is the game? I'd like to go, just for the laughs."

"You'd be interested in another game?" Arnie asked.

"Sure, why not? Being sober now, I like watching people slurp drinks and make fools of themselves. Makes me feel noble."

Jayne stared at him. He was not the mild-mannered athlete she thought he was. "We wondered if Noreen ever received a note with a weird poem," Jayne said.

"Note?" His freckled face frowned.

"Yes, like the haiku I got the night we played Scrabble."

He thought for a second. "The killer and golf course, right?"

"Yes, that's right. Did she ever get one?"

Nick hesitated. Jayne and Arnie exchanged glances.

"Not that I know of."

"Did you?" Arnie asked. "Did you ever get a note like Jayne's?"

"No, I didn't," he said. He took the towel from around his neck and started to wring it. "And if Noreen did, she never told me about it. Why don't you ask her?"

"That's a great idea. We'll do that," Jayne said, taking Arnie by the arm. "You've got a fabulous place here, Nick."

"Thanks." He looked proud. "Business is good. If you two ever want a complimentary training session, give me a call."

"Thank you," Jayne said. "That would be cool, wouldn't it, Arnie? Maybe we could box." Arnie looked at her in shock. "And, Nick, if we set up a Scrabble game, do you think you can get Noreen to play?"

"I can get Noreen to play," he said. "No problem. She loves the game."

As they left the gym, Jayne looked over her shoulder. Nick was standing with a funny look on his face. He pulled his cell phone out of his pocket and hit the call button.

CHAPTER NINETEEN

Romantic—13 Points

"How kind of you to come and see me," said Robin York, sitting in his enormous, sun-drenched living room, all silver and white décor. The view from the sixty-sixth floor was breathtaking. He was wearing a pale gray cashmere tracksuit and drinking mint tea. He had a blanket wrapped around his knees and looked even paler than usual. "The fruit is such a thoughtful gift."

"You look good, Robin, considering everything you've been through," Jayne said.

"It's been a nightmare for you," Arnie said. "I'm glad you're taking off a few days from work."

"It's been unbelievable," Robin agreed. "Tea?" They both shook their heads. "Losing Marion so tragically, getting poisoned by some unknown madman at the beautiful luncheon, and now feeling so very weak and tired, where will it all end? And do you know if the police have any answers? And do you?"

"Do we what?" Jayne said, surveying the room.

Pictures of Robin and Marion, displayed in Art Deco frames were sitting on every table and placed on the white baby grand piano in the corner.

"Have you any answers as to who killed Marion? And how it was done?"

Jayne and Arnie exchanged glances. "Not really, not yet," Arnie said. "We were wondering if you have any ideas? Did Marion have any enemies that you know about?"

"I've been thinking about that," Robin said, picking up his cup. "And no, I can't think of anyone who had a grudge against him. But that's rather a moot point, isn't it? The question is, who among us really had a grudge against Marion? It had to be one of us, the Scrabble players, didn't it?"

"It does look that way, doesn't it?" Arnie agreed.

"But the police can't find any connection among us, can they?" Jayne asked. "Of course, in an Agatha Christie novel, it's usually the spouse who's the murderer or murderess, if I can use the old-fashioned term."

"You are such a romantic, Jayne," Robin said, "for all your athletic, pro golfer, 'I am woman, hear me roar' ways. That only happens in books."

Jayne bit her lip. "Only in books? Do you ever watch the news, Robin? Lots of spousal abuse going on."

"What are you driving at?" Robin sat up and glared. "Are you accusing me of killing Marion?" There was a long silence.

Arnie coughed. "I'm sure Jayne is just speculating about possibilities," she said. "No one would ever think that. You two were so…devoted to each other."

"Except when you were bugging each other like mad," Jayne said.

Robin looked at them both and shrugged. "Okay. I am one of the suspects. Schultz keeps hanging around and I'm sure I'm being followed whenever I go out. That make you happy? And here—" He fumbled in a drawer in the coffee table. "You better take a look at this. I wasn't going to say anything but maybe it would help shed some light on who killed poor Marion."

STRAIGHT, GAY, BI—ROBIN?
DID YOUR LOVER FIND THE TRUTH?
POISON DOES THE TRICK

Arnie read it quietly with Jayne peering over her shoulder. "You see," said Robin, "someone thinks I killed Marion. I keep expecting another letter any minute, demanding money or threatening me with something vile. Do you think I killed Marion?" He appealed to them, hands clutching his chest.

"Of course not," Arnie soothed him. "We don't think it's you for a minute."

"Are you okay, Robin?" Jayne was concerned. "Should we call an ambulance? Is it your heart?"

"I get tachycardia from nerves," he explained. "When I'm upset my heart beats all over the place. I'll calm down," he said, with a wan smile. "I don't need an ambulance, Jayne, my dear. But thank you for worrying about me."

"Naturally, we are worried about you." She studied the pale man, drinking tea, huddled under a blanket.

Arnie waited a moment and then continued, "But who could it be? Who sent this to you? We know you did Fred and Ethel's taxes. Did Marion know them before?"

"I don't think so," Robin said.

"And did either of you have any connection with Nick and Noreen before meeting at Jayne's for Scrabble?"

"Marion worked out with Nick a couple of times and did a photo shoot at his gym. Noreen I didn't know. And I never met Jayne or you, Arnie, before Marion insisted we show up for Scrabble one evening. And I was so glad we did. I had such a good time playing Scrabble with you all and enjoying all the amazing food and cocktails. It was such an escape from my very dry, often boring day as an accountant."

"We're so glad we met you, too," Jayne said. "May we show the note to Detective Schultz? He's collecting them."

"Do tell," Robin demanded. "Who else got a note?"

"I probably shouldn't have said anything." Jayne knew she had made a gaffe. Arnie was looking at her, dismay on her face.

She sighed. "Fred and Vanessa Harding got notes and you know I did, too."

"What did they say?"

"Robin, I don't think we should talk out of turn," Arnie said. "Not yet, anyway."

"Still sleuthing?"

"Yes, we are," Jayne said. "I think Arnie should solve the murder. That would give her detective agency lots of good publicity."

"It would indeed," Robin said, looking at Arnie.

"How's your sister?" Arnie changed the subject. "Sarah. Is she still staying with you?"

"She's fine, thanks. No, she's not here. She went home this morning. She lives in the northern suburbs and wanted to check on her horses. She'll be back this week to check on me."

"Horses, how nice. She married?" Jayne wondered about the hostile woman with the big eyes who looked like she was ready to slay dragons for Robin.

"Sadly, she's a widow. No children. I'm afraid her horses and me are her interests in life." He looked embarrassed. "We both lost the loves of our lives."

"It's wonderful to have family to be with during times of stress and sorrow," Arnie said.

Jayne looked at Arnie. She was a widow and her daughter lived far away. Could she see her as family? At that moment Arnie turned and looked at her. Her deep blue eyes were alight with affection. Jayne smiled. Robin, missing nothing, nodded. "I see you two know what I'm talking about."

"Yes, we do," Arnie agreed. "Love is everything, isn't it?"

"Absolutely," said Robin.

"We should leave you," Arnie said, "so you can relax and rest. How are you feeling after your ordeal?"

"My stomach is better, but I'm still exhausted. I sleep a lot and try not to brood."

"That's very wise," Arnie said.

"Jayne, would you consider having a Scrabble game in the near future? I wrote to Vanessa Harding and asked if she would like to be my partner. I feel terrible that she was poisoned at Marion's luncheon. She hadn't seen him in years and I had never met her before. I feel so responsible. So, what do you think? Can we set a date for a game?"

Jayne nodded at Robin. "Okay. Sounds like a plan. Sound good to you, Arnie?"

Arnie nodded in agreement, but her eyes met Jayne's with that bland look, that meant suspicion.

Suspicion? *How did the letter get delivered to Vanessa's house?* Jayne reflected. She had a lot to discuss with Arnie. *To mail or not to mail, that is the question.*

CHAPTER TWENTY

Intrigue—9 Points

Jayne took her pitching wedge out of the bag and surveyed the hole. It was early the following Friday, one week after the disastrous memorial luncheon at the Drake and two weeks after the demise of Marion Wayne. Tonight she was hosting a Scrabble game, in his honor, as requested by Robin. "Am I nuts, or what?" she asked the geese who sat by the edge of the water hazard, looking at her with cautious eyes. They had been struck by too many wild golf balls in their short life. "Another game, two weeks after a murder at my house? What is wrong with me? And what is wrong with Arnie for agreeing?"

She hit the ball laying by the edge of the green and neatly knocked it within inches of the cup. "Well, at least I can do something right," she told the birds and walked up to the hole. The course was about to open. It was seven a.m., but as Jayne had special privileges, she had teed off at six and was almost done with the nine holes. She played power golf, walking quickly, not thinking much about her shots and just aiming for the hole.

She was working off steam and trying to find some Zen place in her heart. She was failing miserably. Even after getting up at five, walking and feeding Lucia, and tearing off to the golf course to play a lightning-fast nine holes, she still felt edgy. Too much energy, adrenaline and nerves. "What's the matter with me? Arnie seemed to think the game would go well and with Detective Schultz showing up unexpectedly, nothing could go wrong." She wished she had her confidence.

She finished the nine holes, stopped to talk to the golf pro in the pro shop, who she had mentored a few years ago, and walked to her car. She put her clubs in the trunk and thought about getting a cup of coffee at the just-opened snack shop. A piece of white paper in the windshield caught her attention.

At first, she thought it was an ad paper, or some notice from the Chicago Park District about parking. But when she opened it, she stopped cold.

EARLY MORNING GOLF
CAN'T DISGUISE THE VILLAINY
OF LOVE GONE SO WRONG

Another haiku? At this hour? Whose love? What villainy? She spun around and looked at the almost empty parking lot. Nothing. No one. A few sparrows and pigeons lurked by, hoping for crumbs. She felt violated. Who was following her? Which one of the Scrabble team was stalking her? A car pulled up close. Two cheerful men grabbed their golf bags and headed off for the pro shop to sign in for their round. It all seemed so peaceful and serene. Someone was watching her every move. With shaking hands that she attributed to the morning cold, Jayne got in the car and drove downtown to her home, her pup, and she hoped—sanity.

"Jayne, where did you put the ice tongs?" Arnie asked. They were preparing for the imminent Scrabble game. Two card tables were set up with the deluxe revolving Scrabble boards placed exactly in the middle. She had decided not to make a big fuss with the food and drink. Wine and beer, soft drinks, seltzer water, and coffee would accompany trays of small sandwiches, veggies and dip, cookies, and fruit.

"They're in the drawer next to the fridge," she said. "I still think this is a bad idea, Arnie, inviting Vanessa Harding here tonight."

"Robin wanted another game with us," Arnie said, shrugging. "And he already invited her. How could we say no?"

"Very easily. We could say N-O and tell Robin we'd do it another time. I get a bad feeling that something drastic is going to happen with that woman in my house."

She placed the sandwiches which she had cut into heart, spade, diamond, and club shapes on the silver platter. She hadn't told Arnie yet about the note on her car, she was still thinking about it. If it was about their relationship, she didn't want to upset her.

"Nice. Love the shapes," Arnie said, forgetting the mystery for a moment.

"They are cute, reminds me of my mother and her bridge games," Jayne sighed. "She made such lovely lunches. But back to tonight. Are you sure Schultz is coming?"

"When I called to tell him about the game tonight, he insisted. He said he would show up and maybe play a round or two. I said he could take my place."

"Or mine," Jayne said. "I can't believe Vanessa Harding is coming to my home. That's unbelievable. She'd better not try to smoke in here and I hope she's not wearing so much perfume. Between her and Ethel, I'll have to open the balcony door for some fresh air."

"I'm sure it will work out," Arnie said, polishing the wine and beer glasses. "Don't worry."

"Worry? I wasn't going to show you this, but you know I'm not good at keeping secrets. I'm about ready to burst." She took the note out of her backpack and handed it to Arnie. "What do you think about this?"

Arnie read the note aloud.

EARLY MORNING GOLF
CAN'T DISGUISE THE VILLAINY
OF LOVE GONE SO WRONG

Arnie's forehead broke out in sweat. "Jayne, when did you get this?"

"This morning, after I played golf. It was on my windshield. I thought at first it was an ad or a parking ticket, but I was wrong."

"Why didn't you call me right away?" Arnie mopped her brow with a kerchief.

"I didn't want to upset you, dear one."

"Well, I'm upset now. That means someone is following you," Arnie groaned. "Did you call Schultz?"

"I didn't call him," she replied, shrugging. "What could he do about it?"

"He could have you followed to see who's stalking you."

"He might have canceled our Scrabble game tonight and I know how much this means to the Elsinore Detective Agency. I want you to solve this case, Arnie."

"That's very noble of you, sweetheart, but I don't want to see you getting hurt."

"I could have been hurt at Marion's luncheon," she protested. "I think it was random, which three of us got sick."

"Don't you mean four?"

"I think one of you was the intended target and the other three were random decoys to make it look good. It could have been me or Nick or Fred and Ethel. We were all sitting together."

"But what was the point? To kill one of us? I don't have anything to do with Marion or Vanessa Harding."

"Exactly. You were poisoned to throw us off the scent of who it really was intended for," she said, throwing Lucia a bit of broken chicken sandwich. "Maybe the poisoning was a warning for the intended victim. Or maybe the killer knows one of you is in bad health and thought a bit of rat poison would finish him or her off."

"I'm not in bad health," Arnie said.

"I know that and I know you were not the intended victim, but the killer doesn't know what shape you're in. It makes my blood boil, Arnie, to think you could've been seriously injured by this stunt. Maybe all four of you would've died." She bit into a celery stick with vigor.

"That would've made the national news," Arnie agreed. "But it didn't happen. Four of us got sick and we still don't know who the poison was meant for and how it got onto our plates and glasses."

"And by whom. Someone was walking around the room sprinkling rat poison."

"We all walked around the room at one time or another," Arnie said. "Every one of us."

"Except Vanessa," Jayne said.

"Except Vanessa. So maybe we should cross her off the list?"

"Fat chance of that. I don't trust that painted pink trollop one little bit."

Arnie chuckled. "Tonight is going to be very entertaining."

Jayne pelted her with a grape. "I'm sure it will, Sherlock."

CHAPTER TWENTY-ONE

Knit—8 Points

"Par," said Fred, frowning. "Five points. I have terrible letters."

"I'm sure they'll get better, Freddie," Ethel said, studying her tiles. She was very quiet tonight and kept dabbing at her eyes with a lace handkerchief.

"What does that mean, par?" Vanessa Harding squinted at the board and sighed. "These tiles are so little." She had arrived almost on time, claiming her chauffeur was late, wearing a flamboyant magenta pantsuit, clutching Tutu, and blowing kisses to all of the Scrabble players.

"It's when someone makes par, like in golf. The hole is a par five and you take five shots," Nick explained.

The pink glitter scattered across her forehead moved as she frowned at the word. "You are all so smart! I declare," she said. "How did y'all get so smart?"

"And when did you get so southern?" Jayne remarked at the next table. "Oh, wait, she's from the south side of Chicago."

Nick and Noreen smirked. Arnie gave her a tap on the wrist. "Jayne, behave."

"What did you say, Judy, dear?" Vanessa asked, sucking on an empty cigarette holder. Tutu, who had not been invited, but had been brought anyway, raised his head and growled. Lucia, nestled on her cashmere throne, picked up her head and barked, infuriated that the Pomeranian had returned, invading her space.

"I said nothing of importance, Vanessa."

"I am sure of that," the rhinestone goddess sniffed.

A small guffaw sounded from the sofa. Schultz was watching the players, drinking a soda and knitting.

"What are you making, Perry?" Vanessa said. "I just love seeing a man knitting! It's so special."

"Making hats for the homeless," he replied, counting stitches on long, silver needles.

"That is so admirable," Arnie said. "Where did you learn to knit?"

"A long time ago, when I was a rookie cop, I was shot in a robbery. The bullet went through my little finger. I didn't want to quit the job, I liked being a cop, so I did a ton of physical therapy. Part of the therapy was using my hands, like knitting. Most men don't want to knit, but I found it also very good at relieving tension at the end of the day."

"That is so cool," Jayne said, arranging her tiles again.

"Very impressive," Fred said, but he looked like he wasn't sure.

Schultz pulled more yarn out of a duffel bag at his feet. "Who's winning?"

"It's too early to tell," said Robin.

"How do you play in teams?" Schultz asked. "I thought you would play two people together and be able to help each other."

"No, we all wanted our own tiles. So, at the end of the evening, each team adds up their scores and that's how the winner is decided," Robin said.

"And Robin is my partner," Vanessa gushed. "Isn't that sweet?"

"Very sweet," said Noreen, rolling her eyes.

"I'm glad you decided to come tonight, Noreen," Jayne said. "I wasn't sure you were up to it."

"Nick insisted," Noreen said. "I'm not sure why, but he did and here we are."

"I'm so glad we could all get together again," Robin said. "And having Vanessa here is so special."

"Very special," said Jayne.

Robin sat up and smiled. "A-D-O-X." He added those tiles to Fred's word. Paradox. He swiftly counted up the points. "Twelve for mine, added to five for Fred's word and"—he beamed—"a triple word score. That makes fifty-one points."

"Excellent word," Fred said. Ethel sniffed and wiped her eyes.

"What's a paradox?" Vanessa asked.

"A paradox is someone or something that acts one way but really is another," Jayne said. "You know, a phony."

Arnie cleared her throat and got up to get a glass of wine. Fred stood and grabbed a beer.

"Are you calling me a phony, Judy dear?"

"Marion would be so proud of me making that word," Robin cut in. He patted Vanessa's hand. "You are doing a great job, Vanessa, since this is your first time playing Scrabble."

"Yes, I guess I'm a virgin when it comes to Scrabble," she exploded with a raucous laugh. She took out a package of cigarettes from her purse.

"Oh, brother," Jayne muttered. Nick and Fred laughed. "No smoking in here, Vanessa," Jayne reminded her.

"Oh, pooh," she said. "I'm going out on the balcony."

"That's not allowed in this building," Jayne said stiffly. "It's against city of Chicago housing laws. You need to go downstairs and go outside."

"Just one little teeny tiny puff—or two," she said. "No one will know." She stood up, clutching her cigarettes and put Tutu down on the carpet. The little tangerine puffball immediately ran over to a puppy pad in the corner and peed. "Why look, how cute is that?" Vanessa asked and strolled out on the balcony.

"I'd like to lock her out there all night," Jayne said, "but with the police here, I would probably get arrested."

Schultz looked over at her. "Knit one, purl two," he said.

"Why don't we all take a break," Arnie suggested.

"Good idea," said Robin. He grabbed a sandwich and sat down at the piano. "*Strangers in the night*," he sang softly, "*exchanging glances—*"

"*Wandering in the night*," warbled Fred. "*What were the chances—*"

"*We'd be sharing love before the night was through?*" Arnie sang loudly and a bit off-key.

"Marion just loved this Sinatra tune," Robin said, misty-eyed.

"It's very romantic," Jayne said.

"How can we be singing?" Ethel asked. "It seems very disrespectful."

"Marion loved music, Ethel, so he wouldn't mind," Robin said, but stopped playing.

Vanessa walked back inside, picking up pictures from Jayne's life. "I just loved Sinatra! I went out on a date with him, when I was a model back in the day. He was so much fun!" She frowned at a picture of Jayne and Arnie. "He was so, so sexy." She sighed. Her jacket fell open. A tight, low-cut top revealed breasts that stuck out like torpedoes.

"Is she telling the truth or is that another fantasy island tale she's pitching to us?" Jayne whispered to Arnie. "And where the hell does she get her clothes? Frederick's of Hollywood?"

"I don't know, but I could see her as a young woman dazzling Sinatra." Arnie kept staring.

"Quit looking at her boobs before I smack you," Jayne hissed.

"Yes, dear," Arnie said and squeezed her thigh under the table. Jayne responded with a pinch to Arnie's butt.

The Scrabble players grabbed a snack, a drink, or went to powder their noses. Schultz strolled onto the balcony to enjoy some fresh air and to appreciate the lights on the lakefront. The Ferris wheel at Navy Pier was spectacularly lit up tonight in Halloween shades of orange and black. Noreen and Jayne followed him. They stood at the railing enjoying the nighttime view.

"How are you doing, Noreen? Are you feeling better?" Jayne asked.

"Sort of. I still have a sensitive stomach and a headache at times, although I think the headache could be from stress."

"Could be," Schultz agreed. "The past two weeks have been very upsetting for you." Her posture was tense and she was holding the railing tightly. "Is there anything you wanted to tell me?"

Noreen looked over her shoulder, saw that Nick was talking to Arnie in the kitchen and furtively pulled a paper out of her blazer pocket. "Here," she said. "I'm not supposed to share this with anyone, but I'm tired of pretending everything is okay. I think you ought to know that Nick got an anonymous note, too."

Schultz took his phone and shined the phone's flashlight on the note. He read it softly aloud and then whistled.

I'M A DANCING QUEEN
YOU ARE WHAT YOU EAT, RIGHT NICK?
YOU WILL PAY UP SOON

"Is this referring to when Nick was a dancer at the ladies' clubs?"

Noreen was stone-faced. "You know everything about us, don't you? Are you enjoying this cat and mouse game?"

"We are only investigating the people who were present the night Marion Wayne was murdered," he said. "No cat and mouse game, and I am not enjoying this." He put the paper in his pocket.

"Hey, I need that back!" She stuck out a shaking hand.

"I need it for our inquiries," Schultz said. "I appreciate you coming forward with this. I can see why Mr. Pappas would want this to be kept quiet, considering his past dancing career."

She sniffed. "If it were only dancing."

Jayne watched Schultz's face remain impassive. Wow. He already knows Nick was more than a dancer. He knows all our dark secrets.

"If Nick gets upset with you, send him to me. Tell him you were afraid." He looked her over. "Are you sure this is the only note you want to show me?"

"What are you driving at?"

"Maybe you got one, too?"

"I have nothing, I repeat, *absolutely nothing* to hide. I never got a note," Noreen said and stormed off. Schultz opened up a fresh package of mints and followed her back inside to the game. Jayne gave one last look to the silent river and the Ferris wheel, and joined her guests.

The Scrabble match continued. Jayne and Arnie played steadily, if not brilliantly. Arnie said with a frown, "Jaynie, I'm not playing very well tonight. My apologies. I'm too nervous."

"I hear you, my sweet one," Jayne replied. "I'm worried something is going to go wrong before the night is through."

"Courage," Arnie whispered.

Nick came up with some good words, trapeze and windy. Noreen seemed bored. Ethel was having some luck and Fred cheered her on, although he was not his usual chattering self. Robin was on a roll and being very gracious to Vanessa with her three-point words.

"C-A-T, cat," she said, smiling at everyone, putting the tiles down in the middle of the board.

"Vanessa, my dear, remember, you must put your letters next to letters that are already down on the board," Robin corrected her.

She squinted. "I keep forgetting, silly, little ol' me." She moved the tiles over and hesitated.

"Take your T away and then you can make cat right here," Robin said.

"I see, thank you, Robin darling, but what a strange game," she said. "Arnie, sweetie, can you bring me a drink, I'm parched."

"White wine? Red wine? Beer?"

"What, no martinis?"

"Not tonight," Arnie said. "We're not in a festive mood in honor of the memory of Marion."

"All right, then, wine. Something strong. None of those sweet, girlie, fruit punch wines."

"Heavens, no," said Jayne, as Arnie poured a large glass of cabernet sauvignon. "We only drink real wine here, Vanessa."

"Thank you, darling Arnie," she cooed, and took a big sip. Tutu raised his head and yipped. "Can you pwease bwing me a plate with some sandwiches? Tutu is famished, and he didn't eat his dinner tonight. He was so excited that we were coming here, weren't you, little snookums?"

Arnie, ever the host, did as she was told. Jayne made the word TROLLOP. "Eight points, but double word, so sixteen. Sorry, Arnie, it's not more."

Noreen laughed at the word. "How appropriate," she said, watching Vanessa feed bits of ham to the dog. She shook her head and studied her tiles. She put down a D next to the word anger. "Danger," she said. "Ha, it's a double letter on a triple word score. Another appropriate word."

Nick counted up the points. "Good one, Nor," he said. "That's thirty points."

"Read 'em and weep," she said, and got up to refill her wineglass, her third drink of the evening. Nick watched her anxiously. "Nor, slow up a bit?"

"Why? I've got you here, my big, strong, handsome protector," she said, pouring white wine liberally into her glass. "Nobody will poison me again, will they?" She turned around quickly and splashed some wine onto the head of Lucia, who woke up with a snort and a growl.

There was an uncomfortable silence. Everyone looked at Detective Schultz, who was knitting, needles flying. "I don't think so," he said. "We think that was a one-off, to scare you."

"Scare me? How about almost kill me?" Noreen was losing her icy demeanor. "My stomach is still upset. I can barely eat a thing without discomfort." She glared at everybody. "You're all responsible. I don't care who did it, but you're all at fault. Especially you, Jayne, you should have known better."

"Noreen," Nick said. "Don't blame Jayne. How could she have known someone wanted to murder Marion?"

Vanessa shrieked and clutched Robin's arm. "Oh, don't say that word! It reminds me of my ex-husband trying to strangle me! I can't concentrate anymore. Robin, do you mind if I quit playing?"

"Of course, my dear," he said, patting her arm. "How about it, everyone? Should we finish the next round of play and tally up the scores?"

"Great idea, Robin. I think I've had about enough Scrabble for tonight," Fred said.

"I agree," said Nick. "I've had enough."

"Sure, why not?" Jayne said, scrutinizing the faces of her guests.

Schultz sat knitting, watching them for a few minutes. He put down his needles and stood. "Maybe it's a good idea to call it a night. I've got officers downstairs to escort you to your cars, Ubers, or however you got here."

A shocked silence followed. "Cops? Here?" Nick looked worried.

"Police?" Ethel clutched Fred's arm.

Fred patted her hand. "It's all right, Eth, he's just being careful."

"Were you expecting something to happen tonight?" Noreen asked, her body rigid, her face taut with tension.

"We're just being careful, ma'am," he said.

"I want to talk to you two, after your friends leave," Schultz told Jayne and Arnie.

The winners of the night were Robin and Vanessa and they were both beaming with the news. Vanessa embraced Robin, smashing him to her bosom. "Robin, darling, how wonderful. We are winners! Stick with me baby, and I'll be your good luck charm."

Robin smiled and extricated himself from her perfumed embrace. Tutu growled. Arnie draped Vanessa's pink cashmere pashmina around her shoulders. "Thank you, Arnie darling," she cooed.

Jayne put a leash on Lucia. She and Arnie helped her guests find their coats and then they all exited with Schultz. In the lobby, three uniformed officers were waiting. Vanessa proclaimed her chauffeur had the rest of the night off, so she was deposited in a

Flash Cab in front of the building. Nick and Noreen, and Fred and Ethel, were walked to their cars. Robin insisted that he was going to walk home by himself.

"Are you sure that's a good idea?" Schultz asked. "You were just a victim a week ago."

"It's only two miles, and I need some fresh air," Robin said. "It's still early. I want to think about Marion while I walk and focus on my grief. My therapist said it would be beneficial."

"All right, suit yourself," Schultz said, but as Robin strolled away, he gave a signal to one of the officers. Both men vanished into the night.

Jayne walked Lucia and then she and Arnie went upstairs. They cleaned up the remains of the party. "Do you want another sandwich?" Jayne asked, looking at the tray of food, hardly touched.

"No, thanks, I'm not very hungry tonight. I guess everyone felt the same way," she answered, looking at the half-eaten trays of sandwiches, cookies, and veggies and fruit.

"Yes, murder and poisoning can put a damper on one's appetite," Jayne agreed, popping a grape into her mouth. "But they sure put a dent in the liquor." Three empty wine bottles and four beer cans sat on the kitchen counter.

"I hope Fred can drive all right," Arnie said with a frown. "He can sure pack away the beer."

"He always says he has a hollow leg, and we have to believe him," Jayne said. "He never seems impaired."

"I hope you're right," Arnie said. "At least Nick was driving Noreen home, and he never drinks, so that's all right."

"True. Noreen seemed in a very bad mood, tonight," Jayne said, placing plastic wrap around the sandwiches. "More than usual."

"She was very sick last week, Jayne," Arnie reminded her. "Being poisoned isn't a fun thing to endure." She patted her flat stomach.

"Sorry, Arnie, I don't mean to be so callous. I know how sick and scared you were and so was I, believe me, but she seemed even edgier than usual. I wonder if she got a note that she won't tell us about."

"Do you think so? Do you really think that could be it?"

"Someone has gone to a lot of trouble to find out about us," she said. "Finding out about Fred's funeral home mishap and then—"

"And then what?" Arnie's nose began to quiver.

Jayne went to her bedroom and came out with her knapsack. She took out an envelope. "Ethel called me today and asked if she could show me this."

"Another haiku?"

Jayne nodded and handed her the note.

WHERE IS THAT BABY?
GOOD CATHOLIC GIRL, REALLY?
PRAYERS WON'T SAVE YOU NOW

"Wow," Arnie said, "this is serious. Did Ethel have a baby she gave up for adoption?"

"Her sister did," Jayne said. "Almost fifty years ago when they were teenagers. Ethel said her sister never got over the guilt of giving up her baby, but she was only sixteen and they were strict Catholics and her family wouldn't allow her to keep the child. Her sister was never the same after that. Very depressed, guilt-ridden, and died of heart trouble twenty years ago. Ethel was devastated."

"What happened to the child?"

"Ethel doesn't know. She asked me if I thought you would look into it since you're a private detective. She wants to know who sent the note. The child would be about forty-five now. Did the child send it? Or someone from the adoption agency? Or someone from their church? She hasn't told Fred and she's sick about it."

"The child would be late forties? Robin and Marion would be about the right age."

"And so would Noreen."

There was a rap at the door. They both jumped. Lucia barked. "Schultz," Jayne said, stuffing the envelope in her back pocket. "Don't say anything about Ethel's note."

She opened the door. Schultz entered, raincoat unbuttoned, unlit cigar in hand. He eyed the food on the kitchen island. "Can I have a sandwich? I'm hungry."

Jayne pulled the plastic off the sandwiches. "Please, help yourself. There is so much left over. Coffee?"

"Yes, please," he said, helping himself to one of each—ham, chicken, tuna, and roast beef. He looked at the heart-shaped chicken sandwich before he took a bite. "Cute," he said. "You do this, Jayne?"

"Yes, I did. My mother used to make sandwiches like this for her bridge club. Maybe too cute for the occasion?"

"I don't think so. They're kind of pretty actually," he said, taking a sip of coffee and finishing the sandwich. "I'm sure Marion would have enjoyed them. Although I never met the man, from everything I've heard, he was into design and fashion."

"I was thinking of him when I made the sandwiches," she admitted. "And Robin, too. He seemed in fairly good spirits today. I thought he and Vanessa were getting along very well."

"They sure were," Schultz said, finishing a ham club and starting on a diamond roast beef. "Better than the rest of them. Ms. Charles seemed on edge. And Mrs. Woods—"

"What about Ethel?" Jayne's hand stopped petting Lucia. She braced herself.

"She kept giving you meaningful looks and she looked very upset. And you kept touching your pocket. Another note?" Arnie and Jayne exchanged glances. "Out with it," he demanded, picking up a tuna spade. "You can't keep hiding evidence!"

CHAPTER TWENTY-TWO

Evidence—14 Points

"What evidence? What note?" Jayne pulled herself up to her full six feet and looked down several inches at Schultz. "What are you implying?"

"I haven't been in this business for twenty-five years without knowing something about human behavior," Schultz said. He picked up another sandwich, chomped it quickly and smelled his coffee. "You sure make good coffee, Jayne. French roast?" He took a big gulp and put it down with a thump on the counter.

"Yes, it's French roast. Why can't you leave us alone?"

"I can't. It's my job. I believe Mrs. Woods has something to hide."

"What would make you say that?" Jayne was indignant.

Schultz looked out at the lights shining on the Chicago River. He sighed. "We have received some information."

"From whom?" Jayne demanded.

"Ma'am," Schultz said at his most official, "I am not at liberty to say."

"Jayne," Arnie said, "this is no time for subterfuge or anger."

"I'm not angry! Just pissed that the Chicago Police Department is stalking our every move!"

"Hardly stalking," Schultz murmured, taking a cookie off the tray. "We don't have the resources for that."

"Jayne, Marion's been murdered, four of us were poisoned, and you need to talk to Perry. Right now. And if you think about it, dear heart," Arnie said, "Fred must have told him. How else would they know? Unless they had a search warrant for our mail and I don't think it's come to that."

Both Jayne and Schultz looked at Arnie with respect. She was being rational and taking charge. She looked at Jayne for a very long moment. Jayne sighed and pulled the note out of her pocket.

"Have it your way," she said and tossed the envelope to Schultz. "But I don't have her permission to share this."

Schultz grabbed gloves from his pocket. "I don't know why I bother with these. Everybody and his momma must have handled this note by now." He inspected the envelope, the stamp, the postmark and then read the haiku. "Fred only told me Ethel had received a letter that made her cry. He hadn't seen it because she hid it. He didn't want to ask her about it. He was waiting for her to tell him." He scanned the poem and exhaled in aggravation. "So, who had the baby? Ethel?"

"No, her sister," Jayne said. "When she was about sixteen. Ethel is a year younger. They grew up in a very strict, religious family and the baby was put up for adoption. There was never any possibility of her sister keeping the child."

"And the child would be about what, late forties now?"

"Something like that," Arnie said.

"So, the question, among many, is—who sent the note? And did it come from the child, who is now a grown man or woman? Is the intention blackmail or extortion? And how are these notes connected to Marion's death?" Schultz ran his hands through his shaggy hair in frustration. He needed a shave as well as a haircut.

"Those are very good questions," Jayne said. "Who could it be? Robin is about the right age. So was Marion."

"So is Noreen," Arnie added. "Nick is too young and Fred and Ethel too old. So are we."

"Detective Schultz is about the right age," Jayne said, with a touch of malice. "Maybe you got assigned to this case because you know more than you're saying."

Schultz put the note in a plastic bag in his pocket, picked up his knitting and gave them both a curt nod. "Thanks for the sandwiches," he said. "I'll talk to you both later." He walked out.

"Jayne, you offended him," Arnie said. "Like me, he didn't think it was funny, you including him in the list of possible suspects."

"Well, he is about the right age and he's been so darn snarky to us, to me, about the notes and hiding evidence. Who does he think he is?"

"He's the police, and he has every right to ask us questions, demand information, and get mad if we go off on our own," Arnie said. "I really think you should text him an apology."

"Why should I? We're on his list of suspects, don't think we're not. Professional courtesy, my eye."

"You do have a tendency to make jokes at the most inopportune times," Arnie said.

"Are you referring to my ill-timed comment about you being the right age for an affair with Vanessa Harding?"

"Why yes, I am," Arnie said, making smoochie sounds, and they burst into laughter.

"This is like an episode from *The Twilight Zone*," Jayne howled. "It's just too darned weird. Surreal. Vanessa and her pink boudoir, Marion getting poisoned, please forgive me"— she put her hands to the heavens—"funeral luncheons with rat poison and anonymous haikus! When this is all over, I'm going to write it all down and sell it to the tabloids."

Arnie carefully wiped her eyes and forehead with a napkin. "As horrific as this is, I agree, my dear, it's unbelievable. And yet, it all happened. It's happening. It's not over. We still don't know who the killer is."

"I have my ideas," Jayne said, studying her nails.

"What are you keeping from me?"

"I don't want to say anything yet. Arnie, you're so close with Schultz, I don't want to jeopardize your standing with the law enforcement community. You have your detective agency to think about."

"And you have your neck to think about," Arnie said, frowning. "You don't want to get poisoned or get your neck squeezed by an irate husband."

"I still have my doubts about that," Jayne said. "How do we know it was her ex-husband? Or any of her husbands? She's very vague about those twins. More like some dude she met on Silver Swingers dot com."

"Jayne," Arnie groaned, "you do have an imagination."

"I need an imagination to visualize my golf shots," she retorted.

"Sure, you do. You're the Picasso of golfers. A great golfer and a great lady. A little nutty but a great lady. Sexy, too."

"Ah, shucks, sweetie, you are too kind."

They gave each other the eye.

"What should we do now?" Arnie asked.

"All this murder and mayhem has given me an appetite," Jayne said with a smile.

"For more food?"

"No, dear one, it has given me an appetite for you."

"Dear heart…"

She took Jayne by the hand and they strolled off to the bedroom. Arnie very firmly closed the door on a growling Lucia.

Hours later, their phones rang, hers and hers. The sky, still black with a few stray glittering stars, was in the last phase of night. Jayne fumbled for her cell phone, while Arnie groped for hers and dropped it.

"Darn," she mumbled, still wrapped in the warm cocoon of sleep.

"Got it," Jayne said, with a raspy throat. "Yes?"

"This is Schultz. You two had better get down here."

"What? Where? What's going on?"

"Who is it?" Arnie demanded.

"Quiet!" she croaked. "Yes, Perry, I hear you. Yes, Arnie's here. How did you know?"

"I'm a good guesser," Schultz said. "You two are inseparable, anyone can see that. But can we shed the romance and get down to business? Is Arnie able to get to Mrs. Harding's house? There has been another attempt on her life. And she's asking for her private investigator."

"There has? Wow, okay, we'll be right over. Soon as we're dressed," Jayne said.

"Wait, she didn't ask for you," Schultz said but Jayne hung up and jumped out of bed. She gave a glance out the window. In those few minutes, dawn was emerging. Over the lake a small ribbon of pale gold heralded the sun.

"Are you going to tell me what happened?" Arnie demanded. She opened the bedroom door and Lucia trotted in demanding attention.

"You're not going to believe this," Jayne said, giving the Chihuahua a treat. "Someone tried to murder Vanessa Harding—again. And she's shrieking for you, Arnie, my love."

CHAPTER TWENTY-THREE

Cigarette—12 Points

The ribbon of gold had fanned into a brilliant banner of morning sky as they arrived at Vanessa Harding's townhome. Birds were singing above the police cars in front. One of the officers moved a patrol car so that Arnie could pull in. "You're getting special treatment today, sweetie," Jayne observed.

She expertly parallel parked into the small space. "Do you think so? Am I that special to this investigation?"

"Vanessa Harding wants you and *whatever Vanessa wants, Vanessa gets*," Jayne sang to the old Lola tune.

Arnie looked uncomfortable. "I seem to recall that in *Damn Yankees* somebody sold their soul to the devil."

"I think she just wants your body, not your soul," Jayne said, as they walked up the stairs.

"Thanks a lot."

They looked at each other with the memory of last evening's embraces. Arnie's head turned pink. Jayne took off her gloves and fanned her face. "Hot stuff," she murmured.

"Behave, please," Arnie said, as a uniformed officer opened the door.

Upstairs, the combined aromas of stale perfume, spilt whiskey, and dog vomit made a terrible stench. Jayne wrinkled her nose and coughed. Arnie fanned her face with her Cubs cap. The doorway to Vanessa's room was blocked by an officer who looked to Schultz for instructions.

"It's okay, let them stand in the doorway," he said. "Don't come in, you two, we're not done here." Two paramedics, one old, one young, were standing by the bed. Two officers were sorting through the chaos on the floor. They looked very young and seemed a bit embarrassed as they handled Vanessa's frilly lingerie. The gilded white desk had been knocked over and papers were strewn everywhere. The ivory armoire had been opened and ransacked, and mounds of exotic pink garments were scattered everywhere. A pink, leopard-spotted bustier sat on top of a statue of Cupid. A garter belt covered in rhinestones was in Schultz's hands.

The bed looked like a tsunami had hit, with silk sheets and satin shawls twisted up in waves and tangles. The little dog sat growling on the edge of the bed. As an officer walked by Tutu, the pooch snapped and barked. In the middle of this rose-colored hurricane lay Vanessa Harding. This time she was silent. This time her mouth was not flapping because she had an oxygen mask attached to her face. The smells, the mess, the people crowded in the stuffy room, assaulted Jayne's senses, and in the middle of this wreckage, lay the diva.

"How is she doing?" Arnie asked. "What happened?"

"Someone broke in again during the early hours and tried to strangle her, after destroying her room." Schultz told them.

"Looking for the jewelry?" Jayne asked.

"Not sure," Schultz said, looking under the bed. "Some of it's still here."

"Maybe this time the intruder took the real stuff," Jayne suggested.

"Maybe," Schultz said, as he wriggled under the bed. There were some grunts and groans and then he came up with a handful of papers.

"It's about time!" Vanessa gasped and sat up, wracked with coughs that elevated her lacquered bouffant hairdo. She swatted at the mask. "That was awful! What were you trying to do to me?"

"Ma'am," said the middle-aged, sad-looking paramedic. "When we got here, you were about to pass out. So, we gave you oxygen. Did you take any medication before you went to sleep last night?"

"Medication? I don't take any medication. I'm as healthy as a horse."

"And she whinnies," Jayne muttered.

"What did you say, Janet?"

"I said, 'no kidding.'"

Arnie pinched her arm. "Be quiet."

"Will not." Jayne pinched her butt and choked back a laugh.

"What are you two doing over there?" Vanessa demanded. "What are you standing there giggling about? Arnie, you're supposed to be taking care of me. Where's my cigarettes?"

The sad paramedic picked up a pack and held them way out of reach. "Sorry, ma'am, no smoking. Oxygen is flammable."

"Well, take it out of here, then," she demanded. "I want a smoke!"

Schultz nodded at the paramedics. "You can go now. I'll take it from here."

"We need her to sign off that she doesn't want to go to the hospital," said the younger one.

"Why should I go to the hospital? I'm fine." Vanessa pouted.

"Your vitals were slow when we got here," the older one said. "As if you might have taken sleeping pills."

"I already told you that I didn't take any pills last night. Why won't you believe me?"

The paramedic handed her a paper and pen. "Sign here, please."

Vanessa squinted and made some scratches on the paper. "Here, I signed it, you can leave me now. Oh, and thanks for coming," she added.

"Not the most gracious thanks," Jayne said, "but it will have to do."

The two paramedics smiled at Jayne and left.

Schultz looked over at Jayne and Arnie as he unrolled some mints. "Kind of makes you wonder, doesn't it? What the hell is going on around here?"

"What if Vanessa was drugged last night during the Scrabble game?" Jayne asked.

"Maybe you ate or drank something last night that didn't agree with you," Schultz said to Vanessa.

"Well, if I did, it would be Janet's fault! Seems like people start dropping like flies whenever she's around."

Jayne opened her mouth to protest, but then thought, why bother? She gave Vanessa the most bored look she could manage.

Schultz chomped a mint. "Okay, you guys," he said to the young cops, "you can go. I'll finish up."

One of the officers spoke up. "I found this under the bed," he said, and handed something small to Schultz. His eyebrows raised as he put it in his pocket.

"What was that?" Jayne asked.

"Tell you later," Schultz said.

"How are you feeling, Mrs. Harding?" Arnie asked with a look of concern, and the diva lost some of her attitude.

"I feel terrible. Arnolda, such a pretty name. Someday you must explain it to me." Vamp turned into vampire. "How do you think I feel? Someone broke in again and tried to kill me. And look"—she exposed part of her chest—"my diamond necklace is gone! The jerk stole it! That rat! Poor, poor Vanessa and my widdle, widdle sweet snookums were so scared!" She patted Tutu's orange feathery, curved tail. "Why can't the police find whoever it is? For what am I paying all these exorbitant tax dollars?"

"For having five city employees in your bedroom this morning," Jayne said, "and two more outside. Your constant emergencies are costing the city a fortune."

"Emergencies? I was almost murdered—again!" She shook out a pack of cigarettes and dove under the covers for a lighter, and once retrieved, she lit up and sighed. "Bliss, sheer bliss. Jill, dear, hand me that ashtray, will you? The one next to Tutu. Poor little thing."

Jayne walked into the room, grabbed the flamingo ashtray, and handed it to Vanessa. She looked the woman up and down. "I don't see any red marks on your neck, Vanessa."

"I'm sure I'll look like hell later on," she sniffed. "The bastard really grabbed me this time!"

Arnie looked puzzled. "What made him stop? Why didn't the burglar alarm go off?"

"The control for the alarm had been turned off on her phone," Schultz said.

"Did you do that, Vanessa?" Arnie looked at her phone on the nightstand. "May I check?"

"Of course, Arnie." She took a long drag on the cigarette and coughed. "I didn't turn it off."

"What's your password?"

"40DD," Vanessa said.

"Unbelievable," Jayne said. Schultz made a strange noise in his throat and Arnie's hands paused over the phone. "If you didn't fiddle with your phone, then who did?" Jayne asked. "How would anyone know your password?"

"Probably someone at your famous Scrabble game last night, who heard me talking about it and wanted to come back, kill me and steal my jewelry. I've used that password for years. I might have mentioned it. I'm so bad at remembering things like that." She blew a smoke ring up to the ceiling. Jayne watched its flight. Vanessa was as frustrating and mysterious as the caterpillar in Alice in Wonderland.

"I thought your ex-husband wanted to kill you and steal your jewelry? Now you say it could be someone from our Scrabble game or another ex-husband?" Jayne asked.

"He does—he did—but now any one of you might have done it, now that you know about it." She pouted, dropping ash on her bosom. "Except dear Arnie. I know she would never do anything so awful to dear, widdle Vanessa, would you, Arnie baby?"

"Give me a break," Jayne muttered.

"What did you say, Judy?"

"I said," Jayne screamed at the top of her lungs, all self-control gone with the wind, the early hour, and the lack of sleep, although she could blame Arnie for that, "GIVE ME A BREAK! I'm tired of your baby talk! I'm tired of your cigarettes and smelly dog, and I'm tired of your innuendoes!"

"Don't get so worked up, dear. You need some estrogen or Valium to tame that temper of yours." Vanessa smirked. "What's an innuendo?" Vanessa asked Schultz. "Is it something fun?"

"Heaven help me," Jayne muttered and stormed out of the room.

She clattered down the stairs to the front hallway, where the young officer was admitting Tanya into the house. "Hello, Tanya," she said to the immaculately dressed and coiffed personal assistant. Tanya looked at her in both shock and suspicion.

"What are you doing here?" Although barely six a.m., she was wearing a mint-green Chanel-type suit, and darker green stilettoes, probably Manolos, or good knock-offs.

"Your boss called us after she was attacked," Jayne said. "Arnie—I mean Ms. Palmer—and I are working on her case. We arrived right after the police."

"Really?" She looked at Jayne through her unbelievably green eyes. "I thought only Ms. Palmer was the detective."

Jayne peered at her. "Don't those lenses hurt your eyes? Although they are a perfect shade of emerald green. I bet you're a big hit on St. Patrick's Day."

"I don't know what you're talking about," she snapped. "These are my real eyes." She walked away, striking her heels on the parquet floors—rat-ta-tat-tat.

"So, green-eyed kitten found her claws," Jayne said. The young officer at the door stared at her. "Pardon me, officer. Old ladies always talk to ourselves. May I exit, my young officer of the law?"

He smiled and opened the door. Jayne walked outside and took a gulp of fresh air. Again, the boudoir, its odors, and the smoke made her want to vomit. But she wanted to be as professional as Arnie so she took out her phone and dialed her. A thought had occurred to her.

"Yes, Jayne, are you okay?" Arnie whispered.

"Fine, just peeved at the woman. She's too much for me."

She heard her gentle chuckle. "What do you want to tell me, honey," she asked.

"Ask Schultz if the red-lacquered box with all her love letters and personal effects was found. I bet something important was in there."

"Great idea, I will ask him. I'll be outside soon."

"I'll be waiting for you…snookums," she said, purring.

It was good to hear Arnie laugh.

CHAPTER TWENTY-FOUR

Insurance—11 Points

"So, what's in your pocket?" Jayne asked.

They were sitting by the river at Schultz's request, drinking coffee and eating breakfast.

"This is delicious," Schultz sighed, taking a big bite of chocolate cake donut and washing it down with a long swallow of highly sugared and creamed coffee. "Gee, I needed that."

Arnie was eating a coconut vanilla donut, and Jayne had decided to be reckless and get a bagel with salmon cream cheese. The coffee, strong and bitter, tasted of chicory. There were a few early morning joggers and pet owners walking their pooches, and some people were strolling along the river, looking meditative.

"So, what's in your pocket?" Jayne repeated.

"I heard ya, I heard ya," Schultz said. "Man, you never let up, do you?"

"She never does," Arnie said.

"Part of my charm," Jayne said.

"I guess if you want to be a successful golfer, you have to have drive and nerve."

"Drive, that's accurate," Arnie chuckled.

"Quit it." Jayne scowled. "Get to the point."

"Okay. Here it is." Perry pulled a small plastic bag out of his pocket. In it, a Scrabble tile, the letter J.

"J," Jayne said, staring at the little tile. "Was it found under her bed?"

"Yup," Schultz said. "Now who do we know whose name starts with the letter J?"

"You got to be kidding me," Jayne said, sitting up and splattering bagel crumbs to the waiting sparrows under their table. "You think I broke in and tried to strangle that witch? Arnie, tell him. You're my alibi."

Arnie took off her Cubs cap and dabbed at her brow which had started to glisten. "We were together last night," she explained.

Schultz chuckled. "I know that," he said. "We were watching your building. Neither one of you came out."

"Gee, you're sneaky," Jayne complained, and threw the rest of her bagel to the birds.

"This is a murder inquiry," he said and finished his donut. "I would love another one but my wife says I got to cut down on the calories." He patted his stomach complacently. "When I retire, I plan to join a gym."

"You look in fine shape to me," Arnie said.

"You're too young to retire," Jayne groused. "Way too young."

"In two years, I will have twenty-seven years in and I might retire," he said. "The hours are killers."

"What would you like to do when you retire?" Arnie asked.

"Maybe I'll open a private detective agency," Schultz mused. "Arnie seems to be having a good time with her agency. Lots of action."

Jayne studied the Scrabble tile. "J. Dropped under her bed while she was being assaulted. Now which one of us dropped this letter? Had to be one of us from last night, doesn't it?"

Arnie frowned. "Or someone wanting to implicate one of us. Someone who knows our every movement."

"Who could that be?" Jayne demanded. "Who's left?"

"There's Tanya the assistant and Sarah the sister," Schultz said. "They have to be included."

"I don't see either one of those women, trying to kill Vanessa," Jayne argued. "What would be their motive?"

"Sarah could be defending her brother, and Tanya—"

"Tanya could just be plain nuts," Jayne said. "Speaking of pockets, Arnie, what's up with yours? You've been nervously patting your pocket since we left the house this morning. Did you find another Scrabble tile? Vanessa writing you love letters?"

Arnie took out a note and placed it on the table. "I got one yesterday in the mail. Another haiku. Odious and mean-spirited, if I may say so." She looked uneasy.

Jayne and Schultz both read the note at the same time.

HOW DID SHEILA DIE?
MERRY WIDOW ARNIE
INSURANCE MONEY?

Arnie's lovely pale face reddened and started to shine with the sweat of misery and embarrassment. "My wife died suddenly. There was an autopsy. She had a blockage in her arteries that was never diagnosed. I don't know why someone would want to attack me and the memory of my dear wife." She grabbed a bandana from her pocket and mopped her brow. "I'm so embarrassed."

"Don't be," Jayne said, patting her hand. "It's just another sick joke. And I'm so dang tired of these stupid haikus."

"But the others were true, so far," Arnie protested. "Fred did have a mix-up at the funeral home, Ethel does have a sister who gave up a baby, and you—"

"I throw a Scrabble party and someone gets murdered," Jayne said. "I suppose I could have sent the note to myself to cover up that I was going to kill Marion, right?"

"That's one scenario," Schultz said, swilling coffee from his second cup. He stared at a second donut. Long and hard. After a few moments of inner struggle, he unwrapped it.

Arnie stared out on the river. She looked miserable.

"Arnie, my dear, no one would ever think for a moment that you had anything to do with your wife's passing. That's crazy," Jayne said.

"We did have insurance policies on each of us. Sheila insisted on that. She said if something happened to one of us, the other one should be well provided for. She didn't want our daughter to have to take care of us or worry unduly."

"How much money?" Jayne asked. Schultz chomped on donut number two, a vanilla sprinkle. He was silent. "You already know," she said to him, "don't you?"

"We do our background checks," he said. "Part of the job."

"I don't want to know," she said, throwing up her hands. "It's none of my business, Arnie. Shame on me."

"Five hundred thousand," Arnie said, looking forlorn. "A tidy sum."

"But not a fortune," Jayne exhaled. "Why, the cost of senior homes today is outrageous."

"Still, someone took a shot in the dark and hit home," Schultz mused. "There is danger in that type of speculation."

"What do you mean?" Jayne asked.

"Often times the letter writer gets it," Schultz said, making a slashing sign across his neck.

"Stop! You're making me sick," said Jayne. "I know that happens in books—"

"Like your Agatha Christie?" Schultz raised his eyebrows.

"Yes, but this is real life," she said. "When does that ever happen?"

"Now you're changing your tune? You can't have it both ways, Jayne. Either life is like a mystery novel or it isn't. And blackmailers are murdered more than you know," Schultz said. "It just doesn't make the papers. Or it's described in another way. Domestic disturbance, home invasion, when really, it's someone out to get someone who knows too much about their business."

Arnie shook her head. "Like my business."

"Like all of them," Schultz said. "You're not alone." He turned to Jayne. "Since this is cleanup time, maybe you want to tell me what you picked up at Mrs. Harding's on Monday and stuffed in your pocket."

"What? What are you talking about?" Jayne tried to look innocent. But she knew he knew by the way he looked at her.

"What is he talking about, Jayne?" Arnie was shocked.

She sighed and opened her backpack. "I can't keep anything away from the long arm of the law. I wondered how long it would take you to ask me about it."

"Mrs. Harding told me about the note, but couldn't find it since she had scattered the contents of the box on the floor. So, she assumed it was missing in action. I, on the other hand, saw you stuff a beige paper in your jacket, so I guessed that was it. Then you made a nice diversion about the invitation to play Scrabble that Robin wrote, so I let that go."

"You're very sly," Jayne fumed, and tossed the note on the table.

HUSBANDS THREE AND FOUR
TWINS IN NAME, TWINS IN THEIR GAME
YOU'RE NEXT VANESSA

The detective read it aloud and looked at the two amateur sleuths. "So, what do you make of this?"

"Her husband wants to kill her? One of the twins?" Jayne hazarded a guess.

Arnie looked thoughtful. "Or someone knows about the twin ex-husbands and is trying to scare her into thinking one of them wants to get her. For her jewelry or something else?"

"Or someone wants to wring her neck because she's a lousy human being and does nothing for the planet except stink it up and coo at men, and talk baby talk to that little puff of a dog?" Jayne fumed. They stared at her in surprise. Suddenly the absurdity of the notes, the murder and the poisoning attempt hit her hard. She finished her coffee and tossed her long legs over the picnic bench, ready to escape. "I've got to go check on Lucia. She needs a walk."

"Now calm down and sit down," Schultz said mildly, patting the bench. "I know you're upset with all this, more than you let on, and I know Vanessa Harding is the type of woman you most detest. She's overpainted, over-sexed, and culturally ignorant, but still, someone is trying to kill her. And I think I know who."

Jayne sat back down. She and Arnie exchanged looks. "You do? Who? Tell us!"

"Now, that would not be fair, as you two said you wanted to solve the case yourselves so the Elsinore Detective Agency would make the news," Schultz said.

"Jayne has an idea about who did it," Arnie said.

"Does she now?"

Jayne ran her hand through her platinum spikes and gave Schultz a challenge. "Let's make a bet," she offered.

"What kind of bet?" Schultz asked.

"Let's stage one more Scrabble game. Let's get everybody over to my place and we can put forth our ideas about the murderer's identity and see who's right."

"That sounds crazy," Arnie complained. "And dangerous."

"You're dealing with a killer," Schultz said. "A dangerous man or woman, who has murdered one man and poisoned four other people. And you think you can trap one of them into confessing? Do you have proof?"

"Of course, I have proof," she lied.

"Right," Schultz said. "I will have to bring uniforms with me. And this showdown should be at the station, not in your lovely home. Still, there is a certain amount of stealthy romance and intrigue about this situation. All right," he sighed. "When? But it'd better be soon. I'm about to get a warrant."

"I need to invite them over. I'll call them up. How about tomorrow? That soon enough? I'll tell them I have some news for them or something equally mysterious. Something about the mysterious haiku. And that's why we should all get together again so soon. They'll come, no worries."

"I don't think this is a very good idea," Arnie said, mopping her head. "Something could go terribly wrong."

"And what's the bet?" Schultz reminded her.

"If we win, you will endorse Arnie on social media and her website."

"Totally against department regulations," Schultz said. Jayne ignored him. "And when I win?"

"I will make you a tray of sandwiches and goodies once a month for a year."

"Now that's a bet," Schultz said. "We can work out the details later. Make it happen, Jayne. Tomorrow night or I'm moving in and the bet's off."

Jayne swung her legs again over the side of the bench and held out her hand to Arnie. "Come on, Hercule Poirot, let's get this game going. This is going to be so exciting."

"Jayne Marple," said Arnie, shaking her head. "I hope you're right."

"This is going to be a blast," Jayne said. "You'll see."

CHAPTER TWENTY-FIVE

Entrapment—14 Points

"Another note," Arnie complained, as she and Jayne walked furtively down the eighth hole. "We should have definitely called Schultz."

A short tricky hole to play, it was surrounded by water hazards on both sides, and they were afforded privacy from the bike path and the street traffic by magnificent weeping willow trees on either side of the fairway.

Late last night, while they were watching the movie *Murder on the Orient Express* for the fifth time and discussing the clues, the desk staff had called Jayne. There was another messenger-delivered note. They had rushed downstairs to retrieve the message. And this morning, they were acting upon it.

"How could we win the bet if we told Schultz?" She sidestepped a lone goose and kept looking around her. "Something has to be hidden here."

"Read the note again," Arnie pleaded.

CANDY IS DANDY
WHEN DISPOSING BAD GARBAGE
WATER IS QUICKER

"No candy here," Jayne said. "Or bags of garbage. There are two dumpsters over there." She pointed to the gravel cart path that ran between holes number eight and nine.

"A dumpster would be good for disposing a dead body," Arnie said, pulling her cap down and her jacket collar up. It was five-thirty a.m. and the morning dew was damp and heavy upon their shoes. "I'm cold."

"Quiet," she said. "Quit complaining." She ran over to the dumpsters. She opened the first one.

"Anything?"

"Just garbage," she complained, holding her nose. She tried to open the other one but it was stuck. "Arnie, come help me. I can't open it. I don't want to fall in."

She walked over and together they yanked and pulled. Sticky stuff was oozing out on their hands. "Yuk," Jayne complained. "Smells like ketchup."

"It is ketchup," Arnie said, as the lid popped open. Inside, mounds of half-eaten hot dogs, fries and pickles—garbage from the snack shop—filled the dumpster. The aroma of ketchup and onions hit them in the face.

"Smelly," Jayne complained. She took a closer look, her platinum head disappearing briefly. "No dead bodies in here."

"Too bad," said Arnie, wiping her hands on a clean bandana. "Then we could get out of here."

"Let's keep going," Jayne said. "Let's check out the water and then the green."

They walked up to the water pond to the left of the green. Nothing was amiss except for a few floating candy wrappers and dragonflies zipping along the surface. "Clear," said Jayne in her best CSI voice.

"Yes, I can see that," Arnie said. "I'm cold."

"Quit complaining."

They continued over to the pond at the right side of the green. The placid water, a dark green from algae and lily pads, seemed undisturbed except for a frog who hopped out of their way. The sun, as it came up from the east over Lake Michigan, caught something and reflected a small pool of light on the pond. Jayne jogged over and stood dead still.

"What is it, Jayne? What do you see?"

She pointed silently and Arnie joined her. Nestled under the lily pads and blanket of algae was a body, a very dead body.

"Arnie, we're in for it now," Jayne said, and fell into her arms.

CHAPTER TWENTY-SIX

Cadaver—13 Points

They were both wrapped in blankets, drinking hot coffee, sitting in chairs at the back of the pro shop. Jayne had the shivers. Arnie's head had stopped sweating from the shock of finding a dead body. "So, you're sure you never saw the man before? But you think he looked like somebody you might know," Schultz asked Jayne and Arnie.

"No, never," Arnie said.

"No, no," Jayne hesitated.

"But you thought he looked familiar," Schultz said. "How familiar?"

"As familiar as one can get when he's dead and covered in pond algae," Jayne said, her voice raised in agitation. "We just found a dead man!"

"I know you did," Schultz said, unwrapping a mint. "Now why am I not surprised?"

"Don't be funny," Jayne said, scowling. Her shoes and socks were soaked and her jeans were wet from the knees down when she had almost fallen into the water.

"Me? I'm not being funny." There was a warning and a challenge in the detective's baritone voice. "How did he look familiar?"

"There was something about the eyes," she said. "I feel like I've seen those eyes somewhere before. And the shape of the face. Something about the lips and the chin. That's all I can tell you. Maybe he looks like someone who lives in my building." She sat up, knocking the blanket to the floor. "Maybe it is someone who lives in my building!" She sat back, appeased at her brilliance.

"That's a good idea, Jayne," Arnie agreed. "Someone we know slightly from the building or from playing golf? He does remind me of someone we saw last week out on the course."

Schultz watched them both. "Sorry to disappoint you, but it isn't someone from golf or your building. Does the name Donald Harding ring a bell?"

"Donald Harding? Ex-husband of Vanessa Harding?" Arnie was stunned.

"Yes, husband number three, divorced ten years ago, spent time in prison for embezzlement, just released this year and whereabouts unknown until today," Schultz said.

"Does Vanessa know?" Jayne demanded.

"Not yet, Jayne. She's not the next of kin, his brother, David Harding, is, but we can't locate him either. You know where he is?"

"How should we know?" Arnie frowned.

"I thought you were looking for him as Mrs. Harding is your client," Schultz said.

"Yes. I have been looking for him, but he seems to have vanished out of the system," Arnie explained. "No bank accounts, no DMV records, credit reports—where did he go?"

"Indeed, where did he go?" Schultz mused.

Two uniforms entered the pro shop. "Sir, can they take the body away? They're done with the prelims."

Schultz snapped out of his thoughts. "Yes, okay, take him. I'll see the coroner later."

"Coroner?" Jayne mumbled into her coffee.

"Naturally, a postmortem will be done. How did he die? Was he drowned, shot, hit with a blunt object…" He looked at them. "Or poisoned?"

"That's it, I'm going home," Jayne said, standing up. "I've done my civic duty. We reported the body, we waited for you and the team to show up, and now I need a hot shower and time with my dog."

"Ah yes, the dog," Schultz said. "And there's nothing else you want to tell me?"

"What else could there be?" Jayne challenged him.

"How did you figure out to come here this morning?"

"We often play early before the course opens," she said, shrugging.

"So, where are your clubs?"

"We decided it was too cold and we decided to take a walk instead."

"Really," Schultz said. "I'm about to arrest you for impeding the progress of an investigation."

"What do you mean?" Jayne was never hysterical, but she felt a shriek coming on. Hands on hips, she glared at Schultz.

"Jayne," Arnie admonished her.

"What?"

"Give me the note, please," Schultz stuck his hand.

"What note?"

"Jayne," Arnie pleaded.

"The note your desk staff said was delivered to you last night by messenger," Schultz sighed, and looked disappointed. "Do you think you can fool the Chicago Police Department?"

"Jayne, he knows. Give him the note."

"All right," she said, and pulled it out of her coat pocket. "Here." She thrust it at Schultz. "You figure it out. I'm going home."

He read it through.

CANDY IS DANDY
WHEN DISPOSING BAD GARBAGE
WATER IS QUICKER

"So, someone led you right to the dead body," he said. "They knew you two couldn't stay away. You're lucky you weren't plugged and pushed in the water."

"So, he was shot?" Jayne's face lit up.

"Ma'am," Schultz said, his craggy face impassive, "I am not at liberty to say. I'll see you tonight for this infamous Scrabble game."

Jayne groused all the way back to the car. "He's got a lot of nerve, that Schultz. Saying he wants to arrest us and demanding the note and implying we act suspiciously."

"Jayne, he has every reason to suspect us. We did find the body." Arnie unlocked the car. "And we keep producing threatening notes. And then stealing Vanessa's haiku—"

"I did not steal it! I included it in your—our—investigation." She pulled down the sun visor, opened the mirror and arranged her spiky hair. "Dang, I look awful! Dracula's grandmother comes to mind."

"You do not look awful. Where to now, home?"

A look of glee spread over her face. "Arnie, I think we should go pay a visit to Vanessa Harding and tell her husband number three is dead."

CHAPTER TWENTY-SEVEN

Escape—10 Points

"I don't think this is a good idea," Arnie complained, as they stood on the steps at Vanessa Harding's front door. Stone gargoyles grimaced down on them from the second-floor balcony.

"Those statues give me the willies," said Jayne, looking up with her own grimace. "It's a great idea," she disagreed. "Getting to her first before Schultz gets here. Maybe she'll spill some pertinent information."

Arnie, finger poised over the doorbell, frowned. "You're going to get us arrested, Jayne. I can feel it."

"She jests at scars—"

"We've already done *Romeo and Juliet* and *Macbeth*," Arnie said. "What we're doing is pure pulp fiction."

"Ring the bell," Jayne said, through clenched teeth. "Hurry!"

She pushed the bell. Once and then again. "She's probably asleep."

A wheezy, raspy voice spoke through the intercom. "Yes? Who is it? Tanya? Did you forget the code to the door?"

"Mrs. Harding," Arnie said, "it's Arnie Palmer and Jayne Marple. We're so sorry to bother you at this early hour, but we have something important to tell you."

"Arnie." Her voice dropped an octave. "How nice of you to call. Come in, darlin'." The door buzzed and Arnie pushed it open, Jayne close on her heels.

The house was silent as they walked up the stairs to the bedroom. On the bed, there lay Vanessa, in all her pink splendor with Tutu eating breakfast out of a china bowl. It looked like chopped filet mignon and the little pooch was chomping down in ecstasy. Jayne was fascinated to see Vanessa all made up, hair in place, eyelashes attached, hot pink lips glossed and outlined, and sporting bling that was blinding. Did she ever take the stuff off?

"Come in, Arnie dear, and you too, Jill, if you must." She pouted. "Arnie, you bad girl, you should've come all by yourself, like widdle Vanessa keeps tewwing you."

"Barf," Jayne said.

"What did you say, Judy dear?"

"I said, 'scarf.' That's a lovely scarf around your neck."

"Yes, it is." Vanessa preened. "Why, my latest boyfriend, Antonio, gave it to me last night. He's ever so fond of me. And look—" She pulled back the scarf. "I still have marks from when that madman tried to strangle me again."

"Last night?" Jayne said. "You had company last night?"

"Don't look so surprised, Jackie dear. As you know by now, men find me irresistible."

Jayne looked in the empty crater between Vanessa's breasts. "Did you ever find your diamond pendant?"

"It's gone! I told you it was ripped from my neck when my ex came back to kill me. And it was worth a fortune," she said.

"Did you ever get that insured?" Jayne asked.

"I don't know." She shrugged. "Why do you care?"

"Maybe it's not worth what you think it is," Jayne said.

"Are you calling me a liar?" Vanessa snarled. "Where are my cigarettes?"

"Of course, she's not," Arnie said. "Here, they are." She found her a pack from the mess on the bed. "Vanessa," Arnie said, "we're not doubting your veracity, even for one moment."

"Ver—what? Virility? Arnie, darling, women aren't virile, men are."

"What a dummy," Jayne muttered.

"What did you say, Janet?"

"I said, aren't we chummy? All sitting here together in your bedroom."

Vanessa gave Jayne an evil look. "I know you think I'm dumb or something, but I'm smarter than you think. I got all these gifts, didn't I?" She held out wrinkled hands covered in gaudy gemstone rings.

"Vanessa," Arnie said, forestalling more comments from Jayne, "I'm afraid we have some bad news."

"You and Jayne are getting married?" She gasped and then broke into a wicked chuckle, rumbling low in her enormous chest and shrouded with years of endless cigarette smoke.

"Very funny," Jayne said.

Vanessa cackled and Tutu yipped. "I think it is. What is the news, Arnie dear?"

She sat down on the edge of the bed. "I have something to tell you about your ex-husband, Vanessa. When did you see him last?"

"David? When he tried to strangle me Sunday night. If it was him."

"I'm sorry, I should've been clearer. I mean your previous ex-husband, Donald Harding. When did you see him last?"

"It's been years. I don't know...at court when we got divorced? I'd have to check with my attorney. It's been a long time. What have you got to tell me about Donald?"

"Donald Harding was found dead this morning. I'm sorry."

"Dead? Donald dead?" Her big baby blues widened in shock and with a touch of enjoyment. "How? Where?"

"He was found floating in a water hole at the Lake View golf course," Jayne said, watching her reaction.

"At the golf course? In the water? Did he fall in?"

"Something like that," Jayne said. "We think he was probably murdered."

"Murdered? Are you sure? That's terrible. Even though he was a bastard. Holy Saints preserve us. Help me, I feel faint," she gasped, and without further ado, the diva fell back upon her mound of pillows and passed out.

"Not again," Jayne said. "This is getting boring."

"Get the smelling salts from the nightstand," Arnie ordered, and fanned Vanessa's face with her Cubs cap. Jayne took the opportunity to search through piles of pills, makeup, and rosaries. "And stop looking at her stuff. Really, Jayne, you are such a snoop."

"That's rich, coming from you, Ms. 'I'm a professional licensed detective,'" she sniffed, slamming the drawer shut. "Here, Jack Reacher, here's the stuff. Sal volatile, ammonium carbonate, scented with lavender. She must pass out a lot. Knock yourself out."

Arnie pulled out the stopper and waved it under Vanessa's nose. The smell of ammonia and lavender filled the air. The diva started to cough, and opened her eyes. Tutu and Jayne sneezed simultaneously.

"Feeling better, Vanessa?" Arnie asked.

"Mother Machree, I don't know what came over me," Vanessa said, clutching Arnie's hand. "I can't handle all these deaths, on top of being poisoned. It's just too, too much."

The doorbell buzzed. Arnie and Jayne jumped and looked at each other. *Schultz?*

Vanessa pressed the intercom console next to her bed. "Yes? Who is it?"

"Mrs. Harding, you changed the code again. I can't get in," said Tanya.

"We don't want to be seen here," Jayne whispered. "Let's go!"

"Go where? How?" Arnie hissed back.

"Out the back balcony, no one will see us."

"I'll buzz you in, Tanya, and give you the code later," she sniffed. "I have guests. And where are you two going? Don't desert me in my hour of need! Arnie, please!"

"Sorry, Vanessa, but we've got to run," Jayne said, grabbing Arnie by the arm. "We'll just go out quietly." She opened the door to the balcony and pulled Arnie out. "See you later!"

"Jayne, you're crazy," Arnie groused.

"Jump, Arnie, jump!" And like two teenagers, who were caught in the schoolyard smoking, they both jumped, with a grunt and groan, and ran through the yard, laughing like fools.

"Come on, keep up with me," Jayne called over her shoulder. She passed a Streets and Sanitation garbage truck in the alley and waved at the startled driver.

"Jayne, slow down, what's the rush? I'm going to fall over a dumpster!" Arnie stopped running. With hands on her hips, she walked slowly, taking deep breaths.

"Come on, hurry up before the police get here," Jayne urged.

"What's the worry? We parked two blocks away at your insistence."

"That was a good idea," she said. "Now Schultz can't find us."

"Jayne," Arnie sighed, as they got into the car. "Schultz always finds us. And, I think, dear one, that it's your turn to buy the omelets at Eggy's."

Over Denver omelets, waffles and two pots of hot coffee, the sleuths discussed the latest developments. Arnie was writing in a small notebook. "We need to ask Schultz about Donald Harding. I'd like to know more about his prison term and who he worked for in the past. Also, if he'd been in contact with his twin brother, David."

"Fat chance of Schultz telling us anything," Jayne said, stabbing a piece of green pepper with her fork. "He wants to win the bet."

"Jayne, your sporting spirit is getting in the way of conducting a proper investigation. This is not a game. Perry can't tell us everything. It's against police regulations."

"If you say so," she said, pouring more coffee into their cups. "But when he wants to know what we know, then he lets go with some information. He's wily and slick. And having us followed all the time, he knows where we are and what we're doing."

"Surely, we're not being followed all the time," Arnie protested. "The police don't have enough resources for that. We're not that crucial to the case."

"What are you talking about?" Jayne ran agitated hands through her spiky hair, making it even wilder. "He probably thinks one of us did it! He probably thinks I dressed up like a man to strangle Vanessa or you're David Harding in disguise."

"You watch too many crime shows, Jayne," Arnie said. "It's not that easy to change one's appearance and get away with it."

"Oh yeah? How about your lady friend, Vanessa Harding? She has managed to change her appearance from a one-hundred-year-old banshee to a seventy-year-old one."

Arnie chuckled. "Jayne, you're totally adorable and I am mad about you."

"Oh yeah," she repeated, but blew her a kiss. "Arnie, let's get out of here and take Lucia for a walk and solve this case."

Out at the park, the morning air was cool and refreshing. Fluffy clouds like parachutes dotted the brilliant azure sky. Jayne took a deep breath of the sweet air into her lungs and sighed. "I always need air after a visit with Vanessa Harding," she said. "How can she breathe in that hothouse? We had quite a morning, Arnie. Ketchup on our hands, dumpster diving, smelling salts and running down alleys—"

"Not to mention a dead body in the pond," she reminded her. "Don't forget that, dear one."

"I will never forget that." Jayne shuddered. "I don't think I'll be able to play that hole for a very long time. It would be too stressful. I keep seeing his face all green and slimy, floating in the water. And look at that," she said. "Talk about slimy. Are you sure you don't have a GPS monitor stashed about your person? One that maybe Pericles Schultz attached to you when you weren't looking?"

"Jayne, what are you talking about?"

She pointed. Sitting on a park bench, drinking coffee, wearing his raincoat, and facing the sun without a care in the world, sat their Greek police nemesis. Schultz waved. Jayne made a face and waved back. "Now behave, Jayne," Arnie admonished her.

"Why?" she challenged and walked up to Schultz.

"*Kali mera*," she said in her best Greektown Greek.

"Kali mera," he answered. "And good morning to you, Arnie. How was Eggy's?"

"Delicious as always," Arnie said. "You should have joined us."

"I didn't have enough time," he said, unwrapping a peppermint. "By the time I got Vanessa Harding to tell me what you two were doing there, you were probably halfway through the eggs and waffles."

"Is there a camera attached to me?" Jayne looked around her clothes.

"What do you mean?"

"You always know what we're doing and where we are."

"You leave a trail of breadcrumbs for me a mile wide."

"And being watched by the police, twenty-four-seven, helps a lot." She frowned. "I'm tired of being followed."

"Then behave yourselves," Schultz replied, but with an edge to his voice. "Turn in those damn haikus, immediately, when you find one, and don't rush off to see grieving widows—"

"She wasn't grieving," Jayne said.

"Causing them to faint," Schultz continued.

"She wasn't out very long," Arnie assured him.

"She was talking about suing you, Jayne, for being the bearer of bad news and coming to her home uninvited," Schultz said. "Again."

"What about Arnie?"

"Mrs. Harding has a soft spot in her heart for her and wouldn't want to cause Ms. Palmer any trouble. That's almost an exact quote, without the baby talk," he said, and cracked a smile while Arnie laughed.

"I'm glad you two find her funny," Jayne sniffed. "She's absurd. And does she really have a boyfriend named Antonio?"

"Yeah, he's a dance instructor. He's about thirty-five. They dance around her living room to Sinatra records. And he sleeps over some of the time."

"I don't believe it," Jayne said, shaking her head. "She could be his grandmother."

"Give or take a few years," Schultz said. "Love is strange. But back to business. You went to tell Vanessa about Donald Harding. What did she say?"

"She was surprised," Arnie said. "She said she hadn't seen him in years and didn't know anything about him. We didn't tell her anything about his being in prison."

"That was big of you," Schultz said. "What else?"

"Nothing much," Jayne added. "She hadn't seen him since their divorce. She couldn't remember when that was. And, she admitted that the big, gaudy, diamond necklace, which has got to be fake, that she wears dangling on her big chest, was stolen."

"Yes, she did mention that." Schultz nodded and threw some donut crumbs to a squirrel. "I can't believe that rock was real, and if it was, that it was uninsured. That dame might act like a dumb blonde but I bet she's very shrewd about money."

"Has she paid out anything big lately?" Jayne asked.

"Like for blackmail? We're checking on that," Schultz said.

Jayne nodded. "That's one scenario, and why she won't let the insurance company know about her losses. Because she sold the gems for cash."

"Why, if she's being blackmailed, would the blackmailer try to strangle her? Twice?" Arnie conjectured. "That would be killing the proverbial golden goose, wouldn't it?"

"Who said it's the same person, the blackmailer and the killer?" Jayne suggested.

"Hold on, now," Schultz cut in, "you're getting ahead of yourselves. Who said anything about her being blackmailed?"

"Well, the note, Jayne, er—"

"Stole?"

"Borrowed," Jayne corrected Schultz. "I only borrowed it for our investigation."

"Okay, borrowed. The note threatened her, but it didn't allude to any blackmail. She hasn't taken any large sums out of the bank. We thought one of her recent husbands was out to get her."

"Now it appears there's only one to worry about," Arnie said. "And where can David Harding be? And what does he want from Vanessa? If he was after the diamond pendant, it's gone now."

"If it was real," Jayne said. "It was too big to be real."

"Like other parts of Vanessa," Schultz said and Arnie chuckled.

"You guys," Jayne said, rolling her eyes. "I thought you two thought she was hot stuff and all that?"

"She's okay," Schultz said. "At times, you can see why Sinatra dated her."

"She has vestiges of a pretty woman about her," Arnie agreed. "But she's very artificial and staged. Like a soap opera queen. It's hard to take her seriously. Actually, she makes me nervous when she starts to vamp me. My head starts to sweat." She looked at Jayne. "I prefer my women to be natural beauties."

The natural beauty in question, blushed.

"Okay," said Schultz. "Gotta run. Keep me posted about the game tomorrow. Time, et cetera." He stood. "And you two…" Jayne and Arnie looked up at him like little kids. "Try to stay out of trouble before then, will ya, please? No more dead bodies, cryptic notes or strangled women. I'm tired of Vanessa Harding and her little dog."

"Tutu won't like you," Jayne called after him. Schultz wiggled his fingers over his head at them and kept walking. "Come on, let's make some calls."

"I hope this is the last Scrabble game, Jayne, where the police are present," Arnie said, and crammed her Cubs cap over her moist head.

CHAPTER TWENTY-EIGHT

Skirmish—17 Points

"It's a beautiful night for a Scrabble game," Jayne said, bustling about her condo. She was humming a Sinatra tune "Fly me to the Moon," as she arranged hors d'oeuvres on trays and opened the Scrabble boards.

Arnie was inspecting the liquor cabinet and polishing glasses. "Are you sure this is a good idea, Jayne? I keep getting a feeling something is going to go very wrong."

"Schultz will be here. What can happen?" She opened the balcony door. "The boys in blue will protect us. What a gorgeous warm evening." She inhaled. "I just love these warm autumn nights when the air is fresh and you don't need a jacket."

"It has been warm lately," Arnie agreed. "Good for your golf game."

"I did play every day this week, except for today," she said. "It's been great." She gave Lucia a dog treat and patted her head. "One more game, Lucia. Tutu promised to be good." Lucia gave her the eye and snuffled. "Did you get a lot of work done on your other cases? Or is the pink diva taking up all your free time?"

"No, she's not. I had a lot of smaller jobs that I was able to finish. It felt quite good to be efficient," Arnie said.

"I'm sorry you got behind in your cases. That was my fault. I didn't expect so much to happen in so short a time."

"Me either," Arnie said, taking out a bottle of vermouth. "Martinis? Are you sure? That's an awful lot of alcohol."

"That was Robin's idea. He's thrilled we're hosting another game in Marion's honor. He's having filet mignon sliders delivered from Gibson's. And jumbo shrimp cocktail and crab cakes."

"Fancy stuff," Arnie said. "That Rush Street steakhouse costs a fortune."

"It sure does," Jayne agreed, "but Robin wanted to thank us for being so attentive to him after Marion's death."

"Two weeks ago," Arnie said, getting olives, onions and lemon wedges out of the refrigerator. "Marion was murdered two weeks and two days ago. It seems like two months. And we aren't any closer to the truth, are we Jayne?"

"Arnie, we need to talk."

"You know who did it?"

"I have a very good idea. Listen, I'll tell you what I think." A rap on the door startled them both. Lucia barked. "Dang, it's Schultz. He's early."

"Can you tell me now?"

"I don't want him to hear," Jayne said, heading for the door. "We're going to win that bet." Schultz stood at the door, raincoat-clad, mints in hand. Two uniformed officers were standing in the hall behind him. "Detective Pericles Schultz," Jayne drawled, "why, little old me is so happy to see you!"

"Is that more southside talk?" Schultz asked. "Wait here," he said to the officers.

"Come on in," Jayne said, bowing.

"So, everyone is coming tonight, right?"

"Yes, they all agreed," Jayne replied. "I guess they don't want to miss anything."

He walked into the living room. "Hello, Arnie, I see you're the bartender again."

"Hello, Perry. Mixing drinks is my lot in life lately."

Schultz looked at the bottles of gin, vodka, and vermouth and raised his eyebrows.

"Martinis?"

"I thought martinis are a bit strong, given the situation, but it was Robin's request," Arnie said with a shrug.

"Do you think the booze will loosen someone's tongue? In vino veritas?" Schultz asked.

"Alcohol does loosen inhibitions," Jayne agreed. "And makes one speak the truth."

"I see beer for Fred," Schultz said. "Any pop for me?"

Jayne opened the fridge. "There's cola, diet cola, and iced tea, if you'd like something."

"Thanks, I'll have a diet pop." He walked around the room. Lucia picked up her head and looked at him, her little tongue hanging out of one side of her mouth. "Hello, little baby," he said to her. She wagged her tail and nestled back down in her bed. "Cute pup." He studied the Scrabble boards. "I never got into this game. I'm slow at word games, although I like crossword puzzles." He looked at Jayne. "So, what's your strategy?"

"Strategy?"

"Yeah, are you going to wait until everybody is hunkered down at the table, martini in hand and then say, 'you're the murderer, you rascal you,' and call for handcuffs?"

"Very funny," Jayne said. "I have a plan."

"Jayne, you're dealing with dangerous people here," Arnie said, wiping her brow.

"Only one is dangerous," she said. "Only one."

"I'll be on the balcony with my radio, standing by, as needed," Schultz said. "I can hear you from there. You all speak clearly."

"You mean loud?" Arnie asked.

"Something like that." Schultz nodded.

"I'll keep the door open. It's so warm out, no one will notice," Jayne said.

There was a tap on the door. Jayne opened it. The police officers had vanished. So had Schultz as he had disappeared on the twenty-five by five-foot balcony. Fred and Ethel walked in holding trays of cheesecake bites. "Jayne, I made three different kinds," Ethel said, "plain, chocolate chip, and raspberry. Is that okay?"

"Ethel, you outdid yourself again," Jayne said, looking at the perfect mini slices, sitting in crisp bakery paper cups. "Thank you so much."

"I was going to bake a pie, but Fred said this was plenty. I hope it is."

"It most certainly is," Jayne said and put the cheesecake in the fridge for later. "Can we get you a drink?"

"Beer for me," Fred said.

"Coming right up," said Arnie. "I've made pitchers of martinis. Ethel, can I pour you one?"

"Just a tiny one," she said. She sat down on the sofa and arranged her skirt. Tonight she was wearing a lavender print silk shirtwaist with matching lavender shoes with kitten heels. Strands of white and pink pearls hung down her torso, tightly encased in shapewear. "Is everyone coming tonight?" She stroked her pearls with nervous fingers.

"Yes, everyone," Jayne answered from the kitchen.

"Who is going to be Robin's partner?" Ethel asked.

"Vanessa Harding," Arnie said, handing Ethel her drink.

"That vulgar woman? Coming here again. Jayne, how could you?" Ethel sipped her drink, her little mouth pursed in displeasure.

"Couldn't you find anyone else?" Fred asked, making up a plate of cheese and crackers.

"Robin wanted her to be his partner," Jayne said.

Ethel scowled. "I don't know why. She can hardly spell the word cat. She's terrible at Scrabble."

"I was trying to be kind," Jayne said. "He is a recent widower."

"You're so good to everyone, Jayne." Ethel took out a lace handkerchief and wiped her eyes. "It was terrible about Marion." Jayne and Arnie exchanged a glance. Donald Harding's death had not been revealed to the other Scrabble players.

"It was terrible," Jayne agreed. "And tonight—"

Another tap on the door sounded, this time with more vigor.

"Did you tell the front desk to let everyone up?" Arnie asked, shaking martinis.

"Yes, why not?" Jayne said, and headed for the door. In the hall, stood Nick and Noreen. The redhead was smiling, the icy blonde was glowering. "Hi, how you doing?"

"Fine, all good, Jayne, great to see you," Nick said, cracking his knuckles as he walked in. He turned to Noreen. "Are you going to stand in the hallway all night?"

She strutted in like a model on the runway, hand on hip. "I don't know why you're having another Scrabble game so soon, Jayne. It's such bad taste! First Marion was killed, then we're poisoned, and then you have another game and Vanessa Harding is attacked—"

"You know about that?" Jayne asked.

"Of course, we know!" the blonde hissed at her. "I've had the police at the brewery almost every day!"

"Not every day," Nick said. "But we've had a few calls."

"There is a crazed killer on the loose and you probably have invited him into your home—again!" Noreen was in high dudgeon.

"Have a martini," Jayne suggested. "Oh, Arnie," she sang out, "I think Noreen could use one of your amazing cocktails."

Arnie handed Noreen a martini glass filled to the brim. She sat down next to Ethel with a thump. Nick got a soft drink and sat down on the floor, next to Noreen, in the lotus position. Jayne watched, thinking of her aging bones, and was very impressed and a bit wistful for the prearthritis days.

"So, what are we waiting for?" Noreen asked.

"Robin and Vanessa," Arnie said.

"That woman is coming here again? What? Is she snagging Robin as her next husband?" Noreen asked, wrinkling her nose, in distaste.

"I thought he was gay," Ethel said in confusion.

"He's everything and anything," Noreen said. "I don't trust him at all."

"Why not?" Arnie asked. She was avoiding the martinis and opened up a can of grapefruit seltzer.

"Something about him," she said. "The grieving widower wants to play Scrabble? So soon? And wants Vanessa Harding to be his partner? I wouldn't put it past them if they poisoned Marion and then poisoned us." With her teeth, Noreen pulled an olive off the swizzle stick and devoured it in two bites.

Nick looked up in horror. "Noreen, don't say those things. Those are terrible accusations."

"Somebody here poisoned Marion, it had to be," she said defiantly. "And I just bet Ms. Arnie Palmer and Ms. Jayne Marple are going to show us who did it and how."

Fred opened another beer and looked horrified. "Is that true, Jayne?"

A series of taps sounded on the door—quick, staccato, woodpecker raps in sets of three. "Coming," Jayne called. She opened the door as a gust of musky perfume hit her straight in the face.

"Darling, Jill, so we meet again," Vanessa Harding gushed, and sailed past her, a pink Titanic of a woman. Robin, with an apologetic smile on his face, holding Tutu, followed the diva inside.

"That woman has a lot of nerve, bringing her dog again," Jayne said, taking Robin's jacket. She picked up a silk scarf, a cashmere pashmina, and a bag of dog treats off the floor where Vanessa had dropped them.

"I know"—he shrugged—"but what can we do?"

"Find another Scrabble partner?"

Robin smirked, stuck out his chin, and winked.

In that moment, Jayne had a revelation that rocked her world and verified her suspicions. Inside, Arnie was giving Vanessa a martini and helping her to a chair. Lucia eyed Tutu and barked frantically until Arnie threw the pup a couple of treats. Robin, smiling at everyone, took a drink and sat down. Jayne pulled Arnie out on the balcony. Schultz gave them a thumbs-up.

"Arnie," she whispered frantically, "I was wrong!"

"Wrong about what?"

"I thought I knew who killed Marion, but I was wrong! I can see it now. The faces, the bones, the eyes—"

"What are you two doing out there," Vanessa called out with a throaty laugh. "Making out?"

Jayne took Arnie by the hand and pulled her back into the room. "I just can't keep my hands off the girl," she oozed. Arnie gulped, Vanessa squinted to take a better look, and the rest of the company sat staring. "Shall we start to play?"

"This food is so yummy," Vanessa sighed, as she devoured another filet mignon slider an hour later. "Robin, that was so, so extravagant of you to provide us with these goodies. And Arnie, your martinis are to die for."

"Don't say that!" Ethel shrieked. "We don't want someone to die again."

"Just a figure of speech, Eth, don't worry." Fred patted her little hand.

Vanessa put down one letter. "Y, added to sex. Sexy," she said. "That's a good word, isn't it, Robin?"

"Very good word, Vanessa," he said, counting the points. This time Jayne and Arnie were their partners.

"You two are hitting it off rather well, after all that's happened," Noreen observed suspiciously from the next table. Her third martini was half empty.

"I have always loved the company of younger men," Vanessa said, sucking on an unlit cigarette. "So invigorating. You know what I'm talking about, don't you, Noreen honey?" she rumbled with a smoky laugh. Tutu raised his head and yipped.

Jayne watched Noreen scowl and looked at the board. "My turn and it's—" She looked at the tiles on the board. "If I add MURD to the ER here, why it spells, murder."

Ethel gasped at the next table. "Don't say that word!"

"How many points, Jayne?" Robin asked, unfazed by the word or Ethel's hyperventilating. Noreen glowered and Nick patted her back.

"Eight points, double word, sixteen. Quite an appropriate word, don't you think, David Harding!"

There was that dead silence in the room that precedes a tornado of turmoil.

"What did you say, Janet? His name is Robin, not David." Vanessa squinted at them both. "Why are you calling him by my ex-husband's name?"

"Yes, why, Jayne?" Noreen demanded. "What do you know, that we don't know?"

CHAPTER TWENTY-NINE

Exposure—17 Points

Jayne stood and straightened to her impressive six-foot height. With her spiky hair, she towered over her guests and dominated the room. Taking a deep breath, she smiled and nodded to Arnie. "Shall I, Arnie? Or would you like to do the honors?"

"I think you should start, Jayne," she said, but her eyes were pleading, *What's going on?*

Jayne gave Arnie a thumbs-up, implying *It's all right, I got this.*

Schultz appeared at the doorway, quietly talking into his radio.

"He's here?" Ethel gasped. "Is there going to be another murder?"

"Stay calm, Ethel," Fred urged.

"What's going on?" Robin asked, getting up from the table. "Who's David Harding?"

"I'm going to tell you," Jayne said. "As you all know by now, Arnie"—she gave her a gracious nod—"after a successful career as a Chicago public schoolteacher—"

"Hear, hear," said Nick.

"Oh, get on with it," Noreen muttered into her martini.

"As I was saying, when Arnie retired and began her Elsinore Detective Agency—"

"Elsie who?" Vanessa squinted, and took a bite of cheesecake.

Nick laughed. Noreen popped an olive into her mouth. "Give me a break from her ignorance," she mumbled.

The pink volcano erupted and pointed at Noreen. "Listen, Little Miss High and Mighty, you think you're so much better than everyone else. I knew your parents and I know your story! Oh yes, she acts so special! Miss Blondie thinks she's Grace Kelly, but she was adopted after killing somebody in an orphanage or something." Vanessa picked up her empty glass. "I'm exhausted with this bull. Arnie, dwinky, pwease?"

"What is she talking about?" Fred demanded.

"Noreen? A murderess?" Ethel started fanning herself with a napkin.

"Do you know this already, Schultz?" Fred asked.

"We know a bit about all of you," he said. His hand was tucked inside his raincoat.

Noreen raised her head from her glass. "So, Nick, what do you think about me now?" She was defiant and tears shimmered on her lashes.

"I know all about your past, Nor," he said softly. "One day I found the letters you saved, totally by accident."

"And you stayed with me?" She was stunned.

"We all make mistakes. You know mine. That doesn't mean that I don't love you. I do, very much."

Noreen stood. "My wonderful Nick," she said, and threw herself into his arms.

Fred looked uncomfortable. Ethel sat open-mouthed. Robin stood stoically like a sphinx. Arnie stared at Jayne in shock. Jayne waited until Nick had settled Noreen in her chair, arms wrapped around her, and then she plunged on with her narrative.

"Let me continue, please," she implored. "Any past history about Noreen, while shocking, really has no bearing on this case."

"Damn right," Noreen said.

"I think maybe Noreen should join Nick at his next AA meeting," Ethel said with concern.

"Quiet, honey," Fred said. "Let Jayne talk."

"As I was trying to say"—she raised her voice—"when Vanessa Harding hired Arnie to find her ex-husband, who she thought was trying to kill her, we never suspected that one of us could be that person. Until the night that Marion Wayne was murdered, poisoned so very boldly, right here in my living room. And Vanessa told us she knew Marion a long time ago."

Ethel sniffled into her hanky. Fred burped and patted his stomach. "Sorry, guys. Those sliders, wow."

Vanessa, Arnie, Nick, and Noreen waited. Robin sat back down and speared a shrimp with a tiny, but sharp, cocktail fork.

"So, what do you know? Spill it," Fred demanded.

"At first, I thought it was an ex-lover, and she seems to have had many, trying to get back at her by breaking into her home and stealing her valuable jewelry, someone not related to our Scrabble family. But there had to be a connection. Why would someone kill Marion and then try to poison Vanessa, Noreen, Arnie, and Robin?"

"Why, indeed?" Noreen got up and stabbed a couple of shrimp.

"Careful, babe," Nick said quietly.

"Why?" She turned around and held the fork out to the room. "Do you think I'm going to stab one of you? Yes, I killed a horrible girl who was bullying me at the foster home. But it was an accident!" She sat down and Nick took the fork out of her shaking hands.

"I think we should leave this story for next time, Jayne," Robin murmured. "Don't you think you have upset us enough? I think we should all go home."

"Robin, I've only just begun my story."

"I want to hear it," Vanessa commanded. "Keep going."

"So, the question is, who could have killed Marion and at the same time wanted to kill Vanessa and steal from her home? Fred has been married to Ethel for many years. Nick is too young.

Arnie is a recent widower. As I see it, the only people the right age to be Vanessa's ex could be Marion or Robin. And"—she looked at them all—"Marion's dead."

"What are you trying to say, Jayne?" Robin stopped eating. "That I killed my husband, Marion Wayne?"

The silence in the room was heavy. Except for the snoring of Lucia and the wheezing of Tutu, the guests could have heard the proverbial pin drop. "That's exactly what I'm trying to say, Robin. You are David Harding."

"What are you saying?" Vanessa turned and looked at Robin in horror. "Don't you think I would recognize my own husband?"

"Vanessa, you suffer from poor eyesight. You're always squinting at everybody and you hadn't seen Robin, I mean David, for two years. And then, David/Robin if I am correct, and I am about ninety-nine percent sure that I am correct, had some surgery on his face. New nose, lips filled out, eyes lifted, dyed hair, lost some weight, didn't you? He started talking in a very soft voice, invented a fake degree and career and voila! A whole new person. Except they couldn't rearrange your chin, could they, David?"

"Are you sure about this, Jayne?" Arnie whispered in her ear.

"It's the only way it makes sense," she said, under her breath.

"And why would I marry Marion? Why would I, a straight man, want to pull off that charade?" Robin seemed amused.

"I don't think you're really a straight man, Robin. Or a gay man. I think you're an amoral opportunist. Narcissists only love themselves. You married Vanessa after Donald went to prison to find out where the money went that he embezzled. You thought maybe it was in the jewelry."

"And I married Marion for a joke?"

"I think Marion was really in love with you. That stoked your colossal vanity. Then, I think you shared with Marion your plan about finding the money and took him into your confidence. He must have thought that was a hoot. He loved intrigue. And he was well-off. He had made a lot of money modeling and designing interiors. You liked the high life. You liked his condo and his cars. You weren't married very long to Vanessa, were you?"

"One year. One lousy year," Vanessa said, squinting at Robin. "David, is this really you? It doesn't look like you. How could you marry me and then marry Marion? Are you really gay? Detective Schultz, did you know all about this? How could you keep this from me?"

"We can't share information when there is a suspect at large," Schultz said. He stared at Robin.

Robin shrugged. "Does it matter, what I am?"

"How could you sleep with me? All that champagne and sex! How could you do it, if you didn't love me, even a teensy widdle bit?" Her eyes filled with tears and the fake eyelashes started to waver.

"I shut my eyes and thought about the money," Robin said with a smirk.

Vanessa gasped. "You horrible man!" She threw the Scrabble tiles in his face. "How dare you try to strangle me!" Tutu flew out of her arms as she started choking him, her charm bracelets jangling violently as she grabbed his throat.

"Stop her, somebody!" Ethel shrieked and fainted into Fred's arms.

"Keep going, girl, no loss," Noreen chuckled.

Arnie and Nick pulled Vanessa off Robin. She fell back into her seat, gasping, her bosom rising and falling rapidly with the exertion.

"How dare you try to kill me?"

"I figured I'd better kill you, Vanessa, before you recognized me," he said. "And after Donald told me where the money was, I had to get rid of him."

"You killed Donald, too? Your own brother?" Vanessa rose, sat down, and then fainted into the filet mignon.

"I don't have any smelling salts," Jayne said to Arnie. "Do you?"

"Jayne, this is not going very well," Arnie moaned, sweat popping out on her head.

"I think it's going great," she said. "So, Robin, what do you have to say for yourself?"

Schultz, talking into his radio, moved toward Robin.

Robin York, a.k.a David Harding, sidestepped the detective. "I have nothing to say." He scooped up Tutu and rushed to Lucia's bed. He picked up the Chihuahua and headed for the balcony. "If you don't let me walk out of here, I'm going to throw these two mutts off the twenty-fourth floor." Schultz pulled out his gun. David Harding laughed, an ugly sound. "Go ahead, shoot. I might just jump with these furballs. If I don't wring their necks, first."

Dead silence. Jayne felt a cold trickle of sweat down her back. Her beloved dog was in the arms of a madman and he looked insane. "Yes, I killed Donald. He hid the money we stole, and he wouldn't tell me where it was. Finally, from prison, he tells me it's hidden with his ex-wife, that over-sexed dragon lady."

Vanessa, recovering consciousness, raised her head from her plate and screamed, "You bastard. Give me my dog!"

"So, I had to marry her to find the money. But even I, the greatest actor in the world, couldn't stomach being married to that bitch. And, in the meantime, I'd found my soulmate."

"Soulmate? What soulmate?" Ethel asked, waking up in Fred's arms.

"Never mind," Robin said. "You don't need to know. I found my soulmate but we needed money. Always money. So, I married Marion. It was a lark, a joke, oh, how we laughed. My spouses, one an ex-beauty queen and one a model for thongs." He sneered at them. "I ask you, can you believe it? You don't know what I've done for love."

"Love?" Noreen said, in disgust. "Sounds like you were in it for the money. Have you ever worked a day in your life? Besides working between the sheets?"

Robin exploded. "Shut up! What do you know about love or needing money? You were adopted and had a good life. Donald and I struggled to get out of the slum where we grew up. We were poor, struggling brothers. No family to help us."

"And yet, you killed him," Jayne said.

"He double-crossed me," Robin said. "He tried to cheat me. He even went to prison and wouldn't tell me where he hid the money. We were supposed to share it. And then he gets out of jail and acts all high and mighty. Won't tell me. Doesn't approve of my marrying Vanessa, says he's going to go to Marion and tell him about her and me. I couldn't let him do that, you see? I wasn't going to let him ruin my life." He moved to the doorway.

"So, you ruined his," Arnie said.

"What else was I supposed to do?" he yelled. "So, am I walking out of here? Let me get to the elevators and I'll give you these damn dogs." Arnie took a step forward. Nick and Fred both stood up. "Don't come any closer!" Robin had a hysterical edge to his voice. He moved toward the balcony, both pooches whimpering as he clutched them tightly.

"Give me my dog back, please, Robin? We'll let you go, I promise," Jayne pleaded.

"Why should I believe you? With this flatfoot here, I haven't got a chance of escaping." He kept inching backward.

"You'll get away. You're so good at disguising yourself," Arnie bargained. "Look how you fooled Vanessa. She didn't even recognize you, a man she was married to."

"Vanessa needs new glasses," Noreen giggled. She was sloshed.

"I do not need glasses!" Vanessa howled.

"Shoot him, Schultz," Noreen urged. "What are you waiting for? Give him the old .38 Special stuff."

"Mr. Harding, put down the dogs and let's have a talk about your options," Schultz said, in a soothing voice.

"Options? That's a laugh," Harding sneered. "My options, at this moment, are twenty-five to life." He squeezed the pups. Tutu yipped. Lucia growled.

"Give me back my dog, you little runt, you!" Vanessa rushed out of her seat and head-butted Robin right in his stomach. He stumbled, the dogs flew out of his arms, and he fell backward on the balcony. Schultz pounced and rushed outside There were sounds of a scuffle, shouts, moans, then silence. Everyone sat frozen. Robin walked in, covering Schultz with a small pink revolver. Schultz had blood on his forehead and his gun was gone.

Ethel woke up, saw the pink gun, the blood, groaned and passed out again.

"That's my gun!" Vanessa screamed.

"Yes, very handy, this little toy of yours, Vanessa," Robin said, covering them all with the pink .38 Special. He pushed Schultz forward with the gun. "No fast moves," he ordered. "Yes, this little gun, ex-wifey dear, put Donald in the water nicely." Fred was rubbing Ethel's wrists. "Stop moving," Robin ordered Fred, "or I might have to kill you." His laughter was tinged with hysteria.

"You really are crazy," Jayne said to Robin. "What a good façade you put on for us."

"I was a drama major," he said. "I loved to dress up and change my appearance. You should have seen my Dr. Frank-N-Furter in the *Rocky Horror Picture Show*." Ethel moaned again and Fred leaned over her. "Stop moving!" Robin ordered, and raised the gun.

"Shut up, you little pipsqueak," Fred yelled, and threw a bottle of Budweiser across the room. The beer bottle hit its mark. Robin slipped sideways and the gun went off, hitting the ceiling fan in the kitchen. Glass shattered all over the floor. Vanessa grabbed her dog. Lucia hid under the piano. Schultz turned and knocked the gun out of Robin's hand. They fought and Schultz wrestled him to the floor. It took all the combined strength of Arnie, Nick, and Schultz to keep David Harding pinioned down. Schultz handcuffed him and he stopped fighting. Harding was pulled to his feet by Schultz, Fred, and Nick. The fight had gone out of him, but there was still a nasty smirk on his face.

Tutu sniffed the gun. Vanessa, wailing like an Irish banshee, picked up the dog with one hand and the gun with the other. "Give that to me," Schultz ordered and snatched the gun from the diva's hand. He ran out on the balcony and returned with his own gun. With one firearm in each hand he looked like a cop, who wasn't playing around.

Ethel woke up, took one look at the mess and Robin in handcuffs and started crying. "What's going on?"

There was a loud banging on the door and then noise in the hallway.

Two uniforms entered. One was holding the arm of an irate, struggling redhead with green eyes. "Let me go, let me go, I haven't done anything!" Her exotic soft voice from an unknown foreign country was gone. She was shouting in pure Chicago-ese. "I said, let me go! I want a lawyer." She tried clawing at the officer's face. He deflected her hands with his arms while the other officer clapped on handcuffs. She spit and cursed at the men.

"It's Tanya! My assistant!" Vanessa said in shock. "What are you doing here? I thought you said you had to go to Romania or somewhere to visit your sick mother." She squinted in suspicion. "You don't really have a sick mother, do you?"

"I don't think she has a mother at all, at least not in Romania, do you, Sarah?" Jayne challenged the woman.

"You figure it out, since you're so smart." The woman scowled.

"Sarah?" Now it was Ethel's turn to squint. "Who is Sarah?"

"Robin's devoted sister," Arnie said.

"She doesn't look like Sarah," Fred complained. "Jayne, you must be making this all up."

Jayne walked over to the woman, who had stopped struggling by now. "If I may be so bold," she said, and with two hands pulled off her auburn wig. "Voila! Red hair gone. Are those really your green eyes?"

"Of course not," the woman said. "Nobody has eyes that green. Are you stupid?"

Vanessa was processing this information. "Tanya is Sarah? Or is Sarah, Tanya?"

"Heaven help us," Jayne said, pulling her spiky hair skyward. "How can any one person be so dumb?"

"What did you say, Jayne?" Vanessa shouted.

"*Now* you know my name? I said, 'how can you be so dumb?'" Jayne, her self-control gone to the wind, shouted, "Of course, Tanya is Sarah, the love of Robin's life, don't you get it? They were in it together!"

"Well, I never," said Vanessa, and sat down in shock. She picked up Tutu and started feeding him filet mignon. "Robin is David and Tanya is Sarah," she murmured. "Why didn't I see it?"

"Because you can't see a damn thing," Jayne said. "Get some glasses."

"Go to Hell," Vanessa sneered. "I'm tired of your insults."

"Ladies, please," Arnie pleaded.

"Where did you two meet?" Schultz asked David Harding.

"When I was visiting Donald in prison, Sarah was visiting her lover. We decided to hook up and join forces. It was love at first sight." David looked at his accomplice with affection.

"Yes, it was," Sarah said. "We were made for each other."

"I think I'm going to be sick," Vanessa moaned, and lit up a cigarette.

"Don't feel bad, Vanessa, they fooled all of us...for a while. Didn't they, Detective Schultz?" Jayne smirked. "And put out that smoke, Vanessa!"

Schultz, mopping the blood off his forehead, where he had been struck with the gun, nodded. "They sure did. And he's stronger than he looks, too."

"Are you hurt?" Arnie asked.

"Not much," Schultz said and unrolled a mint. "Paramedics are on their way, so they can look at me. It will take more than a lying, scheming murderer to get me down."

The lying, scheming murderer, handcuffed with a cop standing over him, was staring into space, quietly muttering. He looked like he had lost his connection with reality. Jayne looked at Schultz.

"They'll check him out," he said. "He might need to be strapped to a gurney."

"Can we go home now," Ethel whined. "I've got a splitting headache."

"Can we leave?" Fred asked Schultz.

He nodded. "Be my guest. We'll check in with you tomorrow for statements."

Paramedics and more uniforms arrived. All of the fight had gone out of the lovers. David rallied enough to look at Sarah in sorrow. "We tried," Robin said to his gray-haired love. He had a wild light in his eyes. "We will be reunited, soon, my love," he promised. "No bars can confine a love like ours."

"OMG," Jayne said. "He's nuts."

"I think you're right," Arnie agreed.

"Can you uncuff me for a moment? I want to take out these contacts and put on my glasses before I go blind," Sarah asked Schultz.

"Go ahead," Schultz ordered.

She was uncuffed. She popped the lenses out and sighed. "Finally, these hurt so bad." Her eyes were a wren-colored gray-brown. She took a pair of thick glasses out of her pocket. "Now, I can see you all." She grimaced. "Not a good-looking one among you."

"You should talk, you mousy hag," Vanessa jeered. "And you're flat-chested!"

Jayne started to choke. Arnie patted her on the back. Schultz saluted them.

CHAPTER THIRTY

Epilogue—10 Points

"I can't believe I was married to a murderer," Vanesa Harding sighed, guzzling a big glass of Irish whiskey. "Live and learn."

Fred and Ethel stood in the hallway, wearing their coats. "We're going now, Jayne," Fred said. "Ethel has had enough and so have I."

"I'm sorry for all the commotion," Jayne said. "I didn't think it would get so wild here."

"I don't think you thought at all," Ethel sniffed. "We could've all been killed."

"Sorry, Ethel," Arnie said. "But the police were here. You were safe."

"Safe? With a gun going off? And fighting?" Ethel was mad, a petite mother hen, with ruffled silk feathers.

"Not that you shared that information with us, about Schultz on the balcony," Fred said, frowning. "And Robin could have killed us all. Some police presence."

"Our people were next door in 2402. It's empty and we used it for surveillance," Schultz offered.

"Some consolation, after the fact," Noreen said.

"Next time—" Jayne began.

"We are not sure there is going to be a next time," Ethel said, using the royal "we" with ease. "Are we, Fred?"

"We can talk about it, Eth, my dear," he said, and put his arm around her shoulders. "Jayne, I'm disappointed in you," he said. "And, Arnie, you didn't come through with any information when I gave you the note. And here, all the time, it was this Robin York or David whatever his name was, trying to scare us, so he could murder Marion and Vanessa."

Vanessa shrieked on cue. "Murder! Don't say that word." She picked up the whiskey bottle and poured another big splash.

"Let's go home," Fred said. "Ethel, I could use a couple of pieces of your pecan pie." They walked out, their sagging shoulders indicating fatigue and disappointment.

"I feel badly," Jayne said to the remaining guests. "I didn't want everyone to get so upset. I guess I didn't think it all through."

"Upset?" Vanessa took another big swig of whiskey and started to cough. "Upset? Jill dear, did you think about us at all? Arnie darling, how could you let her get so out of hand?"

Jayne, red-faced, hands in hair, opened her mouth to blast the diva, but Arnie, ever the peacemaker, cut in to save the moment. "Vanessa, it was my idea, too," she said. "I did agree with Jayne that perhaps a showdown would reveal the killer. And so did Detective Schultz."

"Showdown?" She wheezed out a laugh. "Like the O.K. Corral? And you Wyatt Earp and Jayne, Jesse James, or something like that? And what was wrong with you, Schultz? Agreeing to such a dumb scheme."

"That was not quite our intention, being dumb," Arnie said with dignity.

"I've read too many crime novels," Schultz said, shrugging. "I thought it would work—and it did."

"What a waste of our tax dollars, these shenanigans," Vanessa complained. "I'm going to call the mayor. We're like this." She crossed her fingers and giggled. Suddenly she was drunk. "Arnie baby, widdle Vanessa and baby Tutu snookums, we wanna go home, we very schleepy." Vanessa yawned, slurring her words, as the whiskey on top of martinis hit her like a float in the St. Patrick's Day parade. "I need a taxi. Call me a taxi, Arnie baby."

"No chauffeur tonight?" Jayne asked.

Vanessa squinted and pouted. "I don't really have a chauffeur. I lied, thinking it would make me sound grand. The truth is, I don't have all that much money. I sold off a lot of the jewelry to pay the taxes on my home. I'm not sure that I can stay there." Her eyes filled with tears. She put her head down on the table and started singing, "My Wild Irish Rose."

"You could always sell the diamond pendant," Schultz said. "We found it in Robin's condo, attached to a crystal chandelier. It was cleverly put there to appear fake. It should be yours."

"You moved fast," Jayne observed.

"We had a search warrant for his property the minute he left the house today," Schultz said. "We suspected he was a phony. There were no records of a Robin York anywhere. We were waiting for him to show his hand. The concierge let us in. All in a day's work."

"That's all you found of value?" Arnie was curious. "What else was there of value that Donald gave to Vanessa so David couldn't find it?"

Schultz, about to take a bite filet mignon slider, paused. "This is really out of one of your mystery novels, Jayne," he said. "There were envelopes in the red box of letters that had very valuable stamps on them."

"How valuable?" Nick asked. "Robin used to tell me he was a stamp collector."

"Actually, Donald knew more about that, so he put some of the embezzled money into rare stamps. Some of the envelopes had no postmark. He went to jail before he could retrieve the envelopes from Mrs. Harding. He made the mistake of telling David about the envelopes with the stamps and so David murdered him and broke into her home twice. The stamps were worth about four hundred thousand dollars."

"You mean I was sitting on a fortune in stamps, and I didn't know it?" Vanessa stopped singing at the mention of money.

"I'm afraid so," Schultz said. "But that money belongs to the company that Donald stole it from. The stamps after investigation and evaluation will be returned to the rightful owner."

"Gosh," said Nick. "Right out of Chicago PD."

Noreen gave a little bitter laugh. "It's a good thing she didn't throw them away or burn them up with her cigarettes. Then where would you be?"

"I don't throw my love letters away—ever," Vanessa contradicted.

"You don't throw anything away," Jayne said, eating cheesecake.

Vanessa stared at her for a moment and then smiled. "You're right, Judy dear, I don't throw anything away. I live in my little love shack, surrounded by my mementos of the past. Pathetic, isn't it?" She sighed. "I used to have a life." Jayne looked at her in shock. Vanessa Harding speaking truthfully for once, without exaggeration and imagination? "Well, the years were good to me. I made a few mistakes in my choice of men, but for the most part, I had a good time." She looked at Noreen. "I'm sorry I said what I did about your childhood and your past. That was terrible of me. I should have kept my mouth shut. I was very fond of your parents. I knew them back in the day, when I was married the first time around. I knew your brother, too. He was very sweet and fond of his little sister."

"That's very generous of you," Noreen conceded. "I was as much a suspect as the rest of you. You had every right to know about my life and my past." Noreen started to cry. Nick rubbed her back and then took her in his arms.

"I think we had better go home now," he said, looking at Schultz. "Do you need us for anything else?"

"Not right now. We'll be in touch," said the detective, and picked up another sandwich. "Police work makes me hungry."

"Vanessa," said Noreen, wiping her eyes. "I did know that you knew my parents. I just never mentioned it, because I am a snob, when you get right down to it."

"Aren't we all?" said Vanessa, rising unsteadily. Arnie helped her to her feet. "Don't worry about it, darlin'."

"Can we give you a ride home?" Nick asked. "Maybe you and Noreen want to talk about her folks and her brother."

"That's a lovely idea," Vanessa said. "If Noreen is okay with that."

"I would like to hear more about the time you spent with my family," Noreen agreed. "That *would* be lovely."

"How do you like that?" Jayne asked, after the trio had left. Arnie and Schultz were stretched on the sofas, with fresh coffee. Jayne was sitting in her recliner chair, still eating cheesecake, with Lucia in her lap. "Vanessa as a surrogate mother to Noreen."

"I wouldn't go that far," Schultz said, "but they did seem interested in one another."

"It's hard to believe that Noreen had killed someone in self-defense and spent time in a psychiatric home," Arnie said, shaking her head. "I was shocked."

"Yes, she kept that very well hidden," Schultz agreed. "What were the chances that Vanessa Harding knew her parents and knew all about her past?"

"Slim to none," Jayne observed, "and yet it happened."

"Small world and truth is stranger than fiction," Arnie said.

"As an English teacher, can't you come up with anything more original to say than that?" Jayne demanded as she put Lucia back in her cashmere dog bed. She stood up and stretched. "What a night. I'm beat."

"'Out, out, brief candle!'" Arnie rose up, extended her arms and quoted Shakespeare in a very dramatic, loud, dynamic voice. "'Life's but a walking shadow, a poor player that struts and frets his hour upon the stage and then is heard no more.'" She lowered her arms. "Tell that to Marion Wayne and Donald Harding. Their hour is over and they will be heard no longer on this earth. Maybe somewhere in another realm."

"Arnie Palmer, on that note, I'm going to bid you adieu," Schultz said, standing up. He found his raincoat crumpled under one of the fallen Scrabble tables. "Jayne Marple, you have lived up to your name."

"What about the bet? We won, didn't we?"

"Yes, you did," he conceded. "I will definitely recommend the Elsinore Detective Agency to anyone in need of a private detective. And give a review on social media, if you have a page."

"We will get a page—tomorrow," Jayne said. "Thanks, Pericles."

"My pleasure," he said, unrolling an antacid. "I ate too much; my wife always says I do during a tricky case. My bad. But I've enjoyed the cuisine, chez Marple."

"Come back anytime, come back next time we play Scrabble, and you can join us," Jayne offered.

"Will there be a next time?" Arnie looked worried. "I'm not sure they will come back after what went on tonight."

"They'll come back," Jayne said, putting her arms around Arnie. "If just to hear you quote Shakespeare."

"See you guys," Schultz said. "Try not to get into any more trouble, at least for a few days."

"Remember," Jayne called to his retreating raincoat, "next time your partner will be Vanessa Harding!"

"Saints preserve me," Schultz shouted, and slammed the door.

"Do you think he would play with Vanessa?" Arnie asked.

"If I were his wife, I wouldn't let him near her. She seems to like younger partners."

"Like you do, Jayne," Arnie said, enveloping her in a hug.

"I'm only three years older," she grumbled into her neck.

"Like a fine wine, mellow, delicious and subtle."

"Who me, subtle?" She pointed to the picture on the wall, when she was a rocker, pink guitar in hand.

Arnie looked at the mess in the room. "Want to clean up?"

"Tomorrow," she said. "I have other plans for you."

Arnie grinned. "You're adorable when you smile at me," she said. She looked at the other Scrabble table and the tiles that were still intact on the board. "Look at that."

"Golfer, ten points, how appropriate," Jayne said.

"Diva, eight points, who do we know that fits that word?" Arnie laughed.

"Lovers, nine points, triple word score. Bingo," Jayne said, wrapping her arms around her lover. "That word fits us, Arnie darling, to a tee."

Also by Felicia Carparelli

The Murder in the Library
Killing Mr. Darcy
Hot for Teacher, Shakespeare Made us Fall in Love
The Mysterious Affair at Longbourn
The Ardent Virgin
The Mysterious Case of Jane Fairfax

About the Author

Felicia Carparelli is a retired teacher, writing in Chicago. She has been published in *Tiny Love* in the *New York Times*, *FlexxMag*, *The Rhubris*, *Coping with Cancer*, *Cure Today*, *Psych Central*, *Chicken Soup*, and the *Chicago Sun-Times*. Gotham Writer's workshops have helped shape her writing.

A member of Gilda's Clubhouse in Chicago, she participates in programs and classes for cancer survivors. She is the proud owner of a Chin-Pin, Presley, and two amazing parakeets. She has played her accordion on the Svengoolie TV Show and the WGN morning news.

She belongs to the Romance Writers of America, Chicago Writers Association, and the Wacker Drive Writers Group.

This is her first sapphic novel for Bella Books.

Bella Books, Inc.

Women. Books. Even Better Together.

P.O. Box 10543
Tallahassee, FL 32302
Phone: (800) 729-4992

www.BellaBooks.com

More Titles from Bella Books

Hunter's Revenge – Gerri Hill
978-1-64247-447-3 | 276 pgs | paperback: $18.95 | eBook: $9.99
Tori Hunter is back! Don't miss this final chapter in the acclaimed
Tori Hunter series.

Integrity – E. J. Noyes
978-1-64247-465-7 | 28 pgs | paperback: $19.95 | eBook: $9.99
It was supposed to be an ordinary workday...

The Order – TJ O'Shea
978-1-64247-378-0 | 396 pgs | paperback: $19.95 | eBook: $9.99
For two women the battle between new love and old loyalty may prove
more dangerous than the war they're trying to survive.

Under the Stars with You – Jaime Clevenger
978-1-64247-439-8 | 302 pgs | paperback: $19.95 | eBook: $9.99
Sometimes believing in love is the first step. And sometimes it's all
about trusting the stars.

The Missing Piece – Kat Jackson
978-1-64247-445-9 | 250 pgs | paperback: $18.95 | eBook: $9.99
Renee's world collides with possibility and the past, setting off a tidal
wave of changes she could have never predicted.

An Acquired Taste – Cheri Ritz
978-1-64247-462-6 | 206 pgs | paperback: $17.95 | eBook: $9.99
Can Elle and Ashley stand the heat in the *Celebrity Cook Off* kitchen?